THERE ARE NO GOOD GIANTS

A Novel by
Dennis Torres

ISBN: 978-0-9980824-1-7 (paperback)

To my beautiful wife Averi who has been my muse throughout the writing of this book and our many years together.

Books by Dennis Torres
The Amazon of Ray Goldberg Rivera

Once more the strong reach out. The weapons vary: gold, gun ... a missionary. But the force is there, the force is always there.

Walter Benton, Captain United States Army WWII.
From his poem, "There Are No Good Giants."

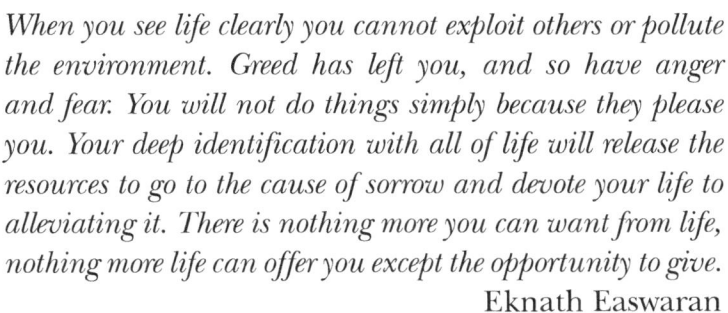

When you see life clearly you cannot exploit others or pollute the environment. Greed has left you, and so have anger and fear. You will not do things simply because they please you. Your deep identification with all of life will release the resources to go to the cause of sorrow and devote your life to alleviating it. There is nothing more you can want from life, nothing more life can offer you except the opportunity to give.

Eknath Easwaran

CHAPTER 1

After flying nearly eight thousand miles in twenty four hours I wake up in a bed dank from perspiration and a sleep so deep I don't know where I am until the fog of recollection clears and I realize I'm a soldier in Vietnam and if I live my life will never be the same.

Intellectually, I know, regardless of age, death is waiting for all of us, but that has nothing to do with emotions. I was reminded of this yesterday when I landed at Tan Son Nhut Airbase with mortars exploding outside the windows of the MATS charted Continental Airways jet that carried me along with a hundred and seventy other GIs from the safety of San Francisco to the war in Vietnam. Trapped inside the plane's fuselage there was nothing any of us could do but hope that our career as a war time soldier wouldn't end before it began.

When the jet's engines shut down so did the air-conditioning and it didn't take long before the cabin was a steam bath scented not with the invigorating smell of eucalyptus, but perspiration and fear. No one dared to speak as if doing so would trigger disaster or worse betray the depth of our fear. Following an eternity of minutes the cabin door finally swung open and a GI with a bull horn rushed in yelling, "The Base is under attack. Egress in an orderly fashion, keep your head low and run to the building on your far right where I'll be waiting with further instructions." Then adding, "Move it, if this bird's hit it'll go up like a bomb!"

In perfect unison one hundred and seventy GIs jumped up and tried to get into the aisle then out of the door. While nervously waiting in the queue I couldn't help but ponder how keeping my head low would save me if a mortar hit the plane; it was the beginning of my questioning everything to come.

By the time we reached the building the mortar attack had ended and we were bussed down the curfew-deserted streets of Saigon to the Hoa Lu hotel, which was under contract with the military for use as a bachelor enlisted men's quarters (BEQ), the term having nothing to do with marital status only that we were unaccompanied by a spouse. As we filed in from the bus an oriental desk clerk handed out room keys and we were instructed by the Sargent in charge to assemble in the lobby at ten hundred hours the next morning.

CHAPTER 2

Lying in bed I ponder how I let myself become one of the faceless cogs in a war machine while so many of my contemporaries turned deferments and dodging into an art form. It's not that I fear death, nobody complains about being dead, but I have no desire to be a disabled hero, or kill another human being, or be on the giving or receiving end of intentionally inflicted pain especially as a tool for the political and financial gain of others. I make no pretense that this war, perhaps every war, is anything other than that.

I feel no animosity toward the Viet Cong or North Vietnamese and don't see them as a threat to me, my family or my country, they didn't invade America. But the only alternatives I saw to the Draft were prison, or lifetime exile in Canada, and in the end I caved in to rationalizing that American was built on the backs of those who had served before me and it was now my turn. It was less a patriotic decision than being up against a wall.

Now lying in a sweat-soaked bed on my first morning in Vietnam, I watch a gecko glued to the wall, motionless until its tongue lashes out and reels in an insect; it makes me wonder if I will be the gecko or the insect.

Right after that, I notice the acrid, sour, putrid smells of decay, of rotting garbage, feces and urine, and the choking fumes of diesel and two-cycle exhaust pouring through the open window accompanied by the cacophony city bustle and humans speaking in a strange language, all of it coming from the street below.

The door to my room opens and a strange man comes in. He doesn't notice me at first, but goes straight to a chest of drawers and starts pulling out clothes. Then, when he sees me yells, "What the fuck are you doing in my room?"

"The desk clerk gave me the key last night when I got in," I tell him.

"Goddam Chinese faggot. I told him a million times no fucking roommates. What's your name kid?"

"Ben, Ben Kovner"

"Well, Kovner, you can call me Sarg, and I really don't give a shit about the room cause I'm never here, just come back once a week to pick up clothes." He then goes into the bathroom leaving the door open so he can continue the conversation.

"Kovner, I've been in Uncle Sam's Army for 28 years. This is my second and last tour in the Nam and I can tell you we're wasting our fucking time here. There ain't a goddam thing here worth fighting for and one American life is worth more than a million of these gooks far as I'm concerned. But that's between you and LBJ, because in less than a month I'll be outta here and retired. Where you being stationed?"

"Tan Son Nhut, I think."

"Then you're a lucky son of a bitch. You'll be living in here in Saigon drawing combat pay and getting a meal allowance too, better than out in the fucking boonies. They tell you where to get breakfast?"

"Nobody told me anything, Sarg."

"Well this joint's got a snack bar on the roof, but it don't open till eleven hundred hours so you're gonna have to go over to the Hung Dao. Got any Ps?"

"What's the Hung Dao? Ps?"

"Piasters son, Nam currency. Never mind, wait a minute." The toilet flushes and he comes out buckling his pants and hands me several bills. "It's only about a buck's worth but it's enough for breakfast and a taxi there and back. The Hung Dao's a BEQ like this one, only it's got a dining room."

"Thanks Sarg, but I don't know how to get there."

"Take a taxi, but if you value your life don't stand in front of the hotel, no one's allowed to stop there and block the guard's view. Go off to the side, hail a taxi and tell the driver 'dee Hung Dao.' That's gook talk for 'go to the Hung Dao,' and when you get there give the driver twenty Ps. If he asks for more just give him the twenty and get out. Then take the elevator if the goddam thing's working, though it never is, up to the dining room and when you're ready to come back just tell the driver 'dee Hoa Lu' and give'm the other twenty. Remember if the son of a bitch asks for more just throw the twenty at him and get the fuck out. Got it?"

"I think so Sarg. Thanks a lot."

CHAPTER 3

S oon as he's gone I shave, shower and go downstairs to
the street where the sun's beating down mercilessly and
the humidity's near hundred percent. The sidewalk's team-
ing with people moving in every direction at once. Petite,
lean men, women and children wearing pajamas, others in short shorts, tropical business suits and traditional
Vietnamese dresses called Ao Dais, long silken tunics over
sheer pants, and on their heads conical straw hats or pith
helmets, and on their feet, amber-colored plastic sandals.
Naked babies, their bodies covered with red sores are crawling on the filthy ground, others riding on the hips of children not much older than they are. Everywhere are food
vendor carts and huge mounds of garbage four to five feet
high with rats and bone-thin dogs, cats, pigs and chickens

foraging for food, and urinating and defecating alongside humans squatting at the curb doing the same.

The street is a gridlock, a jigsaw puzzle of vehicles half chair, half bicycle Pedi cabs called cyclos, and motorcycle-powered ones call cyclo mais, and long black French Renault and Citroen sedans looking like 1920 gangster cars, and countless blue and yellow Renault CV4 taxis half the size of a Volkswagen beetle, and buses and trucks, all of them belching out plumes of choking exhaust, and humans pulling or pushing crude carts loaded with people, food and hard cargo, others being pulled by ponies and oxen, and single bicycles carrying three, four and five people and motor scooters and mopeds loaded the same way; all of them trying to move and blowing their horns in a chorus of frustration.

At the entrance to the Hoa Lu, standing guard behind a bunker of sandbags and steel drums filled with sand to prevent explosives from being driven into the hotel, are an American MP armed with a riot barreled shotgun, and a Saigon policeman known as a Canh-sat (more commonly called a "white mice" because of their diminutive size, tiny eyes and white uniforms) armed with an M-1 rifle; both of them with orders to shoot to kill anyone who fails to keep moving past their line of sight.

I learn early on, for an able bodied VN male, being a white mice is preferred over being a soldier, some even paying for the privilege of working long hours for low pay because it's safer, and they get to go home every night, and are able to supplement their income by extorting bribes from those they're supposed to protect.

When I hail a taxi I'm a little too close to the entrance and the MP barks at me to move out of his line of vision. I immediately move to the side and flag down one of the omnipresent Renault CV4 taxis and fold myself into the back seat, phonetically speaking my very first Vietnamese words, "dee Hung Dao."

The driver turns back to me smiling, his mouth filled with blackened teeth, a tomato red line running from his red gums to the corner of his mouth from chewing betel nut, the tiny fruit of a palm with the stimulating effects of caffeine and more. He speaks to me in Vietnamese saying something I do not understand and all I can reply is "dee Hung Dao," reminding me of the old joke about a foreigner who comes to the United States knowing only one word in English, "coffee," and after weeks of ordering only coffee some well-meaning person teaches him the words "apple pie" so he could have something to eat with his coffee, but when the waitress asks him if he wants cheese with the pie he becomes so flustered he reverts back to just coffee. I repeat the words "dee Hung Dao" and the driver puts one hand on the horn and pulls right into traffic without looking, then winds through all four gears while going only 10 miles per hour, so the taxi's bucking and vibrating like it's going to stall, but his shoeless, leathery foot expertly dances between the bare metal brake pedal, and the bare medal accelerator, the clutch all but forgotten, as he weaves through traffic inches from colliding with others who are driving the same way.

When he drops me off at the side of the Hung Dao Hotel it's right next to a mound of fly-covered garbage, then reaches back and opens my door from the inside, the taxi's that small.

"Hung Dao, Hung Dao," he says, pointing to the building.

It's then that I hand him one of the well-worn twenty P notes that Sarg gave me, worth about fifteen cents in American money, and he nods gratefully before driving off and leaving me to battle the flies as I run toward the Hung Dao, arms flailing.

As Sarg suspected, the elevator's out of order so I climb the stairs to the upper floor dining room where there are tables set with white table cloths on a carpeted floor with young pretty Vietnamese girls serving as waitresses. A sign at the entrance reads "50 cents for breakfast, 50 cents for a lunch, $1 for dinner, all you can eat" and next to it another reading, "Sunday $1.50 all the steak you can eat," and a third "Paid in advance all meals, $45 per month." I find out, most of the food comes from the U.S. and is prepared by local Vietnamese employees under the supervision of American Navy cooks who, before coming to VN, had to do the work themselves and now get to be supervisors and bosses standing around telling the VN workers what to do. This because all logistical support in the Nam is under command of the Navy with the acronym HEDSUPAC, which stands for Headquarters Support Activity, headed by a Navy Captain whom I'm told, likes VN girls, good times and anything that helps the morale of the GIs.

I sit at a table alongside a GI who's already working on a stack of pancakes and order ham and eggs with hominy grits because the combination brings back good memories of the south where I spent summers with my grandparents. It doesn't take long before the GI pegs me for an "FNG," GI speak for "fucking new guy," and he wants to be the first to tell me all about Saigon and the Nam, especially sex and bargirls.

"Soon as you walk into a bar", he says, "they want you to buy them a Saigon Tea, which is a tiny glass of tea that costs thirty-five Ps, and when you do, they drink it down real fast then ask for another, and keep this up by telling you how handsome you are and how much they like you while their hand's on your cock. Then when they got all teas out of you they can, they try to get you to go short time with them for a couple of hundred Ps, which in the States is what we call a quickie, but you got to watch yourself because this town's reeking with the clap."

Then he goes on to tell me how I can get sex for even less money. "A couple of hundred Ps is about a buck, but you can fuck a cyclo girl for half that and it's the same thing only the girl's pimped off by a cyclo driver instead of a bar momason and there's no need to buy Saigon teas."

By the time I finish eating, I'm looking forward to hitting the bars.

CHAPTER 4

When I arrive back to the Hoa Lu, all the GIs who came with me the night before are already assembled in the lobby and they look shocked to see me coming in from the outside.

"Kovner, where the fuck have you been?" the Sargent barks at me. "We've been looking all over for you."

"Sarg, you said to meet in the lobby at ten hundred hours and I'm five minutes early."

"You're supposed to be in your room not wondering around outside. In case you haven't heard, there's a fucking war going on out there and the bus is on its way to take us to breakfast."

"I took a taxi to the Hung Dao and already ate breakfast," I say and can tell he and everybody else is shocked to hear this, and wondering how I managed to do so, then are angry that I did while they're standing around hungry and waiting for me.

"How the fuck did you do that?" the Sarg asks me, and when I tell him how the Sargent in my room gave me some Ps and told me where and how to go they all seem more amazed than angry.

When the bus shows up to take us to breakfast, it's an old, olive drab Army bus with thick wire screens covering all the windows, similar to those used to transport prisoners, only the screens are not intended to keep us in, but other people out, in particular, those who might want to toss an explosive into the bus. To an FNG like me, the subliminal message seems to be, the people we've come to protect want to kill us and it immediately fosters an, us versus them mentality.

Having already eaten, I wait at the Hung Dao bar adjacent to the dining room, watching the Vietnamese waitresses serving twenty cent bar drinks to GIs who prefer alcohol over pancakes and eggs while others sit feeding coins into Las Vegas style slot machines that line the walls.

An easel sign at the bar entrance announces several upcoming events.
Tonight In Your Hung Dao Club Room
"TOP SOIL"
An Earthy Rock Band from Down Under
—

TUESDAY
DON'T MISS MONTE CARLO NIGHT
You're Favorite Games of Chance
Craps, Roulette, Poker
—

FRIDAY
HEDSUPAC BEAUTY CONTEST
Cast your Vote
For
The Most Beautiful Vietnamese Girl
In the Command

Despite being morning, some of the GIs are dancing with VN girls to jukebox recordings of "I Got You Babe," "I Can't Get No Satisfaction" and "Help me Rhonda." At a nearby table a Vietnamese girl is sipping champagne with her GI boyfriend who's dressed in civilian clothes, but still wearing his military boots. I laugh to myself because back in the States they're a dead giveaway for GIs pretending to be civilians in order to get with town girls whose families forbid them to date anyone from the local base.

CHAPTER 5

With breakfast over, we're bussed to yet another hotel only this one's still under construction, the floors have no outside walls and are open to the street below. There, while sitting around folding tables on the fifth floor surrounded by VN construction workers, we're instructed to fill out the first of many Department of Defense (DOD) forms—last name first, first name last, middle initial, rank, serial number, DOR (date of rotation, the date we are scheduled to leave Vietnam) and who to notify in case of death, not something we want to think about.

Following the forms are orientation speeches, only without amplifying equipment they're barely audible against the backdrop of the construction workers, all of them women who are hammering, sawing, mixing and pouring concrete.

First up is Captain Staub who's in charge of the Airmail Terminal (AMT) at the Tan Son Nhut Airbase where I and several others are being assigned. He tells us, unlike the militaries of old, it now takes nine GIs to support each one engaged in actual combat, then continues on about the important role mail plays in that support. When he's finished a staff sergeant named Robbie, who's a shift supervisor at the AMT, takes over, shouting to be heard above the din, in a southern accent mixed with ethnic vernacular.

"Gentlemens, we has three shifts at the AMT, each one gots from 6 to 9 men, dependin' on who's coming in and who's rotatin' back Stateside. The work ranges from pickin' up mail from BEQs, BOQs and US installations, to sortin,' sackin' and sorties. Loadin' and unloadin' conexes and palets is hard work, wooooeeee, I'm sweated up a storm just thinkin' about it." He exhales then pauses long enough to wipe a handkerchief across his sweating face before continuing with, "Your work day will begin when a truck from the AMT picks you up at the hotel and drives you out to Tan Son Nhut and when you're off duty, you're off, but if you're ever late for work I'll presume foul play or that you deserted so you better never be late."

A GI named Snover takes over after him and starts off telling us he's been at the AMT longer than anybody else because he volunteered for a second tour so he could take advantage of an early discharge program for those rotating back with less than three months remaining on their military commitment. He's a short, cocky guy who comes off as arrogant.

"I don't care what you FNGs did in real life," he says, "but this ain't the movies and if you want to leave the Nam in one piece, you better listen up. First some house-keeping bull shit. You can buy Ps anywhere in Saigon—in bars, tailor shops, and from people in the streets—and get one hundred eighty to one hundred ninety Ps to the dollar instead of the one hundred you'd get at a bank, but exchanging money outside of officially approved places is illegal because Victor Charlie, that's the VC to you FNGs, uses those greenbacks to buy weapons from Red China, but everybody does it, even the big Brass so you'd be stupid assholes not to, and I don't want to work with any stupid assholes. Just make sure you don't get short changed by some slant eye son-of-a bitch giving you a quick count.

Next up, pussy. Every girl in the Nam can be had for a couple of Ps so fuck them, but don't marry them, and use a god dam rubber because VD can be a court-marshal offense if you're not able to perform your duties. Watch your ass too, some of the bitches are VC and put razor blades up their pussies to mess you up real bad or they'll take you home to fuck and have one of their VC buddies finish you off while you're busy humping."

He then goes on to warn us about innocent looking street kids who are skilled pickpockets and taxi drivers who say their meters are broken so they can jack up the fare, and drive-by motorcyclists who can slip a watch off a wrist or grab anything out of a shirt pocket without even stopping, and he never gets around to the lifesaving information he alluded to before Sgt. Robbie cuts in and dismisses us for lunch, saying he'll try to get a quieter room when we return for the afternoon session.

CHAPTER 6

For lunch, the bus then takes us back to the Hung Dao dining room, but instead of going in to eat I decide to walk around and see the city. Just a short distance away, flanking both sides of the street, are bars, one after the other, most with American names like The Chicago Bar, The New York Bar, The Holiday Bar, The Playboy Bar, The Good Times Bar, etc., and each one fortified with a double wire cage entry to keep vehicles loaded with explosives from driving in which, I learn, prior to the cages, happened more than once.

Passing The Playboy Bar, I make a U-turn and decide to go in to see what it's all about. After my eyes adjust from the bright sun to the dark interior, I see several Oriental girls lounging around on settees, easy chairs and bar stools, some with GIs, all of them petite teen looking and provocatively dressed, some in skin tight slacks, others in short skirts with low cut blouses, and a few wearing traditional Ao Dais.

"You want?" the bartender asks me.

"Beer, please"

"Mot ba muoi ba," he calls out and another bartender sets down a large bottle of cold beer in front of me that has the number 33 on the label, which is pronounced "bah-moy-bah" in Vietnamese.

He then says, "Fifs-teen Ps," and when I hand him an American dollar he waves across the room to a corpulent, middle-aged VN woman who comes right over and turns out to be the bar's momason, meaning manager and pimp.

"My name Lily," she says to me. "You want change money?"

"How much you give?" I ask, remembering Snover's briefing.

"How much you change?"

"Twenty dollars."

"One hundred twenty," she says, meaning for each dollar I change.

"Two hundred," I counter.

"Okay, one hundred fifty."

"One hundred eighty."

"Okay, one hundred seventy five," and with that her fat one-ring-per-finger hand reaches inside her bra and takes out a roll of Ps.

After carefully counting them, I tell her okay and she says in return, "You say other GI Lily give good change money okay," and pats me on the back, which I later learn is an insulting gesture in VN culture unless carried out by a very dear friend. "You come see Lily fry-day payday," she goes on, "I give number one change money okay." Then, before walking away, signals one of the bargirls to come over using a hand gesture that looks like a child waving bye-bye, only in the Nam it means to come here, and when the girl comes over she is not even five feet tall and looks only twelve or thirteen years old.

"My name Thuy," the girl says to me, "this first night I work bar," she then holds up her limp little girl hand for me to shake. "What is your name?"

"My name Ben. You speak English?"

"Ti Ti," she answers making a diminutive sign with her thumb and forefinger meaning very little. "I can sit with you?"

"Yes, of course. How old are you?"

"Aaaas-teen."

"Eighteen! No, you no eighteen," I say.

"Fa-sure I aaas-teen," she says, resting her hand on my leg. "You number one GI, you buy me one Saigon Tea?"

"Yes, of course."

"Xuan, Xuan, mot le," she calls out to the barboy who sets down a tiny stemmed glass with a few thimbles full of green murky liquid along with a paper marker that's Thuy's receipt for the sale.

"Thanks you too much," Thuy says. "You give Xuan thirty five Ps for Saigon tea."

One sip and the tea's half gone and just like Snover said, her hand is now working my thigh.

"How old you say me?" she asks

"Twelve!" I say.

She laughs. "I no sau, I aas-teen," she says. No sau meaning she's not lying, then shows me her official identification but it's in Vietnamese and I can't decipher it. "You number one, dep hoa, ver-ly handsome," she continues. "Thuy likes too much."

"Thuy very pretty, Ben likes too much," I say back.

"No, Thuy so dep, no pretty," she giggles, pressing her finger to her flat button of a nose. "Thuy have number ten nose, no same, same Amer-lie-kin nose."

"I like your nose"

She giggles again, then moves her hand into my crotch and lets loose with her quiver full of memorized bargirl speak.

"How long you come my country? You have girlfriend? You have married? You buy me one Saigon Tea?" After which I tell her I have to return to a meeting and promise to come back to see her again.

CHAPTER 7

Orientation continues in the same room as before, but without any noise from the construction workers who are on break and sprawled out on the cool concrete floor shaded from the sun by floor above.

Sgt. Robbie begins talking while pacing and wiping the sweat from his face in the manner of the great jazz musician Louis Armstrong who always moped his face with a handkerchief while playing his trumpet, and all of us forced to listen while fighting to stay awake in the intense heat and humidity, me in particular after two large bottles of ba muoi ba. He starts by reading verbatim from a booklet we've all received called "Guide Book to Vietnam," as if we were not capable of reading it for ourselves; something that always pissed me off when teachers did it.

1. "All official United States personnel are accorded diplomatic immunity by special concession of the Government of the Republic of Vietnam.
2. Since military personnel are subject to U.S. Military law, any local incident involving our military people is reported to the Command, U.S. Military Assistance, Vietnam (COMUSMACV), for appropriate disciplinary action. This arrangement has worked out very well. Vietnamese Government officials have expressed their satisfaction with the prompt and fair way such incidents as have occurred have been handled."

He then stops long enough to explain what this means saying, "As soldiers in war we is free to do whatever the fuck we wants until somebody complains, at which time we'll be accorded Diplomatic Immunity, which does not mean we escape without consequences, only that we is governed by a different set of rules than the Vietnamese people."

Skipping ahead he the reads from another section. "Is Nuoc Mam something to wear, something to eat, or the name of an organization?" The answer being something to eat, it's a Vietnamese sauce, and, "Why is it often difficult to tell a Viet Cong from a loyal South Vietnamese?" the answer being "because it's like trying to tell a Democrat from a Republican," and "Who is Ho Chi Minh?," the answer being the Communist leader of North Vietnam, as if we didn't know, then finishing up by reading verbatim the following narrative.

"The Vietnamese have paid a heavy price in suffering for their long fight against the Communists. We military men are in Vietnam now because their government has asked us to help its soldiers and people in winning their struggle. The Viet Cong will attempt to turn the Vietnamese people against you. You can defeat them at every turn by the strength, understanding and generosity you display with the people."

At this point he notices most everybody has nodded off and lets out a loud "WOOOEEE," which gets our attention long enough for him to pass out two sets of cards. One is a "Geneva Conventions Identity Card" that we are told to carry with us at all time. "In the event you get captured, it informs the enemy an agreement was signed in Geneva, Switzerland, that says all prisoners of war are to be treated in accordance with certain standards of decency." To me the idea seems absurd, like reminding a criminal what they're doing is illegal. and not only that, the card's in English and it is doubtful the enemy understands English or has ever heard of Geneva, or even cares what was decided there. I tell the GI next to me, "It would be better for us to carry a fake Communist party membership card written in Vietnamese." The other handout is another wallet-size card entitled "Nine Rules for Personnel of the U.S. Military Assistance Command, Vietnam," which Sgt. Robbie reads aloud.

> "Rule number one. Remember we are special guests here. We make no demands and seek no special treatment.
> Rule number two. Join with the people. Understand their life, use phrases from their language, and honor their customs and laws.

Rule number three. Treat women with politeness and respect.

Rule number four. Make personal friends among the soldiers and common people.

Rule number five. Always give the Vietnamese the right of way.

Rule number six. Be alert to security and ready to react with your military skill.

Rule number seven. Don't attract attention by loud, rude or unusual behavior.

Rule number eight. Avoid separating yourself from the people by a display of wealth or privilege.

Rule number nine. Above all else, you are members of the U.S. military forces on a difficult mission, responsible for all your official and personal actions. Reflect honor upon yourself and the United States of America."

When he finishes reading, Snover shouts out a loud, "Good luck with that!" which turns out to be his response to just about everything anybody has to say about anything. Before dismissing us for the day, Sgt. Robbie reads from three more military booklets entitled "An Opportunity to Serve," "At Home with the Vietnamese" and "Service with Satisfaction," the last one being about the satisfaction we as GIs should get from sharing in the experience of halting the spread of Communism in Asia, to which Snover adds, "Good luck with that."

CHAPTER 8

The next morning we're bused back to the Hung Dao for breakfast. The Sun's barely up but it's already hotter and more humid than I can ever remember experiencing, and sapping whatever energy the night's sleep has provided. After breakfast we're taken to an Army Field Hospital where a team of medics sticks us with hypodermic needles as if the multitude of immunizations we got in the States for small pox, yellow fever, cholera, typhoid, diphtheria, tetanus, typhus, polio, plague and influenza weren't enough. Included in the new ones are boosters for the previous inoculations plus gamma globulin for hepatitis A, injected via a large diameter needle in proportion to individual body weight. Then, before we leave to be bussed back for a second day of orientation, we're given a supply of pills, aspirin-like ones to ward off clinical malaria and large pink salt tablets, each the size of a nickel, to be taken four times a day for the prevention of dehydration and electrolyte imbalance.

Eight more hours of battling fatigue and boredom through a litany of speeches and we're bused back to the Hotel Hoa Lu for dinner at its newly opened roof garden restaurant and bar where even though the sun has set, the super-heated air comes at you like a blow torch and the menu includes hamburgers, French fries, Texas style chili, ham n' Swiss, tuna sandwiches, Budweiser beer, milk shakes and ice cream sundaes. Besides a complete bar, there are rows of slot machines that cause me to reflect if my luck is bad, do I dare risk going to work that day.

Seated at a table on the roof garden I can see across the Saigon River where American planes are dropping hundreds of flares suspended under tiny parachutes to aid in spotting the enemy. I can also hear the distant popping of gun fire and the thud of mortar shells and see the red streaks of tracer rounds, like I'm watching a movie on TV yet separated from it by only a few city blocks and a not too wide river. It's especially surreal when I realize in that very moment human beings are deliberately killing each other while I sit comfortably munching on a burger with a beer in hand, taking it all in.

CHAPTER 9

I learn there are more than 300 GI serving bars in Saigon, all of them advertising "Charming Hostesses," a euphemism for bargirl sex workers, the sheer number being a testament to the steady influx of GIs with discretionary money and an uncertain future, the uncertain future applying to the lives of the bargirls as well.

Besides offering an escape in the form alcohol and the company of a teenage girl to massage your ego, they sell physical release, either limited or unlimited in "short times" and "all-nighters," and for those who feel the need for a relationship they will become your girlfriend for at an additional cost, but unlike your gun, they will leave when you run out of ammo. While pretending to be monogamous and faithful, they will also return to work or another boyfriend when you're not around.

CHAPTER 10

At the Holiday Bar I order a cold Ba Muoi Ba and when a cute bargirl hostess latches on to me, I buy her a Saigon tea and listen to her tell me how handsome I am while staring at her perky breasts strategically peeking out from her unbuttoned blouse and her creamy teenage thighs clearly visible all the way up to her panties, thanks to her short skirt and intentionally shifting legs. Occasionally I divert my attention to my fellow GIs, some of who are dressed in jungle fatigues and flak vests with grenades hanging in double rows like mammary on an old dog. Others in dress-up civilian clothes of linen trousers and custom shirts handmade by local Indian, Chinese or Vietnamese tailors for only a couple of dollars, and a few wearing Texas style cowboy outfits with Cuban-heeled boots, snap button shirts and tie-down holsters with bone-handled revolvers, privately owned weapons being tolerated by the military.

The bargirl hostesses are also in a variety of costumes, some in silk or cotton pajamas, others in Chinese Chung Sams, others in traditional Vietnamese Ao Dais, some in short tube skirts with low cut blouses and push-up bras, and still others in skin tight sausage slacks, the kind movie prostitutes wear, only due to their petite stature and youthful appearance they look more like kids dressed up in mommy's clothes rather than the hardcore sex workers they are.

On this my first visit to the Holiday Bar, a GI who had too much to drink suddenly disrupts the place by calling the Vietnamese people out in a loud boisterous voice, accusing them of being heathens because they believe in Buddha instead of Christ, even though many of them are Christians, and yelling they should kiss his ass because he's risking his life "to save their goddam fucking country from the commies." In doing so he refuses to pay for his drinks and when the momason insists he pay, he pulls out his weapon and challengers her to make him. When this happens the whole bar falls silent knowing that a drunk GI with a loaded gun is a dangerous situation, especially when he's conditioned to kill and may have to follow through to save face. As Snover said in the orientation, "This ain't the movies." After a few tense moments the momason gives him a way out, saying if he puts away the gun and pays for his drink she'll make sure he's happy, and he wisely does just that, but not before declaring if he was president, he'd pull every one of us out, "and let you gooks kill each other off," then throwing a few Ps on the bar and leaving.

Soon as he leaves the bar gets back to normal and all my blood-pumping adrenaline morphs into arousal and I start negotiating for a short time with the bargirl whose tiny little hand has done its job of helping to fuel my libido. When she asks for three hundred Ps, about a buck fifty, I counter with one hundred and predictably we end up at one fifty which is the going rate. She then leads me through a doorway adjacent to the bar, down a narrow hallway with a concrete floor and drain in the middle, into a room that's like a stall in a barn. Once inside, she takes off her clothes and lays down on a soiled sheet, atop a soiled mattress, atop a platform bed and leaves her body for me to work out my fantasies alone and not coming back to life until minutes later, then only to complain that I'm not finishing fast enough. When I finish, she steps into the hall, in full view, and squats down and pees on the concrete floor, letting it run down the drain along with other co-workers who are doing the same, one of them holding a bowl of rice up to her mouth and shoveling it in with chop sticks while she pees, the whole place reeking of urine. After getting into her clothes, we go back into the bar where she tells me that I'm now her boyfriend and I have to come back to see her again and only her, after which she goes off to find another handsome GI to work her magic on.

Later, when I tell Snover about the incident with the drunk GI, he tells me it's to be expected when you mix guns, alcohol, power, fear and sex, and that sometimes, there are actual shootings like in the saloons of the old west.

CHAPTER 11

Saigon, once known as *The Paris of the Orient,* is a city under siege from VC gorillas with shootings and bombings occurring every day against both military and civilian targets. From what I see versus what I read in the military newspaper *The Stars and Stripes* and the English additions of the *Saigon Daily News* and *the Saigon Post,* the governments of both the United States and South Vietnam are deliberately underreporting these incidents and casualties to maintain popular support for the war and keep the funding coming. This fraud is obvious not only to me, but also to many of my fellow GIs when every day we pass the Tan Son Nhut mortuary and see blood unceasingly flowing from an open sewer and the increasing number of shiny aluminum caskets stacked up on flatbed trucks waiting for shipment back home.

One thing the government cannot hide however, is the midday bombing of the My Canh Floating Restaurant that is permanently tied up in the Saigon River in the heart of downtown. The bombing makes headlines not only because it kills and injures more than 80 people, some of them from the American Embassy, but because it proves nothing in Saigon is safe from the VC. Further proof of this comes when the VC blow up the police director's office, killing and wounding 21 people, followed by another bomb in the main business district killing and wounding 20 more. Even more notable, is these deadly hit and run raids are not being carried out by a modern, well-equipped military like ours, but by bone thin men, woman and children who hide explosives inside a variety of everyday items from watermelons and vendor carts, to the wooden boxes carried by shoe shine boys, or strapped under the pajamas of little children who are then told to run into buildings and crowds, or tossed from motor scooters that also shoot at people as they drive by, or loaded into cars then driven into buildings. In many ways, Saigon is more a combat zone than the one in the jungles, mountains and rice paddies up and down the country. It's a different kind of combat, but the result's the same.

The strategy of most wars is to take control of enemy-held territory, but in Vietnam it is simply to kill more of the enemy than they kill of us, which makes sense to those in Washington who believe in statistics and believe our side will win because we have a bigger stick. In doing so, however, they ignore Vietnam's long history of expelling foreign domination, first the Chinese, then the French, then the

Japanese and again the French. To implement this strategy, Washington sends the Air Force's Strategic Air Command (SAC) and its huge 14 million dollar B-52s to carpet bomb the country and nobody could be happier about this than the bomb manufacturers. It's Goliath vs. David, the most powerful military in the world against the skinny, underfed, poorly equipped VC and North Vietnamese Army (NVA) in a country less than half the size of California. Only the strategists discount the fact that the VC and NVA will fight to the very last man and, like a metaphoric David, they have downed our multimillion dollar helicopter gunships by hitting the rotors with arrows fired from a crossbow.

CHAPTER 12

The Air Mail Terminal (AMT) at Tan Son Nhut is housed in a large corrugated metal building that looks a lot like an oversized aircraft hangar. Inside are makeshift bins and racks used for sorting incoming and outgoing mail. I'm assigned to floating shifts that sometimes begin early in the morning when a VN national who works for the AMT, picks me and my fellow workers up after breakfast at the Hung Dao and delivers us back eight or 10 hours later. On the same shift with me are Sgt. Robbie and fellow grunts Henry Snover, Ray Reynolds, "Poncho" Sanchez, Robert E. Lee "the general" White, Jacob "Alphabet" Yzakrzewski, Dennis Wong, aka "Charlie" because he's of Asian descent and looks like a VC, and a big, barrel-chested German national named Zoffa Bartl who joined the U.S. military so he could apply for citizenship in a shorter period of time than otherwise required.

It is Zoffa and I who become instant friends, perhaps because we are unalike in many ways but alike in others. He's bold, impulsive and restless, always huffing and puffing and dripping sweat to my more subdued and measured personality. But we share a mutual distrust of government and power, his driven by the history of his native country and mine by comparing current events and lifelong observations to history. We are also united by our ethnic sensitivities, me being Jewish and he unfairly carrying the burden of what the Nazis did to the Jews. This sensitivity revealing itself when, as an avid reader of the Saigon Daily News and the Saigon Post, he sometimes reacts to stories about VC atrocities with comments like, "Dis is the same madness like da Nazis," though once explaining to me the stain of the Third Reich through the post-war conditioning of German culture, "Vhile I don't condone vhat da Nazis did, vhen you study da economic situation in Germany at da time, da Jews who vere in da minority, and not really Germans, controlled all da money and just about everything else. Imagine if da Negros in America ran da country and everybody had to vork for dem."

Knowing Zoffa's a great guy, and we are all more than our perceptions and opinions, I do not take offense.

CHAPTER 13

S ince Zoffa and I have become such good friends, Sgt. Robbie sees us as a natural choice to work with Snover on sorties replacing two GIs who are rotating back to the States. The word "sortie" ironically comes from the French, meaning exit, and is an overused term in the military for the dispatching of anyone or anything on a mission. At the AMT, sorties involve the personal delivery of classified and/or time sensitive dispatches to remote camps up and down the country.

On our very first sortie as a team, the three of us are charged with carrying a classified communique to a Special Forces commander in Duc Co, a military camp just west of Pleiku in the Gia Lai province of the central highlands. Following protocol, we first sign out weapons and gear from the AMT armory, that includes an M16 rifle and Colt 45 automatic for each of us along with extra clips, flack vests and helmets, then head over to Tan Son Nhut Base Operations for a flight up to Duc Co. When we get to Operations, however, Snover gets into an argument with the Air Force load master who cautioned us to be careful because of a recent VC attack on Highway 19 not far from our LZ (landing zone). But Snover, who Zoffa and I suspect was just trying to impress us FNGs, flippantly responds to him with, "No shit, that's why we get Combat pay." This response offends the load master who then decides not to let us board the Air Force plane using the excuse we're not properly manifested and not in full uniform, which is true since the sortie was short noticed, and the mixing of uniforms with civilian attire is tolerated at the AMT. Snover then tries bullying the guy by telling him we're carrying timely classified documents. But the load master refuses to back down and we end up having to go out on the flight line and search for a plane or helicopter heading up to Duc Co, and end up running after an Army Caribou going only as far as Pleiku, hopping on the tailgate while it's still taxiing, with Snover declaring, "we're never going to use Air Force transportation again."

After landing at Pleiku Airbase, we catch a Huey over to Duc Co, deliver the dispatch, then hang around talking to the GIs stationed there while waiting for a ride back to Tan Son Nhut. It's my first time meeting combat GIs and I listen with interest as they tell us how they're bored shitless 90 percent of the time, spending the majority it securing the camp, and scared shitless the other 10 percent when out on so called search and destroy missions.

"We're supposed to be searching for Charlie, but we're really decoys so Charlie can find us and when he does, we call in for air support that may or may not come. It's a fucked up strategy."

They also tell us that sometimes these missions are solely for the American Press so they can take film back and show it on TV, the proof of this being the photo journalists ask for volunteers who haven't been on TV before so the viewers don't see the same faces.

"This war's a fucking joke," they say, "we're risking our lives for people who don't give a shit. All the ARVN want to do is go home. They even sleep on fucking guard duty for Christ sakes. As far as they're concerned, it's not their war, it's ours."

We also her stories about *fragging*, which is the killing a superior officer by tossing a fragmentation grenade at him, or rolling one under his tent, and blaming it on the VC, justifying such action as necessary to save lives put in jeopardy by incompetent leadership.

When we get back to Tan Son Nhut, we have the rest of the day off plus the following day this being a perk in exchange for the extra risk sorties entail, and to me, well worth it to escape having to spend hours tossing around heavy mail sacks in the heat and humidity.

After celebrating our first sortie together as a team with a couple of cold beers at the Hung Dao's roof garden, I decide to visit Thuy at the Playboy bar and invite Zoffa and Snover to go with me, but Snover says he's got other plans, and Zoffa says he's got to write a letter to his wife and three year old daughter, though he confesses to me in private it's really because as a father and married man he doesn't want to be around the sexual temptation.

CHAPTER 14

When I get to the Playboy, Thuy's nowhere to be found and I consider hooking up with one of the other bargirls, but then think better of it because I'm really attracted to Thuy and don't want to ruin my chances of getting her into bed. So I head over to the Good Time Bar and go short time with one of the attractive bargirls there, who thankfully turns out to be into it more than the first bargirl I had sex with, and wants me to have a good experience.

The following day at work, Zoffa asks me to describe what goes on at the bars so he can share the experience vicariously without guilt. But not wanting him to get all worked up, I temper the actual sex episodes and tell him mostly about Thuy, how we haven't had sex yet and how she claims to be a cherry girl, meaning some level of a virgin, and wants me to give her money so we can get an apartment together. And this is just enough for him to feel like he's not completely missing out.

CHAPTER 15

O nly weeks into my tour and I'm feeling at home in Saigon, mostly because the people and the city have become familiar sights to me and I've amassed enough phrases in Vietnamese when mixed with English and hand gestures, I can communicate on a pragmatic level. In addition, I've settled into a routine which, when I'm not working, usually includes a stop at the *Pole Nord*, a popular French ice cream and pastry shop on Le Loi Street in the central shopping district. True to its name, it has the best air conditioning in the city and is a spotlessly clean place, frequented by upper-class Vietnamese, Chinese and French who can be seen sitting at tables eating ice cream or sipping demitasses while consuming one of the Pole Nord's superb miniature pastries like fruit tarts, custard-filled Napoleons and flaky butter croissants. A place where I can linger and stare at the fashionably dressed, snobbish daughters of the wealthy while they stare back at me with contemptuous looks that tell me, despite my civilian clothes, they know I'm a low-life GI foreigner and that it's only their third world economy that puts me in an economic class where I can sit anywhere near them.

My favorite thing to eat at the Pole Nord is a bowl of their delicious French vanilla ice cream that comes with a triangular shaped cookie-like wafer, the cold ice cream tasting heavenly and the sweet wafer adding just the right amount of crunch. After enjoying the ice cream I usually explore the city on foot and end the day with dinner in one of the many interesting restaurants; more about them later.

Once settled into this routine, I decide it's the right time to contact Mark Breslin, a high ranking government official with the US Embassy in Saigon and friend and client of my aunt Pauline who lives in New York City and is his literary agent. When she learned I was going to Vietnam she insisted I look him up and say hello for her. With this in mind I head over to The Caravelle Hotel on Lam-Son Square, the premiere hotel in Saigon, knowing they have a telephone, and ask them to place a call for me to the Embassy. Even with their prestige, it takes them nearly half an hour just to get through to an operator because, with the increased US presence, the old switching equipment is overtaxed and you have to continuously dial the number for either "Tiger" or "Lion," the code names for the US-run switchboards, in hopes of breaking through between busy signals. The system is so bad it's often faster to take a taxi to the place being called, even with Saigon's grid-locked traffic.

When the hotel finally reaches the Embassy, I ask the Marine guard for Mark Breslin and he tells me that it's Saturday and all offices are closed.

"Can you call him at home and tell him Ben Kovner just got in from Washington and it's important that I speak with him." I say, deliberately trying to sound like someone important on official business.

"Yes sir!" the Marine guard says back, then comes on a few minutes later and tells me he can't reach him but gives me his address suggesting I go by his home, leaving me aghast at the lack of security.

Before heading to the house I go back to the Hua Lu to shower and change, something you can never do enough of in hot humid Saigon. There are two faucets in the hotel shower but only one temperature—cold. And I hate cold showers no matter how hot it is outside. In addition, there's a sign over the faucets that reads "Water Not Potable" in four languages—English, Vietnamese, Chinese and French—as a warning not to ingest any of the water because it is unpurified and unfiltered with dirt and hair coming right out of the shower head. To me, the shower alone justifies the hazardous duty/combat pay we receive.

Back downstairs I stop at the Paris Tailor Shop across from the hotel to change some US dollars into Ps. The shop's owner, Mai, is one of the nicest people I've ever met anywhere. Thirty-four years old and always elegantly dressed in a white silk Ao Dai with her hair twisted into a bun on top of her head. A pretty mother of three, she speaks enough

English to communicate effectively and is a curious person who has lots of questions about life in America. We have a deal, in return for my answering her questions, she tutors me in the Vietnamese language, customs and culture. In contrast to Mai's outgoing personality, her husband, who sometimes helps out in the shop, is a shy quiet man who used to be a captain in the South Vietnamese army, but got wounded and was fortunate enough to get an administrative job with the Saigon government.

Mai runs her shop much like the immigrant shopkeepers of early twentieth century America, warm and friendly, but always with an eye on business, and what she sells is laundry service, custom tailoring and money changing. Most of the actual tailoring work is done by her Chinese employee Mr. Ton who, along with his teenage daughter, sits behind a small counter off to one side of the entrance while Mai's counter, a glass showcase stuffed full of fabrics, directly faces the entry so she's the first person you see when you go in, along with her youngest child, an infant, who's usually crawling on the floor being watched over by Mai's 13-year-old daughter and 11-year-old son.

"Hello Kovner" she greets me, unused to the Western custom of putting the given name first and the family name last, it being the opposite in Vietnam.

"Chao Ba manh gioi," I say in return, phonetically using the greeting she taught me on my first visit meaning "Hello, how are you?"

"Manh gioi cam on, you speak Vietnamese ver-ly good, you come for lesson today?"

"No, I can't, I'm going to meet a friend."

"Ahhh, girlfriend?" she says, smiling.

"No, American friend, later I go see girlfriend."

"You like Vietnamese girl?"

"Very much, Vietnamese girl dep hoa," meaning pretty, another word she taught me.

"Maybe you marry Vietnamese girl?" she says, laughing.

I then lean forward and whisper "Change money" and discretely press a small roll of dollars into her hand even though no outsiders are in the shop, all this secrecy being necessary because for a Vietnamese, changing money, even the mere possession of foreign currency, is a serious offense punishable by many years in prison; although the law is rarely enforced and the police are easily bought off, but there's no need to be careless. Mai then disappears into the backroom and returns with a tightly rolled wad of Ps that she discretely presses into my hand. Knowing Mai there's no need for me to verify the count, she's as honest as they come.

As I turn to leave, a deafening explosion rattles the building and stops me in my tracks. At first I think it's a VC bomb, but when I look outside golf ball size drops of rain are falling with the intensity of a 6,000 rounds per minute M134 machine gun, and I realize the explosion was just a burst of monsoon thunder from a passing cloud. There's no umbrella or rain coat that can keep one from getting soaked in a monsoon, so I decide to wait out the usual twenty minutes until it passes, during which the streets flood, knee high in some spots, and the trash and surface dirt get washed away before the strong tropical sun returns and evaporates all traces of rain within minutes.

Mr. Ton, seeing my captivity as an opportunity, comes over and shows me some cloth samples.

"I make you number one pants, shirt, army suit, no cost too much," he says in a humble voice, and before I can respond his daughter, a plain-looking girl with a bad complexion and disarming smile, is measuring me with a tape and calling out numbers in Chinese to her father who is writing them down vertically in Hanzi characters, on a small pad.

"Thank you just the same," I tell him, "perhaps some other time," but he persists without being pushy and by the time I leave he has my order for two pairs of pants, two shirts and a silk smoking jacket with free monogram, smoking jackets like the ones worn by Playboy Magazine founder Hugh Hefner, somehow being all the rage among GIs in Saigon.

CHAPTER 16

When the taxi driver asks me "Di dau?" meaning "where to", I hand him a piece of paper with Mark Breslin's address. He stares at it for a few moments then nods his head and drives off, taking me out of the familiar downtown area for the first time and through unfamiliar sections of the city, which is both exciting and disconcerting because I'm unarmed and VC are everywhere.

Twenty minutes later he stops across the street from an impressive looking villa surrounded by a concrete wall topped with chards of broken glass. There are no house numbers anywhere, but he motions for me to show him the address again, and when I do he gets out and rings a bell next to the villa's metal entry door. A moment later a small window within the door opens, words are exchanged, and the driver returns indicating to me it's the right place. He then points to the meter and I hand him the fare, tipping him generously for his service. Not until he drives off does it occur to me that I should have had him wait to make sure Mark was home, and I'm wondering how I will find a taxi this far out to get back to the city center.

Then VN woman on the other side of the door sees me approaching and lets me in without question, presumably because I'm Occidental, then using the now familiar VN bye bye gesture, signals me to follow her through a small tropical garden in front of the two house compound, with a porte-cochere, where an American car is parked.

A large dog comes rushing at me barking menacingly as the woman leads me through a sliding glass door into a room with a terrazzo floor and black lacquer furniture. On one side of the room are shelves of books, a record player, a tape recorder and a large Oriental tapestry hanging on the wall behind a well-stocked bar. She then gestures for me to sit on the sofa and disappears upstairs, and minutes later a man who looks like "Papa" Hemingway comes down the steps.

"Are you Mark?" I ask him.

He nods.

"I'm Ben Kovner, Pauline Silverman's nephew. She told me to look you up and say hello."

Just hearing her name, his eyes light up and he pumps my hand excitedly, saying how amazing my aunt is and praising her as both a friend and literary agent.

"Can I get you a drink?" he asks, and not waiting for an answer says, "I'm having Martinis, I'll make us a pitcher."

He then scoots behind the bar and hurriedly fills a pitcher with ice followed by gin poured from a half gallon bottle.

"Tell me about your aunt. How is she? I owe her a long overdue letter."

"She's busy as always."

"Will she ever retire? For my sake, I hope not."

"Never. She believes everybody's got a book in them and it's her job to get it published."

"What brings you to Saigon? Wait, before you answer I'll get the cook to fix us some lunch. Annie! Annie! Where the hell is she?" he yells.

Another VN woman comes in dressed in a white uniform and plastic sandals.

"Annie, you fix lunch, salad, lobster, prawns understand?" She nods, then leaves the room and Mark says, "It's hard to find a cook you can trust and who speaks English, especially now with all the build-up." He then hands me a cold Martini. "I hope you like it. I consider myself a connoisseur."

"It's really good," I say after taking a sip.

"How long are you going to be in Saigon?" he asks.

"A year," I tell him.

"Ah, so you're military!"

"How did you know?"

"Non-military assignments are usually longer. Are you married?"

"No."

"Then you'll love Saigon. The Vietnamese woman are beautiful."

"How about you?"

"I'm married, but the State Department moved all dependent families out of Vietnam due to the war escalating. My wife and kids are in Singapore and I only get to see them one week-end a month. So, like you I'm now a bachelor and there's always somebody—a Congressman, or general or government official—coming here on a bull shit fact-finding junket so we entertain a lot. I'll see that you get on the invitation list."

He then says, "Where's our lunch?" and calls out for Annie who comes shuffling in with a tray of lobster and prawns laid out on a bed of lettuce, enough to feed half a dozen people, and sets it down on the coffee table in front of us.

"You forgot the forks," Mark tells her and she shuffles off again.

"What kind of books do you write?" I ask him.

"I was a war correspondent before joining the State Department and wrote a book about my experiences. Your aunt was the miracle worker who got it published."

After a few hours of conversation, a second pitcher of Martinis, and my fill of prawns and lobster, Mark has his houseboy get me a taxi. My head's buzzing from the alcohol and feeding my libido, so I tell the driver to take me to The Playboy where I'm hoping to see Thuy.

CHAPTER 17

S oon as I come through the door of The Playboy, Thuy comes rushing to my side. "Troi oui, why you no come see me long time?" She says, Troi oui being a VN expression for exasperation.

"I have to work," I tell her.

"Troi oui, work too much. I want you meet sister."

She then takes me over to a settee and introduces me to her sister whose name is Bich. She appears to be a few years older than Thuy and several pounds heavier, and has an eye patch covering one eye that makes her stand out in a room full of flawless younger girls.

When we shake hands, Bich tilts her head slightly to get a better look at me with her good eye, then says, "Thuy say me you number one GI, you live house withs Thuy soon."

"Maybe soon."

"You buy one Saigon Tea for me and for Bich?" Thuy asks.

"Yes, yes of course."

She then signals the barboy to bring two Saigon Teas and I signal nothing for me because I've already had too much to drink.

"Bich no work Playboy," Thuy says. "Bich work number one bar."

"What bar?" I ask, surprised, given her appearance.

"TriMe Bar, Tran Hung Dao Street."

"I've never go there." I say.

"Troi oui, you no go TriMe Bar. You go TriMe, I cock-adau you. You butterfly same, same other GI," Thuy says, both of them laughing. And what she means is "I will cut off your head if you flit from girl to girl like other GIs do. "This being routine bargirl speak for girls trying to hang on to a steady customer boyfriend.

She then tell me her father is very sick.

"What wrong with Popason?" I ask.

"Him ver-ly sick, him die."

"Die?"

"You come house Thuy you see."

"No, no that's okay," I tell her, but the two of them pull me outside where they hail a taxi and minutes later I'm standing in front of their house, a small weathered hovel about the size of an American two-car garage and topped with a shiny metal roof of unrolled and flattened Coors beer cans. It's in a neighborhood of similar wooden shacks on a street littered with trash and garbage and a single hydrant half a block away that's the sole source of water for the entire neighborhood. Like similar hydrants in the city, it's trickling into an assembly line of recycled five gallon oil cans being positioned under the spigot, one at a time, by a queue of women in black pajamas and conical hats, all of them squatting on their haunches, patiently waiting for the cans to fill, then carrying them, one can suspended at each end of a long flexible pole that's hosted atop their shoulder, then carried home where it's emptied into a an earthen cistern set beside the front door. Poor as the neighborhood appears, it's decidedly working class, the metal roofs proof of this, with the real poor living openly on sidewalks and down alleys in cardboard boxes or discarded sections of concrete sewer pipe, subsisting on the castoff waste of others, and the real rich in villas similar to Mark Breslin's.

My appearance in the neighborhood triggers a natural curiosity and everyone stops what they're doing and stares at me as I go into Thuy and Bich's house, pushing aside the soiled cloth that serves as their front door and stooping under the header, which is low because Vietnamese tend to be shorter than Americans. It's dark inside except for a few burning candles, deliberately kept that way to moderate the heat. There are two open windows for cross ventilation, but both of them are draped to block the scorching rays of the sun. Several children come running up to me, all of them Thuy and Bich's younger brothers and sisters, and all of them excited to find an American visitor in their house. They immediately take my hand and lead me across the tiny room to a hammock that's hanging from beams in the ceiling and next to it, when my eyes adjust to the dimness, I see the tiny figure of a man lying in repose in a wooden box, his bearded face ashen, thin and hollow. Thuy proudly introduces him to me. "Him Popason Thuy," then, with tears streaming down her face, adds, "Him die today in morning." A minute later she's composed again and excitedly introduces me to her mother.

"This Momason Thuy," she says, turning her face toward the tiny wisp of a woman dressed in a white blouse with black pajama bottoms, her long greyish yellow hair rolled up into a bun on her head. She looks 80, but given Thuy and Bich's ages and the age of her other children, I guess she must be half that.

I nod and Momason smiles back at me with a mouth full of blackened teeth and red-stained gums that are considered a mark of beauty in lower class VN culture, but to my western eyes look rotten and difficult to observe. This again the result of chewing betel nut, a well-known carcinogen with psychoactive properties that is an obsession among the poor.

"Momason ver-ly happy you come house," Bich says. "Momason want you stay house, she bring you food."

"I'm not hungry," I plead.

"Momason ver-ly no happy you no eat house," Thuy says, sitting me down in the hammock and doing her best to explain when offered food, especially by the poor, a refusal to eat is considered an insult.

It's then that I notice the curious faces of neighborhood children who have pushed aside the curtains and are peering in through the windows staring jaw dropped at me sitting in the hammock next to Popason in his casket. When

Thuy spots them, she yells in rapid fire Vietnamese and they scatter like flies, laughing as they do.

Momason then reappears from behind a beaded curtain that separates the kitchen from the rest of the house, a bowl in each hand, and behind her several of the children with more bowls, and they set them down on a straw mat on the floor in front of me, each bowl filled with rice and topped with a thin slice of something that I guess is fish. Bich hands me a pair of crude wooden chopsticks and the whole family, fourteen in all, squat down on their haunches, bowls lifted to their chins, waiting for me to begin, before they do, then carrying and shoveling the food into their mouths while staring at me in wonder, in part because they've never seen anyone using chopsticks with their left hand, and in part because I'm an American and eating VN food in their house. Little Thuy is squatted directly in front of me still wearing her bargirl tube skirt, her thighs and underwear just the distraction I need to divert my attention from whatever it is I'm eating.

From my lessons with Mai at the Paris Tailor shop, I remember to leave a little food in the bowl so my hosts don't think I am still hungry and bring me more. Thuy then takes my bowl and disappears behind the beaded curtain while Bich, without asking, and ignoring my protests, unties my shoes and slips them from my feet, then swings my legs up and over so I am now reclining in the hammock.

When Thuy returns she's dressed in black pajamas and carrying a small folding fan that she spreads above my face and starts waving away. "Tonight you sleep house," she says. "Tomorrow take Popason to ground."

"No, no I can't. I have to go hotel tonight, work tomorrow," I say, though I'm not scheduled until late afternoon.

"Troi oui, Thuy ver-ly no happy you no sleep house tonight. Momason want too much you sleep house tonight."

I try to reason with her, but she's deaf to the word "no" and I find myself acquiescing to spend the night next to dead popason. Momason flashes her blackened teeth and red gums as she holds up to me the framed photograph of popason as a young man that was propped up beside the casket on a makeshift altar along with a few sticks of burning incense, some red flowers, candles and a small bowl of food. As she stares at the photo her eyes well up with tears until she turns back to me again and smiles.

Thuy then brings out a photo album to show me and flips through it, pointing to a picture of a toddler lying peacefully in a tiny casket, a deceased brother she tells me, and a sad sight to see, but to her and her family a cherished memory. Then another photo of yet another infant in a casket with Thuy saying, "Momason have too much babyson, die too young," followed by a question to me, "You have how much brother, sister?"

"Only one sister," I answer.

"Troi oui, why you have only one?" She then translates this information to Momason, whose face lights up in astonishment, then it's on to more photos of family members both living and dead.

When we're through with the album, Momason says something to Thuy who translates it back to me, "Momason say you can make picture same, same for popason?"

Meaning she wants me to take pictures of popason in his casket for the family album.

"Yes, of course, but my camera's back at the hotel," I say, hoping this will get me out of spending the night.

"Okay, in morning you go hotel get camera, take picture popason," she says.

"Fa-sure," I respond, recognizing I'm stuck there for the night.

Two of Thuy's younger siblings, about four or five years old, then come over and lovingly comb popason's hair and beard, while Thuy lets down a mosquito net over my hammock and, along with her other siblings and momason, sets out their beds on the tile floor, which consist of thin straw mats with mosquito netting suspended above them.

For me the night is endless, filled with rats scurrying across the beer can metal roof which amplifies the sound of their little feet, and more of them foraging on the floor in the shadows of the burning candles, inches from the sleeping family and popason's casket. Watching them triggers in my mind the scene in Eskine Caldwell's book *Tobacco Road*, where Jeter Lester recalls how he stored his father's body in the corn crib to await burial, and when he retrieved it, was horrified to see that rats had chewed on it, and fears this might be his fate someday.

When morning comes, one of Thuy's little brothers takes my hand and leads me to the home's toilet, a terra cotta tile set into the floor with the impression of a foot on each side of a center hole, and next to it an urn of water and a metal cup. He then demonstrates its use to me, squatting down, straddling the hole, urinating and defecating, then dipping the cup into the urn, and washing his bottom. Ceding the throne to me, he steps aside and watches to make sure I know how to use it, only by then, Thuy, Bich, momason and the rest of the family have lined up to wait their turn and I have to battle a lifetime of conditioning before nature can take its course.

For breakfast, the straw mat that serves as a table, is un-rolled upon the floor and I squat down alongside the family, their thighs comfortably resting against their calves, but before long my knees are killing me. Breakfast is a bowl of Pho, a noodle soup with pork, vegetables and burning hot chilies, the bowl tipped to the mouth so the broth can be slurped while chop sticks shovel in the solids.

"You same, same Vietnamese," Thuy laughs, watching me eat, the others laughing with her, me trying hard not to look at momason's blackened teeth or dead popason lying a few feet away, patiently waiting for his big day.

CHAPTER 18

Following breakfast, I take a taxi to the Hoa Lu and return half an hour later with my camera. By then there's a large crowd gathered outside Thuy's house along with Thuy and her extended family who are dressed in traditional VN funeral wear—white robes, white headbands and white hoods that make them look like Klansmen. Thuy runs through the crowd to greet me, excited to see the camera hanging from my neck, then pulls me by its strap to the side of a hearse that looks like a parade float set atop a truck chassis, garishly painted ornately in red and gold with carved dragons and festooned with flowers, candles, images of Buddha and a Christian cross signifying the religious pluralism common in VN culture that holds all religions are right and none are wrong.

Directed by Thuy, the photo session begins with several shots of her immediate family in front of the hearse followed by one with momason in the center flanked by her children in descending order according to age, along with the uncles and aunts with their kids kneeling down in front of them. After each staging Thuy calls out, "Okay Ben, you takes picture okay," and "Okay, Ben, you takes one more picture okay."

Popason is then carried out of the house, his casket open, the family gathered around him and Thuy calls out, "Okay Ben, you takes picture with family and popason okay."

Four skinny barefoot men in conical hats and black pajamas then place popason's casket on the hearse and I hear, "Okay Ben, you takes picture okay!"

The framed photo of popason from the alter in the house is placed next to his casket and the procession begins, with immediate family gathered behind the hearse, leaning slightly forward, hands out front like they're going to push it, and behind them the extended family, and behind them friends and neighbors, including me. The same men who carried popason from the house then pick up an assortment of musical instruments—cymbals, horns, winds and strings—and start clanging, twanging and banging away as the hearse's starter laboriously grinds until the engine comes to life with a belch of diesel exhaust, then starts off slowly down the street, the music drowning out the mournful sobbing coming from family behind it.

As the hearse drives by, people in the street turn to it, hats off, some with tears in their eyes that I sense comes less from the sadness of inevitable death, but more in recognition of the suffering that must be endured before its reward.

A few blocks later the hearse stops, the music stops, and Thuy, looking like a grand dragon in her white hood, runs to my side and says, "Okay Ben, you takes picture okay."

The hearse then continues on and stops a few blocks later so the younger kids can be lifted up to sit with po-pason for yet another photo opportunity, then continues on starting and stopping every few blocks where the family openly cries for a few moments, then openly laughs for a few moments, which I deduce, signifies both the sadness and joys of life and death.

CHAPTER 19

When we reach the cemetery there are more requests for photographs, one with the younger children alone, another with the older brothers and sisters alone, then one with the uncles and aunts alone, then one with the friends alone and then one with family and friends together.

The four pole bearer musicians then lower popason into a grave, pre-dug in a field of headstones engraved with photos of the deceased, something I had never seen before. When the ceremony's over, a VN man wearing horn-rimmed glasses and a white business suit approaches me and says, "I am uncle of Thuy. The father of Thuy was my brother. I speak English and French, because I have worked with your countrymen for many years. I am pleased to meet you."

We shake hands and he goes on, "Now I wish to tell you something about this burying ground you do not know. Many years ago an American just like you came to Saigon to help my country and he got sick and died. His family who lived in the United States say because he likes Vietnam so much he should be buried here. Come with me, I will show you."

He leads me across several grave sites, then stops and points to an inscription on a headstone.

"You see, here is his name Robert Hanson, born 1929, Fall River, Massachusetts, died 1955, Saigon, Vietnam." He then pulls a tobacco pipe from inside his jacket and lights up. After a few puffs he continues, "Now I will ask a favor of you as a friend of Thuy, and you will please do it for me. As you see I smoke a pipe, but it is a very poor pipe. Here in Vietnam you cannot get a good pipe. I know they have good pipes in America and at the Tan Son Nhut military store. You will please get a pipe for me and I will give you the money okay?"

"I will see what I can do," I tell him, and with this he calls overs several others who approach me with hands extended in friendship and start telling me how they are related to Thuy—an aunt, a cousin, a good friend of the family—with the first man translating what each of them wants me to get them from the BX—a carton of American cigarettes, chocolates, a can of hairspray—and, being cornered by them, all I can say is, "I'll see what I can do."

CHAPTER 20

O n the days I work the morning shift, we're picked up at the Hung Dao and transported in the back of a mail truck driven by a VN national who's an AMT employee affectionately named "Dinky," which is short for "Dinky Dao," VN slang for crazy, a name bestowed on him primarily due to his driving. After securing us inside a protective cage built on the back of the stake-bed truck, he drives like a mad man weaving through traffic on busy Tran Hung Do Blvd., narrowly avoiding collision at each turn, then full throttle up less crowded but still perilous Cong Le Boulevard, hand on the horn, swerving around traffic and tossing us side to side in the process. Even though we curse at him through the back window of the cab and pound on the roof with our fists, it does no good; he knows he can get away with it because other than his driving he's an extremely likeable character.

At the AMT our routine begins with loading and unloading heavy canvas mail sacks, tossing them on and off aluminum air freight pallets and in and out of steel Conex shipping containers and the stall-like sorting binds inside the AMT, all by hand, with some of the sacks weighing over 70 pounds, and doing this in near hundred degree heat and humidity. The processing cycle works like this: When we get a call that a mail plane from the States has landed at Tan Son Nhut, usually a chartered Pan American Clipper from San Francisco or a Flying Tiger or World Airways jet, four or five of us truck out to the flight line and wait for the pallets of mail to be off-loaded, then break each pallet down by tossing the individual sacks onto our truck for sorting at the AMT. Once at the AMT, the sacks are tossed into individual bins linked to specific locations within the Nam and from there tossed onto trucks and taken out to the ramp for flights to those locations. Outgoing mail is picked up from military and US government instillations within the Nam and brought to the AMT where the postage is hand canceled before being sorted and sacked according to the appropriate destination. If the mail is designated air, it is loaded onto pallets, netted down and taken out to the flight line. If it is designated to go by boat, which is usually the case for parcels, the sacks are loaded into steel Conex shipping containers, after which the doors are locked and sealed with temper-proof metal bands and Conex's weight and destination are stenciled in white paint on three sides, then fork lifted onto a big rig flat bed for delivery to Khanh Hoi in the Port of Saigon, where it's then loaded onto ships.

Another aspect of AMT operation takes place from midnight to four a.m. when the strict citywide curfew is in effect and the streets are deserted except for specifically authorized military and police. During this time any VN caught outside will be considered a hostile and shot, and any unauthorized GI will face strong punishment. Armed with a 45 caliber automatic handgun and M16 rifle, two of us go out in a panel truck driven by another VN AMT employee named Map, which is pronounced mop, and make the rounds of all the military post office sub-stations and letter drop boxes at US installations collecting mail for postage cancellation, sorting and sacking. It's my favorite duty because the normally congested city is a ghost town and we can drive down Tran Hung Dao Boulevard at 70 without having to stop for red lights or stop signs, justifying this speed as part of a defensive strategy against VC snipers. Sometimes Map will turn off the headlights to see how long he can drive straight in pitch blackness, saying it makes us less of a target, even though this makes us more nervous than the thought of snipers.

The third phase of AMT operations is the sorties which, for better or worse, are run by Snover who's the most senior GI at the AMT in terms of time in country. While he's outranked by Sgt. Robbie and others, he tends to use his seniority to bully anybody he can. Most of the guys just ignore him, attributing his bullying to a Napoleon complex because he's short in stature, but sadly, the VN workers who desperately need their jobs to feed their families, are easy targets. Besides Dinky, who's in his mid-twenties, there's an older gentleman called Popason who has white hair and a white goatee, and two thirty somethings, one called Peanut who at four foot ten is a hardworking dynamo, and Map, who's overweight and lazy and can usually be found "resting" on top of a mail sack in one of the bins whenever you need him. All of them nice guys who go out of their way not to take offense at Snover even when he's ordering them around using loud and abusive language.

With flexible hours, extra time off and an opportunity to get out of the hard work of slinging mail sacks, I have no problem working sorties, but initially Zoffa wanted nothing to do with them and for good reason too. As a husband and father, he felt his primary responsibility was to be there for his family without increasing the risk of being killed or disabled. I suspected too, with all the extra time off, he was concerned about the temptation for inexpensive, readably available sex, and it was only because of our bonding as friends that he finally acquiesced.

Nonetheless, sorties are not daily events and most of our time is spent tossing heavy mail sacks around for long hours at a time, especially with the steady increase in troop build-up that brings with it a corresponding increase of mail. It's a boring job with only an occasional incident to break the monotony. One such event occurs when a GI armed with a 45 automatic pistol on his hip and an M-3 Sten Grease Gun slung over his shoulder pulls his jeep into the AMT hanger to pick up mail for his unit. After he loads the mail into his jeep, he starts telling us how he's an avid gun collector and sending all the weapons he can get his hands on back home. In the process of showing us his latest pride and joy, the M-3 Grease Gun, it accidently discharges narrowly missing Poncho, Ray Reynolds and Alphabet and sending four rapid fire rounds into a bid full of mail sacks. Everybody's freaked out at having come so close to being killed and the GI who's freaked out at almost killing us, jumps into his Jeep and hightails it out of there. When things calm down and we check out the mail sacks, I can't help but wonder what the recipients back home will think when they get a letter from their son in Vietnam with bullet hole through it.

Another boredom breaker occurs one day while we're loading mail sacks onto a truck and a gigantic cockroach-like beetle the size of door knob, comes running out of one of the bins. Charlie Wong instinctively rushes over to crush it under the heal of his boot when old Popason starts yelling, "No, no, number one, number one!" then snatches up the beetle, snaps its wings back and takes a bite out of its thorax saying "number one eat" and puts the remainder of the beetle into to his shirt pocket for later. Most of the guys are so repulsed they want to beat up old Popason for being a sick mother fucker, but instead turn back to tossing the mail sacks with abandon, hoping the physical exertion will shake the image of what they just saw from their minds.

CHAPTER 21

O ne of the many advantages of being stationed at Tan Son Nhut is that when we're hungry we can open up a box of C rations, which are in abundant supply at the AMT or go to the base Dining Hall and eat for free even though being billeted in town, we are paid a separate ration allowance to cover the cost of eating "on the economy," meaning at one of Saigon's many restaurants, or at the BEQs with their affordable meal plans.

This perk being possible because during war time with lives at risk, the only rule is "there are no rules" and it helps too that Snover knows the Navy cook who's in charge of the Tan Son Nhut Dining Hall. In the military, even more than in civilian life, it's who you know that matters, especially when it comes to being generous with government supplies that have no accountability attached to them. For example, beer is frequently bartered "out the back door" for purloined military equipment and supplies and even though we're not supposed to drink on duty, it's overlooked because of our need to replenish the fluids we lose from doing hard labor in oppressive heat. Likewise, food stuffs, including whole turkeys and canned hams, are frequently bartered for a variety of things, including sex, with VN female employees who take the food home for their families.

CHAPTER 22

After work, Dinky drops us off at the Hung Dao so we can eat breakfast before going back to our rooms at the Hoa Lu to get some sleep. But sometimes we're just too wound up and a few of us, Zoffa excluded, skip breakfast and go next door to the Annex, which is what we call the brothel, located in an alley alongside the hotel where we can get a short time for only seventy cents, about half the price charged by bargirls and with no need to buy any Saigon teas.

The girls in the Annex are just as young and good looking, only the place stinks even worse than the bedroom stalls at the bars because the girls pee on the floors of the bedrooms where there are no drains and the place is infested with rats and roaches. But for less than a dollar, we can temporarily cure a bad case of yellow fever, which is what the desire for Oriental girls is called, and along with it, any tension from work.

CHAPTER 23

In the morning when the curfew ends and the sun rises, the streets of Saigon come to life with a palpable optimism that belies the tragedy of war. Perhaps it's because as diurnal creatures we're programed to equate a sunrise with a new beginning and it's fascinating to watch the people come out of the alleys where they retreat during curfew and begin their day's routine. Most all start by squatting with their asses cantilevered over the street curb to toilet, while searching for a scrap of paper, even a discarded chewing gum wrapper, with which to wipe themselves, and doing this next to the bone skinny dogs, diseased chickens, hogs and cats toileting and foraging in the nearby garbage heaps. The hogs are painted with pastel colors to identify ownership and will eat anything, and the cats well fed because of the abundance of rats on which to feed.

After toileting, the poor take their dongs, which are VN coins, some worth less than half a cent, and queue up at the ubiquitous street vendor carts to buy breakfast bowls of Pho for themselves and their children, who are little kids with younger sisters and brothers perched on their tiny hips, and naked toddlers crawling on the filthy ground beside them, their skin covered with sores and insect bites. I gasp when I see a mother lift her naked and crying infant son up above her head and take his tiny penis into her mouth, instantly calming him, something I've never seen before.

Following breakfast, the legion of black pajama-clad women with badly soiled conical straw hats and black teeth begin their day's work of squatting at the widely scattered, trickling hydrants to fill their five gallon oil cans with water, and the skinny leather-skinned men who are cyclo drivers, climb up onto their saddles to begin another long day of shuttling passengers around Saigon while proudly clanking the under seat brake levers to warn people to get out of their way, and those who are taxi drivers fold themselves into their tiny blue and yellow Renault CV4s and head out into the already grid-locked streets, like bees coming out of a hive, while the white mice Canh-sats try to untangle the jam-ups especially at the roundabouts where the cacophony of endlessly beeping horns competes with the distant thud of bombing and exploding mortar.

Within hours the optimism is gone and the new day is choking from the exhaust of diesels and worn out two and four-cycle engines in need of repair, along with the smoke from thousands of wood and charcoal hibachis belonging to the street dwellers and food vendors, and the methane gas escaping from the heaps of garbage with their human and animal waste decomposing under the oppressive humidity and sun, and with the knowledge the worse is yet to come.

CHAPTER 24

A sure sign that I'm becoming a Saigonese is when I pass Orientals in the street and can distinguish one from the other, whereas when I first arrived, they all looked the same. Vo Thanh Street where the Hoa Lu and the Paris Tailor Shop are located is now my neighborhood and Mai, the shop owner, is both a neighbor and friend. When I stop in she always sends her daughter out for two steaming bowls of Pho so we can sit and slurp-in the slippery noodles, hot broth, crunchy vegetables and spicy pork while going over phrases in Vietnamese, with me carefully writing them down phonetically in a little pocket-sized notebook to practice later, and this while GIs are stopping in to drop off and pick up laundry, order custom clothes or exchange dollars for piasters.

On one such visit a big black Mercedes pulls up outside and toots the horn, and when the driver opens the back door, an elegant Vietnamese woman gets out and enters the shop. She turns out to be Mai's very rich sister, Madam Binh, whose husband is in the import export business and together they own several large villas, with a staff of servants, and three expensive cars. My meeting her later plays an important part in my journey.

CHAPTER 25

Two blocks from the hotel is a tiny shop with a sign reading "Hot Toc." which means "haircut" in VN. Inside, is a single chair facing a small mirror the size of an average picture frame. On a table next to the chair, is a single pair of mechanical clippers, the kind with handles you squeeze together, along with a comb, scissor, straight razor, can of powder and bottle of lotion. The barber, a guy with latigo skin and wisps of white hair growing sporadically all over his head, notices me looking in and motions for me to enter by pantomiming a scissor using his two fingers coupled with the familiar VN bye bye gesture.

Most every GI gets his hair cut at the barbershop on Tan Son Nhut, and for good reasons too, because you never know if a VN barber is a VC or VC sympathizer, or how sanitary his equipment is, or even his abilities, but the barber seems so happy to see me I decide to give him a chance. Once in the chair he tucks a soiled rag of a bib into the front of my shirt then, using the mechanical clippers, trims my neck, and the sides of my head, taking his time, moving slowly like a craftsman who has all the time in the world, cutting the hair methodically then following this up with a scissors and comb.

Part way through the haircut he stops and goes over to a clay pot sitting on a table in the corner, holds a lighted match over the top and inhales through a hollow reed sticking out of its side, exhaling the smoke through his nose and mouth. The substance he's smoking being opium, which many Vietnamese, especially the poor, have grown up using since childhood, and because of this they can still function under its influence while taking the edge off the day's struggles, including physical pain, which with limited access to doctors and medication, they would otherwise have to endure.

A few puffs more and he's back to cutting my hair and I think nothing of it until he moves on to a shave and is drawing a straight razor across my throat. All I can do is make myself a manikin, daring not to move or even breathe, and thinking what if he's a V.C. or accidently slips? On top of this he's doing so without benefit of shaving cream, only a thin coating of bar soap, leaving my face feeling so raw I suspect blood is oozing out of it. Then, when he finishes, he rubs my face with a bar of camphor, causing me to lift out of the chair, and follows this up like the tonsorial practitioners of old, by cutting the hairs in my nose and cleaning the wax out of my ears using a thin bamboo rod tipped with bristles.

When he inserts the rod deep into my ear canal and rotates it, which produces a strange tickling sensation, I'm thinking how one VC-motivated shove could send it deep into my brain and kill me on the spot. The total cost for this adventure being thirty five Ps, about nineteen cents American with cheaper haircuts being available from barbers out on the street who carry their supplies on bicycles and hang mirrors up on the walls throughout the city.

CHAPTER 26

Mai tells me her rich sister Madam Binh, has asked her, to ask me for a favor.

"You can get for her from BX store, machine for making cakes? I no know how you call it, buts Binh write it on paper." She then hands me a piece of paper with the word "Mixmaster" on it. "If you can get, Binh pay you much money and be ver-ly thanks," Mai tells me.

"I will do my best," I say, "but only because you and I are friends, and I will not take any money." My reason for this being I want Madam Binh to appreciate her hard working sister and by making it a gift I hope it will stem other requests and not get out of hand like what happened at the cemetery with Thuy's family.

But being the humble sweet woman Mai is, she feels a need to explain. "No, Binh pay you, she have ver-ly much money, buts no can buy cake machine in Vietnam."

Mai then goes on to tell me how her sister and brother-in-law have been preparing for a worse case outcome for the war. "Binh and husband go Nippon and Aleman, buy ver-ly much pearls, diamonds, gold, buts now South Vietnam government makes too hard and no can do."

And while she's saying this I can tell she has genuine sympathy and concern for her super rich sister, even though she herself has to work hard every waking hour of the day just to feed her family and I find it particularly rewarding to be around someone who's so appreciative of their own situation they are capable of real compassion for others who are far better off.

CHAPTER 27

In preparation for his rotation, which is still months away, Snover tells me he wants to sell his motorbike so I ask him to bring it around so I can see it and it turns out to be a decrepit-looking red Sachs moped with two flat tires, a missing chain, broken light and broken seat.

"It needs a little work," Snover says, "but I'll give you a deal. You can have it for only twenty-five dollars."

"But it's worthless," I say. "It'll cost me a fortune just to get it running."

"No way," he says. "The gooks here do that kind of work for next to nothing. Tell you what, I'll let you have it for only fifteen dollars. Now where can you get a good German motorbike for only fifteen dollars?"

Knowing nothing about how much it will cost to get repaired, Snover and I wheel it across the street to the Paris

Tailor Shop so I can ask Mai and she tells me she knows someone who can fix it for "No too much money," then leads us a few blocks away to a street corner, where out in the open, a man and young boy are working on a number of bicycles and motorbikes from a tool box chained to a wall of the adjacent building.

After the man examines the Sachs, he talks to Mai and she translates to me, "Him say he fix same, same new, withs new this (pointing to the cables), and new this (pointing to the seat), and new this (pointing to the head light), and new this (pointing to the chain), and new this (pointing to the wheel), and new this (pointing to the tires), and paint same, same new for four thousand five hundred Ps," which is about twenty-six US dollars.

"He do good work?" I ask her.

"He ver-ly good work."

I then turn to Snover and hand him the fifteen dollars. Only after hearing how little money it will cost to make it like new, he wants more. But when I refuse he takes the fifteen dollars and walks off happy to be done with it. Mai then asks me to give the man a few thousand Ps so he can buy the needed parts, saying he's too poor to lay out the money himself.

CHAPTER 28

When I get back to the Hoa Lu I go straight to Zoffa's room, all excited to tell him about the motorbike, and find him sitting on the bed reading his favorite magazine from Germany called "Der Spiegel" that his wife sends to him.

"Guess what, Zoff. I just bought a German Sachs motorbike."

"Vhy, vhat for? Vhere can you go?"

"What do you mean, Saigon's the old Paris of the Orient and there's lots to see. There are parks, a zoo, pagodas, the palace, not to mention the Buddhist Institute, which is world famous though I've never heard of it, and Cholon, the Chinese section, and just riding around Nguyen Hue Boulevard, the street of flowers, and Tu Do Street, which means Freedom Street in Vietnamese in case you're interested. You got to get out of this room and explore the city with me."

"But I'm married."

"Who said anything about girls?"

"But there's a var going on and my family vants me to come home in von piece."

"Zoff, the war's in this hotel as much as it is outside or in the boonies. Every day the VC are blowing up places like this and shooting people in the streets. You can't escape it, so why not get out and enjoy yourself?"

After thinking for a minute he jumps up, puffs out his chest and says, "You're right, you're vone hundred percent right."

"And we don't have to wait for Sachs either. Let's go out right now and explore the city together."

With that we go down the stairs and head toward the huge central market, which is in the heart of the city, but on the way the sun's too hot for Zoffa's German blood so he stops in a shop and buys a VN-made Panama hat for protection. That hat turns out to do more for his psyche than it does for the heat, becoming a symbol of his emergence into Saigonese life as demonstrated by his stepping out lively and tipping it to almost everybody we pass along the way.

As we discover the city together, curious and interesting things catch our eyes like a sign in English across a store front that says, "Televisions Repaired" when there are no television sets or broadcast stations in the Nam (they come later). And a Cadillac car dealer with only one old Caddy parked in the showroom looking like a museum piece, and an outdoor market place with rows and rows of vendors selling military contraband and black market goods including American cigarettes, American hair spray, US military underwear, unopened boxes of C rations, US military-issue helmets and flak vests, and jungle boots and ammunition cases, even live hand grenades still in their original boxes marked "Property of the U.S. Government," all of it right out in the open for everyone to see and anybody to buy. Even more astonishing, the paper used to wrap the merchandise is US government documents retrieved from the city dump, some of which are marked classified and confidential. In the same marketplace are handmade Vietnamese crafts such as wallets, belts, camera totes and golf bags made from local elephant hide, and water buffalo horn lamps, and tortoise shell combs, and ivory-carved Buddhas spread out on straw mats with vendors calling out "You buy? You buy?" as we pass and "You sell? You sell?" to every GI in uniform, meaning they want to buy more stolen military supplies.

From there we stop by the multistory Tax Building, the retail and office complex where the Pole Nord is located along with other stores that sell everything from clothes to phonograph records. I've been there many times, but to Zoffa it's all new and he's a wide-eyed kid ordering a big dish of ice cream, an espresso and pastry all at once.

When the sun begins to set, we stop for dinner at a popular Italian restaurant run by a Frenchman who serves real honest to goodness pizza and spaghetti. Zoffa starts off by ordering a bottle of Chianti for us to celebrate our first day of discovering the city together, and when we finish that, a second bottle to have with dinner, calling out a toast with each glass, including one to his new hat and my new Sachs motorbike.

Over dinner, aided by the effects of the wine, Zoffa starts asking me questions about the Annex and I fear from the level of detail he wants, his alcohol-liberated libido is gaining power over the constraints of his guilt. Not wanting to add fuel to the fire, I answer his questions as before by tempering them with things like, "Oh, it's okay, nothing special" and "The girls are okay, but nothing to write home about" and "The sex is okay, but not terrific" and "It stinks from pee and rat shit" and in-between this, try to change the subject. But my efforts to put out his sex flame are frustrated by our strikingly beautiful young waitress, who every time she comes over to the table to serve us, unintentionally stokes this fire. But by the time dinner is over, his guilt or loyalty returns and when we get back to the Hoa Lu, he tells me he going up to his room and write a letter to his wife.

CHAPTER 29

Riding in a cyclo is like riding on the hood of a car because you're sitting in a chair out front of the driver, exposed to everything coming at you while the driver sits behind and high above you, peddling away. But hands down, Cyclos are the best way to get around the congested city since they can travel on both the streets and sidewalks.

They are also pennies inexpensive, though not without their risks because you're completely vulnerable to all the cars, trucks, motor scooters, fumes, bicycles, pedestrians and snipers, not to mention pick pockets who can reach right over and snatch things off your person as you pass by. And since you can't see the driver, there's always a risk he might be a VC or VC sympathizer, though most are decent, hardworking men who take great pride in their work and greatly appreciate that you have chosen them for the important job of taking you where you have to go.

Any astute observer can tell the snapping the cyclo's brake lever by the driver is done as much as a warning to pedestrians to get out of his way as it is to say, "Look, this important person has chosen me to take them to their destination" and it's this sense of pride and the money that can be earned from fares and tips that make being a cyclo driver the number one ambition of poor street boys.

CHAPTER 30

When the cyclo driver drops me off at The Playboy Bar I go in and little Thuy comes running up to me dressed in a pink, western-style dress, her long black hair draped over one shoulder. She's all bubbly and excited to see me and not surprisingly the first words out of her mouth are, "Troi oui, why you no come see me long time?" Quickly followed by, "You buy me one Saigon tea?"

After the tea arrives she says, "I find number one house for Thuy, Ben."

"Where?" I ask.

"Hai Ba Trung Steet, no too far. Tonight, we go house, you give money for house."

"How much money?" I ask.

"Troi oui, you no think Thuy number one, you no want give money?"

"No, no, Thuy number one. I likes Thuy too much."

"You sau," meaning I lie

"I no sau," I say.

"You no sau, you give Thuy two thousand Ps for house."

For me, two thousand Ps is Monopoly money, less than 12 dollars and not worth arguing over, especially when it can lead to plenty of sex with her and when I hand her the money a huge smile crosses her face driven, no doubt, by the knowledge she has just defeated a member of greatest military force in the world. After stuffing the bills into her little girl bra, she then signals the barboy to deliver another Saigon Tea, knowing as the victor there's no longer a need to ask me if it's okay.

We then take our drinks and sit on one of the sofas where our trivial talk continues, punctuated by some light touching and where I can't help but notice her friend Dung has her hand inside a GI's pants and his is under her skirt, and Thuy's friend Noc is similarly engaged. All this stimulation is getting me impatient for some real sex with Thuy, but the problem is, now that I've given her the money for the house it's too late to move our relationship from boyfriend and girlfriend to bargirl and customer for a quick short time, a decision I regret. And when Thuy sees my wondering eye, she pokes me in the side and says, "Troi oui, you no can look other girl."

"I no look other girl. I just thinking," I say, trying to cover for myself.

"What you thinking? You want eat? Okay, Thuy gets you eat."

She then calls out to a shoeshine boy who's buffing a GI's boots under the bar. When he comes over she gives him a few Ps and he runs out, returning minutes later with a stack of metal containers, one on top of the other, secured by a U shaped clamp that doubles as a handle.

After separating the containers by removing a wing nut on the top, she sets them out on a table before us, then goes behind the bar for bowls and chopsticks. Knowing the food most likely came from a street vendor where it's unrefrigerated, exposed to the hot tropical sun and covered with flies, I tell her I'm not hungry, only she won't take no for an answer because in her world no one turns down food when it's offered. I then make the mistake of pointing to each of the containers and asking "What's this?"

"Troi oui, that number one cha ha noi," she says, which I believe is some part of a pig.

"And that?"

"That number one Nuoc Mam!" Nuoc Mam being the pungent sauce made from fermented fish, pungent being a euphuism for a smell no American can go within 20 yards of without gaging, though admittedly it doesn't taste bad.

While we're eating she tells me, "I no wants marry Vietnamese man. Vietnamese man number ten, no have too much money. I want American babyson. American babyson number one dep hoa."

Every GI in Saigon has heard this same thing from every bargirl. To bargirls, coming from poor families, GIs are seen as rich and powerful. After all, we've invaded their country with impunity, are larger in stature than most VN men and have lots of money. We also look like the people they've seen in American magazines and movies who live fantasy lives.

Twenty minutes before curfew which begins at 11 p.m., The Playboy Bar along with all the others, closes and people pour into the streets in droves like when a baseball game is over and the stadium lets out, everybody rushing to get where they're going to spend the rest of the night, because once they're there, they can't leave until the curfew ends in the morning. Some GIs and bargirls go to their own homes, others to nearby hotels for all-nighters, and others to apartments with girlfriends, which is what Thuy and I do, grabbing a taxi to the house she found for us on Ha Ba Trung Street.

When we get there, she proudly leads me up the staircase, then down a narrow hallway and through a curtained doorway into a room with a tile floor, double bed, chest of drawers and a table set with two black lacquered rice bowls and matching sets of chopsticks.

"Okay, you see, I no sau you, house number one," she says, beaming.

Having seen her family home I can understand how she views the room as an upgrade. It's clean, uncluttered and freshly painted, but it's not a house, not even an apartment and it has no privacy, only a beaded curtain for a door and a three quarter partition wall over which anyone coming down from the upstairs can see over and into the room. But like it or not, due to the curfew, we're there for the night so I set aside my disappointment by anticipating the upcoming sex with Thuy.

Only before I can steer things in that direction, she pulls me into the hallway and down a few doors to show me the ornately tiled squat-down toilet that she thinks is upscale, then across the hall to show me the room where her friend

Noc is living with her GI boyfriend, then up to the roof where her friend Dung is living with her GI boyfriend in an army tent with a mattress enclosed by mosquito netting, then finally back down to our room where I can tell from the tour, we really do have the best room in the house even though it lacks privacy.

Before she can think of anything else to show me, I take off my clothes and sit down on the bed, then watch as she steps out of her skirt and takes off her blouse. In bra and panties she looks even younger than she did when she was fully dressed.

"I no sleep GI before," she reminds me, then climbs into bed staring up at the ceiling, waiting for me to begin.

I start off by gently stroking her cheek, then her arm, then her breasts, letting my hand dip into her bra to tease her nipple where I can feel her heart beating rapidly, then down across her stomach under her panties coming to rest between her legs. But when I try to enter her with my finger she winces and is so small I'm not sure I can penetrate her any further. It's then that she slips out of her bra and panties and guides my hand back to where it was, and it's then that her friend Dung comes into the room.

"Troi oi Thuy and Ben fucky, fucky too much," Dung says, laughing.

I'm frustrated and annoyed by the interruption, but to Thuy, it is as if they just ran into each other while out shopping and they carry on a girly, girly conversation in VN until I finally blurt out, "Talk Dung later. I tired, I want sleep," and they both laugh at my obvious lie. Dung leaves but not before saying, "Ben want fucky, fucky withs Thuy."

The moment she's gone I pick up where we left off, but after another attempt to penetrate Thuy she's on the verge of tears.

"I sorry, I number ten girlfriend for Ben," she says.

"No, no. You number one girlfriend," I say, not willing to give up and wondering if she's really a virgin after all.

"I wants fucky, fucky withs Ben," she says, then climbs on top of me and carefully lowers herself down ever so slowly, winching as she does and stopping part way where she collapses into my arms crying. "Girlfriends Thuy sau me, it hurt beaucoup."

With tears rolling down her cheeks she gets back up, more determined to complete what she started, only now I sense it has less to do about sex or me then becoming like her girlfriends.

It's over 100 degrees in the room and sweat's pouring off of us as small gains are made and when I'm finally fully inside her she couldn't be happier. Excited and beaming proudly, she hops off and wants me to go with her up to the roof so she can tell Dung the good news, and when we get there Dung's on top of her boyfriend. She's not at all put off by the intrusion, but her boyfriend is clearly annoyed.

"Get the fuck out," he yells, and I try to get Thuy to leave but she's determined to tell Dung the good news and Dung wants to hear it, so they carry on a conversation in sing-song Vietnamese while Dung continues to grind away until Thuy and I go back downstairs and finish what we started.

CHAPTER 31

For the next two weeks I divide my time between working at the AMT and living with Thuy at the apartment. When she's working I explore Saigon on the Sachs, which turns out to be a great wind-in-the-face freedom machine, and a good looking one too, with its new fire engine red paint job, shiny new head lamp and cushiony grey seat, the kind of motorbike that has automatic transmission with one forward speed and a two-stroke engine cranked to life by rapidly turning its bicycle-like peddles. It's because of this feeling of freedom that I've become possessively in love with it, hell-bent on enjoying my time in Saigon despite the war and loving the ability to weave in and around Saigon's grid-locked traffic with the precision of a surgeon and not having to ride out to Tan Son Nhut with crazy Dinky any more, that in itself being a great benefit. The only downside being the Sach is too underpowered to carry a passenger the size of Zoffa, although the Vietnamese somehow manage to carry three or four people on one, and it's because of this, that Zoffa and I end up spending less time together.

After working the night shift, I drive directly to the house on Hai Ba Trung Street and get into bed with Thuy who's asleep after working her shift at The Playboy, yet happy to be awakened for some sex before we both fall asleep, waking up around eleven for breakfast or lunch and I never think about how many GIs she's been with the night before or will be when she goes back to work later in the day. After all, it's her job like mine is at the AMT.

The real problem comes after weeks of the same routine when the excitement has left our relationship, which is based 99 percent on sex and one percent on the same shallow conversation due to our different life experiences and limited command of each other's language. For her, our relationship is mostly, if not entirely, about money, while for me it's about fantasy sex with a beautiful girl, but it's in a city full of beautiful girls begging to have sex with me for what amounts to pennies, even at my low military pay. Exacerbating the problem is Thuy's increasing bargirl persona, which means, all she thinks about is money and whenever we're together it's, "You can buy this for me?" and "You can buy that for me?" and "Family of Thuy need this" and "Family of Thuy need that," and complaining because she suspects I'm seeing other girls, which has less to do with jealousy than the fear of losing income. Based on this, I decide at the end of the month when the rent is due on the Hai Ba Trung house, I will move back to the Hoa Lu and start seeing other girls, only I don't dare tell her this beforehand at the risk of a big fight and loss of whatever sex we have left.

CHAPTER 32

While I enjoy exploring the City on the Sach, I miss spending time with Zoffa and he with me, so I start leaving it at the Paris Tailor shop and we're back to walking around together and hanging out near the flower stalls on Nguyen Hue Street where Zoffa, being the German neatnik he is, is most comfortable because it's the cleanest, most manicured street in the entire city.

From there we peruse the blocks and blocks of sidewalk merchants and check out the latest black market goods and on to night club alley to see what new bars have opened up, then end the day dining at one of the many good restaurants like the Crazy Cow on Dinh-t-Hoang street, or his favorite, the Moulin Rouge on Tran-hung-Dao, or my favorite, the Mekong Floating Restaurant on the Saigon River. Even though the Mekong has been blown up twice by the

VC, we can sit in the shade of its corrugated fiberglass roof and enjoy the breeze blowing off the river, and watch the sampans and freighters, while discussing the news of the day over good food and ice cold beer.

Our discussions usually begin with Zoffa talking about recent stories he's read in the English editions of The Saigon Daily News and The Saigon Post.

"Did you read vat da newspapers are saying about us? Day are blaming us for everything vats vrong vit da country. Day say da GIs is spending too much money and driving up da prices and now da poor people can't afford to eat. And because ve are paying local laborers five times vat da Saigon government pays dem, da city only has 70 garbage collectors to clean for two millions of people and dats vhy da streets are filled with garbage."

"Just maybe, Zoff, it's because the Saigon government is corrupt and syphoning off money to their own bank accounts and won't implement price controls on essential things like rice, fish and gasoline."

"I read vhere students from da Buddhist Institute vas volunteering to clean up some garbage from da streets and dhey moved piles vhat vas dhere for seven and eight years and ve havn't been here dat long. Dhey are even blaming prostitution on us, but forget da French didn't call Saigon da Paris of the Orient for its climate."

"Not only that, Zoff, the government got their corrupt fingers in every brothel and bar in the city."

It should be noted, even though Zoffa was born and raised in Germany, he's a super American patriot and a passionate defender of the USA, which he believes is the greatest country on earth. Because of this, he gets offended and all worked up whenever he reads or hears any anti-American criticism. For example, if I try to argue the VN side of things by saying something like, "Well, Zoff, maybe what the newspapers mean is our being here has compounded an already bad situation," he'll just counter with, "Irresponsible journalism" and then go on defending America like a right wing hard liner, often ending his arguments with, "Just remember dhere's no place in da vorld better den America."

Another place we like to dine is the Capriccio restaurant, which satisfies our craving for an American hamburger or pizza, and when we're in the mood for seafood we head to a restaurant called Hai Cua, which is VN for "two crabs" and where every item on its extensive menu is made from crab. My favorite there being their crab meat corn soup and Zoffa's the crab-filled spring rolls.

After dinner we usually walk back to the hotel where Zoffa goes up to his room to read the newest edition of Der Spiegel magazine or write letters back to his wife, and I get on the Sachs for a quick wind in the face-freedom ride before curfew, sometimes stopping for a short time before heading back to the hotel for the night.

CHAPTER 33

At times when I'm out riding the Sach, I'll stop outside a bar like The Princess Bar on Tu Do Street and wait for a GI to come out and get into a cyclo or taxi, then follow him, knowing the driver will try to talk him into going to a brothel where the driver can get a commission and by doing so will learn the location of new brothels; the typical dialogue going something like this.

"You want girl?"

"No, take me to hotel."

"Number one girl, no too much money."

"No thanks."

"Number one girl, sucky fucky, ver-ly cheap."

"Not interested."

"You no like, you no pay."

"I said not interested."

"You see girl, you ver-ly happy, like too much."

"Don't you fucking understand, I said no"

"Number one Chinee girl, Vietnamee girl only one hundred Ps, ver-ly young you no like you no pay."

"Number one young girl sucky, fucky, I no like, I no pay. Okay, di di."

I know full well, if the drivers persist they will succeed, and by following them, I can compile a resource directory of home-based brothels where the girls are not hustlers, but the children of poor families helping to put food on the family table, and not being part of a commercial enterprise, they can afford to do so at half the going rate, a win, win situation for all; this information being useful in trading favors with other GIs when needed.

But such rides around the city are not without risk as the war continues to escalate and three times in as many weeks, I come face to face with death, reminding me why those of us stationed in Saigon draw hazardous duty combat pay. One of these close calls comes as I'm passing a bus stop and a VC bomb explodes, killing four people and wounding several others who were waiting for the bus. The blast knocks me off the Sach and onto the street, but aside from a few cuts and bruises, I'm unhurt. The real trauma from it comes when I hear the cries and screams of those torn apart by the explosion, and see the body parts and corpses laying in the street that moments ago were men, women and children.

Another occurs when a bomb goes off in a bar where literally minutes before I was enjoying a cold beer, and a third while I was enjoying a coffee at the Continental Palace

Hotel's outdoor cafe and two VC go by on a motorcycle spraying machine gun fire, killing and wounding people just a few yards from where I'm sitting. These incidents and other close calls make me wonder how much destiny and fate play in my survival. The most surprising revelation however, is how quickly the shock and fright moves on and things get back to what passes for normal. Something I attribute to the human need to adapt in order to survive, and how we do not function well in a constant state of fear. The VC bombing of the Mekong Floating restaurant is a prime example of this. After being blown-up and killing and injuring scores of American and Vietnamese, it was simply towed down river, rebuilt, then towed back to the same place, and everything returned to the way it was before as if nothing had happened.

CHAPTER 34

Besides death and injury, the culture of war threatens our humanity, as reported in the numerous newspaper accounts of daily confrontations.

One of these stories recounts the killing of a 12-year-old VN boy who skirted the sand bag barrier in front of a BEQ and grabbed the MP's transistor radio. The boy was subsequently chased down and shot to death by a white mice who justified the killing by declaring the boy to be a VC. Another recounts the killing of an angry, unarmed VN man who jumped the barricade in front of the Hung Dao and punched the MP with his fist. The much larger MP was completely unhurt and easily knocked the VN man to the ground where the white mice guard shot him to death, also justifying his actions by declaring the man to be a VC. In both these incidences, it was a VN killing one of his own for a petty offense, but they exemplify how the war has changed consciousness and cheapened life and desensitizing us to it through a process of polarization where we're the good guys and most everybody else is bad and deserving of destruction.

It is well known we become like those we associate with and this is the basis of military training in addition to religious and political indoctrination, as can be seen in the numerous reports of VN family members killing one another over political differences, one sympathizing with the North, the other the South, and of GIs shooting taxi drivers over fare disputes, and shooting street kids for stealing a wrist watch or hustlers for short changing them in a money exchange, and sex workers demanding more money for sex, and fragging fellow GIs over perceived incompetence or in fits of rage, and the killing of defenseless, innocent village civilians, including the elderly and infants, caught between the forceful demands of the VC/NVA and our scorched earth policy. When you train somebody to kill, they lose their connection with humanity and the one thing that scares me the most, is the unspeakable torture of human beings and animals. More than anything else, cruelty exposes an evil and depravity that's inside even those of us who wouldn't hurt a fly, and it's brought to the surface through indoctrination and polarization unless we guard against it.

At a brothel in Cholon, I witness four heavily armed, intoxicated GIs abusing the girls and committing rape rather than pay the few pennies they want for sex. And when I try to intervene, they threaten to kill me and won't let me leave for fear I will summon the MPs. Concerned for their safety and not wanting any trouble from the Canh Sats who they know will either extort them for money or arrest them for prostitution, the girls had no choice but to submit to what amounted to a brutal rape, one that had less to do with sex or money, than the intoxication of power without consequences, as evidenced in how the GIs passed them around by their ankles, lifting and lowering them while their heads hit the floor.

CHAPTER 35

When I return to the Hoa Lu after working the night shift, there's a message waiting from Mark Breslin asking me to meet him for lunch at the Eskimo Restaurant in Cholon. After catching a few hours' sleep, I shave, shower, dress in my civilian clothes and head out on the Sach.

"I've been meaning to contact you," he says to me, "but I've been in Singapore visiting the family," then proceeds to order for both of us, telling the Chinese waiter, "We'll have the roasted pigeon, beef in black bean sauce, thousand-year old eggs, boiled crab, steamed rice and two bottles of LaRue beer." The waiter jots this down in Hanzi and signals a Chinese boy to set the table with bowls and chopsticks, along with two tiny metal dishes of peanuts and the LaRue beer, while another boy using metal tongs offers us steaming hot wash cloths, so we can wash the dirt and sweat from our hands and faces.

After a gulp of the LaRue Mark continues, "Singapore's a rat race. It's getting harder and harder each time I visit. We're living different lives and my wife and kids are like strangers. Have you told your aunt we've connected?"

"No, but I've told my mother and I'm sure she told her," I say.

"You know, if it weren't for your aunt I'd never gotten published," he tells me, repeating what he previously said, then jumping to, "I'm having a party this Saturday and I'd like you to come. There'll be lots of beautiful women, great food and a band coming in from Hong Kong."

"Thanks Mark, I look forward to it, and appreciate you inviting me."

"Oh, and don't wear your uniform. There'll be some high ranking military and government people there. You'll be the only enlisted."

When I arrive at the villa dressed in my brand new pants and shirt expertly tailored by Son at the Paris Tailor shop, the place is already crowded, mostly with Occidental men and young Oriental women, but a few western girls too, the first I've seen since coming to the Nam. The dining room table's heaped high with caviar, lobster, lots of giant prawns and plates of roast beef, turkey and cheeses and in the over-sized den a bar with two bartenders and a four-piece band. When Mark spots me and comes through the crowd I can immediately tell by his flushed face he's had too many of his famous martinis.

"I'm glad you made it Ben, I want to introduce you to some people." He then leads me back through the crowd to a foursome of men and women.

"Everybody, I want you to meet my good friend Ben Kovner. Ben's aunt is my literary agent in New York and he's here in Saigon on assignment."

After a brief exchange of greetings, he leads me off for more introductions while pointing out different people along the way and telling me who they are and what they do.

"That guy over there in the white jacket's a full colonel and comes to Saigon every month for a day or two just so his entire pay is tax free combat pay, and his military record will reflect that he served in Vietnam. And that guy over there's a congressman on a junket, and that one over there's a reporter for the Miami Herald."

He then introduces me to a Jordanian girl named Nouf from Chicago who's supposed to be a singer and goes off to greet other guests. Nouf is drop dead gorgeous, with olive completion and dark hair and a graduate of the University of Michigan. She tells me she goes on these government junkets a few times a year, officially to entertain the troops but really as a companion to VIPs who in turn open up doors for her professionally in her career as a pharmaceutical sales executive. By the time the party winds down, we've hit it off so well she invites me to go back with her to her government-paid room at the Caravell and in one of the Embassy's chauffeur-driven sedans with a military escort because of the curfew.

CHAPTER 36

Orders come down that all AMT personnel are to move out of the Hoa Lu and into the Hung Dao, and Zoffa and I slip the Hung Dao's desk clerk a couple of hundred Ps each to assign us to rooms near each other on the same floor. By this time we've done dozens of sorties together along with Snover taking us to bases and camps up and down country south of the DMZ, each one more nerve racking than the last due to the escalating war.

An example of this occurs on a sortie to an Army camp near Ban Me Thuot, an area of mountainous jungle known to be infiltrated by the VC and NVA. After driving to base operations in "Ole Grey," the jeep I stole from the Navy during the second week of being the Nam, we catch a flight in an Army Caribou with its tailgate down, giving us a picture window view of the country's rich jungles and mountains, serpentine rivers and checker-board rice paddies dotted here and there by simple thatched roof villages, all of them peaceful sights at altitude belying the tragedy of war. Due to increased NVA and VC activity in the area, we're all on edge, especially Snover because he constantly aware by extending his tour he's pushing the envelope and extending his risk.

After the Caribou sets down on the LZ's PSP landing strip, I can't help but notice how much the escalating war has assaulted nature in the few months since we were last there. The once beautiful landscape, that took eons to create, has been bulldozed down to raw muddy earth and covered with tents, sand bags, trucks, planes, helicopters, mortar, fuel tanks etc. making it look like a massive storage yard rather than a once pristine forest.

And when the jeep pulls up to transport us to the camp, it's not even a standard military one like Ole Grey, but a brand new International Scout, more like a family car and something I've never seen before in the cities or the boonies. Moreover, the driver's a stoned out private who volunteers he recently fucked up and was demoted, but refuses to tell us the reason, then pulls out a bong son bomber, which he offers to share, but we refuse. And when Snover asks him about recent activity in the area all he says is, "Don't worry about the Indians (VC), the little people (ARVNs) are out there mopping things up as we speak." None of this give us much comfort and we're on edge, so when we hear something rustling around in the brush Snover overreacts by firing off a few rounds from his M16 not even knowing who or what it is, and a moment later a massive elephant steps out of the brush onto the road directly in front of us, stops for a few seconds, looks at us eye to eye, then disappears into the brush on the other side. Relieved it wasn't a VC and apparently unhurt, we're beside ourselves at having been so close to such a magnificent wild animal. It's the first time any of us has discharged a weapon on a sortie and a prime example of our increasing concern.

CHAPTER 37

When we get back to Saigon we're still so excited about seeing our first wild elephant we tell everyone at the Hung Dao bar and celebrate with a couple of beers. Afterwards, Zoffa and I continue to celebrate with dinner at the Guillaume Tell restaurant on Trinh-Minh-The Street, starting it off with a couple of ice cold bottles of LaRue beer, which is as good as ba muoi ba but comes in a much larger bottle, followed by escargot in garlic butter the escargot being the size of golf balls, followed by French onion soup, cubes of marinated beef, frogs legs, Coq Au Vin and for dessert, caramel custard topped off with glasses of Cognac.

On the walk back to the hotel we pass by one of the city's countless Steam Bath Massage parlors and Zoffa surprises me by saying, "I treat you to a massage."

"Are you sure?" I ask him.

"Vhat's wrong vit a massage?" he says

Once inside, a VN receptionist collects four hundred Ps from Zoffa and we're led into separate cubicles, each with its own massage table and partition walls for privacy, where a masseur hands me a towel and a plastic bag indicating I should get undressed and put my valuables into the bag. He then leads me to a large steam room with wooden benches and a shower against one wall. A minute later Zoffa enters and the room fills with steam as one of the masseurs watches us through a small window in the door.

When we've had enough steam, our respective masseurs lead us back to the cubicles. My masseur signals me to lay face up on the table and begins the massage by taking hold of my flaccid penis and commenting, "Okay, number one," then releases it immediately with a laugh, when I protest. He then massages my scalp and without warning snaps my head from one side to the other, cracking the bones in my neck and making me realize how close I came to being killed or paralyzed if he didn't know what he was doing or if he was a VC or VC sympathizer. Working his way down my shoulders, chest and arms, he then has me turn onto my stomach and starts slapping my back with cupped hands and kneading it painfully with his knuckles. He then prompts me to turn over again, and when I do he's gone, and in his place is a pretty VN girl who leans over and takes my penis into her mouth, then stands back and points to my wallet inside the plastic bag while opening and closing her hands three times to indicate I must pay thirty P's if I want her to continue. Deferring the decision to my penis, I hand her the thirty Ps.

On the walk back to the Hung Dao, Zoffa tells me how much he enjoyed the massage and doesn't mention anything about sex, even though he knows, that I know.

The next day after work when we're sitting at the Hung Dao bar enjoying a cold beer and running through stories in the daily newspapers, he slips the steam bath sex experience into the conversation in his own roundabout way. "Did you read da story ver dis Indian tailor gets sentenced to death for possessing twenty-five thousand dollars' vorth of checks drawn against foreign banks? First he tells da judge dat he finds da checks, den changes his story and says he collects checks for a hobby."

"Yes, they're going to execute him tomorrow at Execution Square."

"And da story about all da kids dat are drowning in da Saigon River."

"I know, they wade in to cool off, but don't know how to swim."

"And the one about a woman who got raped at a bus stop vile vaiting for da bus. Dat's hard to believe vhen dere are steam baths to relieve da sexual tension."

It's not only his way of confessing something he was struggling with, but now that it's out of the bag, he says, "I treat you to another steam bath."

CHAPTER 38

It's no secret among GIs that the steam baths are not selling massages, but oral sex, and for this reason they're known in GI speak as "steam and creams." But for Zoffa, the proper name along with the fact that the sex is only oral and not intercourse is enough for him to overcome his guilt, and after a few more visits he's so comfortable with this pretense he's able to rationalize the experience as just being a normal part of stress relief. But to me it is not a stretch to see where this will ultimately lead and I wonder how that will affect his life.

CHAPTER 39

One evening, while out for a ride on the Sach, I spot two officers coming out of the Brinks BOQ and follow them to what is undoubtedly the finest brothel in all of Saigon. Located in the Dakao section of the City, it's officially called *The Pleasure Palace*, but more commonly known as *LeRoy's* after its owner, an ex GI who took his discharge in VN, then got some investors together and leased a beautiful villa, where he installed gambling tables, craps, poker, roulette, a bar, a small restaurant and a cadre of the most beautiful well-dressed sex workers, even importing some of them from the Philippines and Thailand. By Saigon standards, his prices are high but being an American his clients, who are mostly wealthy businessmen, government officials and military officers, can trust him to be discrete.

CHAPTER 40

Nearly every week Mark Breslin and I try to get together for lunch either at the Eskimo in Cholon, which is his favorite, or mine, the Mekong Floating Restaurant, near his office at the American Embassy. At both restaurants there's always that tiny dish of peanuts on the table to satisfy your hunger until the food comes, alongside a tiny dish of salt that you have to pinch between your fingers to use because with the high humidity of Saigon it simply won't come out of a shaker bottle, and of course, the hot wash clothes to wipe the grim off your hands and face so there's no need for a wash basin.

During these lunches, Mark pretends we're close friends even though our relationship is based on his admiration for my aunt more than any interest in me. As a result, his conversations tend to be about him and his unsatisfactory marriage, or contempt for the corrupt South Vietnamese government, or his boredom for the unending parties he has to throw and attend for the many government and military officials who arrive and depart each week. Because of this one sided going-nowhere-sameness, I start making excuses why I can't meet with him and we end up seeing less and less of each other.

CHAPTER 41

O n a sortie to Quan Duc in II Corp, I meet a GI who tells me he made a vow to get through his entire tour without firing his weapon unless absolutely necessary to save his life. The reason is, he has no desire to kill anyone and believes the war is immoral and a sham, and that we as a country have no business being in the Nam. He also tells me he considered shooting himself in the foot or leg as others have done so he could be sent home, but was afraid of getting court martialed and thrown into the brig, then dishonorably discharged for deliberately making himself unfit for duty.

Having heard similar stories from others, it occurs to me there are three types of GIs serving in the Nam—those who blindly trust our government and unquestionably believe we are helping to free the South Vietnamese people and save the world from communism, those who don't trust anything the government says and those who don't care about anything but getting home in one piece and getting on with their lives.

For me, I ask myself, when I was born, how would my parents have felt knowing their little baby would grow up to kill the son or daughter of another couple just like them, who had the same hope and expectations for their child. I also look to history to see how future generations might judge us in the way we look back at past events and judge them, such as we have done with slavery and the Jim Crow South, and the Nuremberg Trials. And when I apply this thinking to our involvement in Vietnam, it's not inconceivable, that in the future, society might believe, as Albert Einstein once reflected, "Killing under the cloak of war is nothing but an act of murder." Or Mahatma Gandhi when he said, "What difference does it make to the dead, the orphans and the homeless, whether the mad destruction is wrought under the name of liberty, or democracy?" Or Ernest Hemingway when he reported on the Spanish Civil War, "Never think that war, no matter how necessary, nor how justified, is not a crime."

CHAPTER 42

Nearly every day the headlines of Saigon's leading newspapers deal with the escalating War in the City:

"WAVE OF V.C. ATTACK SAIGON"
"BOMB TOSSED IN CHOLON RESTAURANT"
"SEVENTEEN WOUNDED IN GIA DINH"

Unsettling as it is to live under the sword of Damocles, it drives me harder to look for opportunities to create a routine of normalcy that distracts from the war and makes it tolerable. For many GIs, especially those stationed in Saigon, this often centers on, drugs, drinking, gambling and sex, but these activities soon become more mind-numbing than distracting. For me, one such opportunity comes when a taxi driver overhears me telling Zoffa how I once tutored students from immigrant families, and says, "You can be teacher? Vietnam need teacher too much," then begs me to go with him right then, to see the director of an English language school, adding, "I take you no charge."

He then takes us to a school called "Hoi Viet My," meaning Vietnamese-American Association, whose mission is to teach English as a second language to Vietnamese, French, Chinese and Indian students at its multistory campus in an upscale section of downtown Saigon with a branch in the Cholon neighborhood. My meeting with the headmaster is short and direct, reflecting their desperation for teachers.

"What are your qualifications, Mr. Kovner?"

"I once tutored students of non-English speaking immigrants when I was in middle school."

"That's excellent. You can start tomorrow."

"But I have to work tomorrow and I don't know anything about your program."

"The following day will be fine. You will take over for Major Cushman who recently transferred back to the States. His two one-hour classes meet on the same day once each week. You will be paid three dollars per hour in Piasters by check drawn against the Bank of Tokyo. How about you, Mr. Bartl? We need more teachers"

"No tanks, I'm still working on English myself."

When we get back outside, the taxi driver has a broad grin on his face as though he already knows the outcome of the meeting and then takes us to our original destination where he refuses to accept any money for the ride. What began as a routine taxi ride ends up changing my life in ways yet to reveal themselves.

CHAPTER 43

On the day of my first class the headmaster hands me a file full of papers and says, "Here are the current enrollment sheets and grade records for both classes. Following orientation today, you will teach your first class, English level three. Simply review the vocabulary and be sure to keep attendance records up to date."

He then disappears into his office and I head to the orientation room along with four other newly recruited teachers, all of them Vietnamese nationals.

"This is a table," the orientation instructor says tapping at a picture of a table, "and this is a chair," pointing to a picture of a chair. Simply tell the students "table, chair." Never say this is a "ban," called table in English, or this is a "ghe," called chair in English. Speak English only at all times and never translate from the Vietnamese."

She then holds up a small blue booklet. "This is a student record book. On the first page you will find a picture of the student and his or her name and address, and on the following pages you will enter any comments you as teachers may have about the student, along with the final grade for each class. Never pass a student from one grade to the next if he or she does not come up to proficiency standards."

"What are the proficiency standards?" one of the would-be teachers asks.

"I will cover that later," she says, but never does. Instead, she continues on about record keeping, then takes us into the teacher's lounge and assigns each of us a mail box and locker, mine still labeled with Major Cushman's name.

When I walk into the classroom I feel no more prepared than I did before the orientation. All I see is a room full of men and women, from teenagers to middle age, some dressed in shorts, others in suits with ties, even a shaved head monk in a saffron robe, all of them standing as I enter and waiting for me to take charge. On impulse I bow my head to show respect and when they do not react, wonder whether bowing is only a custom in Japan.

As instructed, I begin by calling the roll. "Tah ran try ech-ooh," and when nobody reacts I read the name again, "Tah ran try ech-ooh." And when there is still no acknowledgement, I write the name on the blackboard.

An older gentleman stands up. "Tran Chee Sue," he says respectfully, then sits down.

When I read the next name, it meets with the same result and I have to write it on the blackboard before another student stands and carefully pronounces her name for me. At that point I realize most of the hour will be consumed by me trying to call the roll so I motion for one of the students to come up to the front of the room and hand him his first assignment, which is to call the role, and when he's finished I write my own name on the blackboard and start the lesson.

Pointing to a picture of a bicycle on a flip chart I ask, "What is this?" And when no one responds, I repeat the question, "What is this?"

A student raises his hand, then stands up. "It is a bicycle, Mr. Ben."

"Very good."

I then point to a picture of an airplane. "What is this?"

Another student raises his hand, "It is an airplane. Mr. Ben."

"That is correct." I say.

When the first hour's over, it's on to my second class and by the end of that class, I am exhausted, but feeling good at having contributed to the students' journey in a positive way as evidenced by the appreciation and respect they show me when they filed out of the room, smiling, nodding and shaking my hand.

CHAPTER 44

That evening, Zoffa and I celebrate my first day of teaching with a dinner at a new French restaurant, recently opened near the Saigon River called Maxim's, after the famous Maxim's of Paris, though it's doubtful there's any connection. And that decision sets in motion yet another serendipitous event that alters my life in a significant way, though it doesn't come until we're heading back to the Hung Dao, and with the long ranges changes coming much later.

The evening begins with a leisurely walk down Ben Bach Dang Street on the way to the restaurant while passing rows of sampans tied up next to the towering black hulls of cargo ships being unloaded by skinny little men in ragged shorts and filthy bandanas scurrying down foot wide wooden gang planks carrying 50 pound sacks of rice and five gallon cans of kerosene. On the same wharf are their homes where they live with their families in discarded concrete pipes, wooden shipping crates and cardboard boxes, where their wives cook dinner on little charcoal-fired hibachi stoves and their diaper-less babies crawl in the heaps of garbage and ride on the tiny hips of their barely older sisters and brothers, and their mangy dogs forage and toilet next to their fellow dirt-poor food vendors selling skewered chunks of pineapple and giant prawns wrapped around thin sticks of sugar cane grilling atop smoking hibachis, and origami cubes of banana leaf stuffed with whatever available animal flesh they can get.

As we pass by, Zoffa greets them all by tipping his Panama hat and calling out, "Bonjour, bonjour," getting in character for our French meal to come, and they smile back with their black teeth and red gums, just happy to be acknowledged, followed by a few to be expected, calls of "sucky, fucky," which speak more to our culture than theirs.

When we get to Maxim's, the maitre'd seats us at a "table pour deux" next to a fountain with a mermaid riding on the arched back of a dolphin that has water pouring from its mouth. For Saigon, it's an elegant dining room featuring a faux wrought iron balcony, terrazzo floor, crystal chandeliers and Vietnamese waiters dressed in formal tuxedos who speak to us only in French.

We begin our celebratory meal with white wine and a starter of escargot in garlic butter and parsley, then switch to red for the main course of bifteck tar-tar and Chateau Brion. I savor each morsel, while Zoffa inhales his like a human vacuum cleaner, sending them straight to his stomach, barely passing his taste buds. To me it's a waste of gourmet food, but he eats with such gusto and delight I suspect his enjoyment exceeds mine. For dessert we order "Omelette Norvege," which is flaming meringue over sponge cake topped with ice cream.

By the time we're finished, the second seating arrives, mostly American government officials wearing white dinner jackets, valuing fashion over comfort, especially in Saigon's heat, though the restaurant is air conditioned, and sweat-soaked American journalists having just dashed over from their air conditioned rooms at the Caravelle, and well-heeled carpet baggers, and high ranking military officers, and along with them, a few GIs like us.

Lingering over Cognac, we hold on to our table, despite angry stares from the maitre'd, so we can listen to the beautiful VN singer named Mai Lin who's vocalizing romantic-sounding French melodies, the kind you don't need to understand the words to know what they mean, only the songs are so emotional they make me sad and I can't help thinking about the poor people living on the wharf just outside the door trying to feed their families from a single pot of rice while Zoffa and I just stuffed ourselves with gastronomic excess.

When I can't bear it any longer, I convince Zoffa to leave, but when we get outside I feel even worse seeing these poor people again. To assuage this guilt, I try to convince myself that the children, having never known anything different, are really happy and Zoffa offers up, "Dere are vorse tings in life den poverty," an intellectual response that almost makes starvation and suffering sound like a blessing. This comment ignites the thought of how those in the US deliberately starve their bodies on diets just so they can eat more, and I envision how it won't be long before the same people might emulate the poor by dressing in tattered clothes to symbolically show others they're so rich they can afford to dress in rags.

As we continue on, the thud of distant bombs and mortar makes me think at least these poor people are not out there killing others, or themselves being blown to bits. That thought being enough to change my mood and allow me to enjoy the garlands of lights in the freighters' rigging and the kerosene lanterns, in the sampans that are bobbing in the swells, making them appear to flash on and off like fireflies, and the shadowy figures on the dock squatting in their improvised shelters silhouetted by the light of a single lantern, and the hot humid air perfumed with the scent of opium, mixed with putrid odor of decay, and the melodic sing-song sounds of Vietnamese conversation, and the laughter of children playing before the curfew sets in, this supporting my theory that children don't suffer poverty to the same degree their parents do. A case in point, I see a toddler pick up a small piece of sugar cane from the filthy ground, put it into his mouth and break into a huge smile of delight.

CHAPTER 45

The serendipitous moment I spoke earlier occurs when a taxi pulls up just ahead of us and two men get out and approach us as we're heading back to the hotel. One of them is short and stocky, dark complexioned and oriental looking, and the other a tall Anglo built like a football linebacker.

"Excuse me, mates," the shorter one says in a British accent. "We're new in Saigon. Would you possibly know of a good brothel? We don't trust the bloody taxi drivers."

"The best one's the Pleasure Villa in Dakao," I tell him. "The owner's American. Where're you guys from?"

"Name's Graham Southern from Australia," the taller one says, holding out his hand, "and me mate here's Jack Wu, from Hong Kong."

After talking, it turns out they're both captains of freighters tied up at the wharf and they invite us to join them for a beer aboard Graham's ship, the *Europa*, which is the larger of the two and docked in front of Jack's ship which is called the *Indo Traveler*. "I got plenty of Fosters aboard," Graham tells us. "It's not the best Aussie piss, but it's decent."

Once aboard we follow them through a catacomb of steel doorways and bulkheads and up a flight of metal stairs to a day room, that for a tired looking freighter, is surprisingly warm and cozy with upholstered settees and chairs, highly polished mahogany tables and original paintings of old sailing ships on the walls.

Graham presses a button next to one of the tables and I hear footsteps running up the metal stairway. A moment later an Oriental man dressed in a white dinner jacket enters the room and bows to Graham.

"Walter, bring up some cold Fosters for everybody," Graham tells him, "and some tinned ham, a couple of good cheeses with biscuits."

A few minutes later Walter's back with four ice cold cans of Fosters and a platter of cheeses along with slices of ham next to a row of crackers, all so fast it makes me think how much being the captain of a ship must be like being a king.

The moment one can is empty Walter replaces it with another while the four of us exchange stories with Zoffa and I listening in awe to their stories about Cape Town, Taiwan, Bangkok, Manila, Singapore, Djakarta, Tokyo and us telling them about America, Germany, Saigon and the war. It's not long we bond like old friends with Graham and Jack kidding us about being Yanks, Zoffa by virtue of his being an American GI, and us kidding them about being subjects of the Queen.

Jack who's 35, has never been married and has been at sea since graduating the Merchant Marine Academy and becoming a captain at 24, a young age for a British Master. And he's fluent in French, Chinese, Portuguese and English, having a mixture of all those nationalities in his blood.

Graham is 42, from Melbourne, divorced with three children, his ex-wife being back in Australia with the kids. According to him, she was tired of his being away at sea and not missing her as much as she missed him.

The two of them have been good friends for many years and now work for the same Hong Kong-based company that owns both freighters. Before the war they ran freight between Indonesia and Vietnam, but now make runs up and down the coast of South Vietnam carrying kerosene, lumber, citrus fruit, food stuff and building supplies. And it's this chance meeting that sets in motion a big change to come in my Saigon soldier life.

CHAPTER 46

The day after meeting Graham and Jack, Zoffa and I are on a sortie with Snover heading up country to Nha Trang just north of Cam Ranh Bay, and hoping to get back in time for a couple of beers with our new friends, followed by dinner. While waiting at the ramp, I catch sight of two jets simultaneously taking off on parallel runways, one a Pan Am Freedom flight taking GIs back home, the other an F-4 Phantom loaded with munitions on its way to inflict death and destruction on some unsuspecting human beings, both pilots briefly glancing at each other from their cockpits before turning in opposite directions on their respective departure routing.

After we land at the LZ, sniper rounds whizz over our heads and we immediately hit the ground and lie there returning fire into the void until a convoy of GIs shows up and assures us the threat has been neutralized, meaning the snipers have been killed or got away. To us, it's yet another example of the war escalating because it's the first time we've come under attack while on a sortie, and what I learn in those few anxious moments is, when it comes to fear, you are always alone.

CHAPTER 47

When we get back to Saigon Zoffa tells me he's quitting sorties because of the incident with the snipers, but once we shower, change into civilian clothes and head to the Europa where Graham breaks out the Fosters and calls over to Jack on the Indo-Traveler to join us, using a bullhorn, he doesn't bring the subject up again. And when the four of us go to dinner at the Au Caruso French Restaurant on Vo Di Nguy Street for another evening of camaraderie, good food and conversation, he tells me he's changed his mind, not only because of our friendship, but because of the opportunities working sorties provide for such good times.

At the end of the meal, while toasting with glasses of Courvoisier to yet another great evening, Graham suggests we all go to the Pleasure Villa and not surprisingly Zoffa begs off with his usual excuse about having to write a letter to his wife, then abruptly gets up and leaves before Graham or Jack can convince him otherwise. Once he had gone, I explain to them the real reason for his departure and while they respect him for it, they find it much too ascetic for their merchant marine mores. The three of us then hail a taxi out to Dakao where we are set up, an American term Graham hates because in his Aussie culture it connotes being duped, with three of LeRoy's finest girls. Instead of staying at the villa however, Graham suggests we bar-fine the girls out and take them back to the Europa so we don't have to cut the evening short due to the curfew. But before we leave Jack, who's an avid gambler, plays a few rounds of Roulette and ends up winning seventy eight dollars' worth of Ps, which he generous uses to pay for all three girls.

The next morning, after a night of great sex in one of the Europa's cabins, I treat myself to a long hot shower, the first since coming to the Nam, not counting the one at the steam and cream, made possible due to the ship's water maker and diesel boiler. Then, minus the girls, the three of us meet up in Graham's private dining room for a breakfast of steak and eggs on elegant china with polished silverware, crystal glasses and linen napkins attentively served by Walter who also serves the girls a VN breakfast of Pho but does so in Graham's day room, making sure they don't take anything with them when they leave.

The reason for this separate dining arrangement is Graham's insistence on formality when it comes to meals served in the Captain's dining room "to preserve a modicum of dignity in the undignified world of the sea," which means no females allowed and dressing properly, insisting we wear dinner jackets that he provides to Jack and me, even though it's only breakfast.

CHAPTER 48

When classes end for the term at the main campus in Saigon, I'm transferred to its branch in Cholon, which is located in three story building with no campus grounds. It's not as nice as the Saigon facility but there I have my own office and get to teach a class I developed that's entirely devoted to American slang, in response to students perplexed by all the GI vernacular they hear such as "Fugazi, ASAP, SNAFU, and no sweat."

With Cholon being the Chinatown section of Saigon, there are more Chinese students than Vietnamese, many of them the progeny of multi-generations of ethnic Chinese born in Vietnam and conditioned by previous generations to believe Vietnam is really Chinese homeland since it was ruled by China for over a thousand years. Conversely, the Vietnamese students are culturally conditioned to look upon the Chinese as foreigners, notwithstanding the fact they have been in Vietnam for more than ten centuries. The French and Indian students are excluded from this bias because they are insignificant in number and do not consider themselves Vietnamese, identifying instead with their ethnic nationality even though they and their parents, and parent's parents, may have been born in Vietnam. This cultural bias comes to light when I ask each student to present a talk on a topic of their choice with the objective being solely to practice speaking English. The essence of those presentations going something like this.

"Hello, my name is Luong Van Tot, I am Vietnamese. My country is beautiful. It has many mountains and rivers. There are Chinese who live in my country. They are not Vietnamese, but we let them live here."

And, "Hello my name is Lao Ying. I am Chinese. I was born in Vietnam where my ancestors were born and ruled for a thousand years. Today we live in our land with the Vietnamese."

It troubles me to hear this, not only because I believe we are all cut from the same cloth, but also because I am trying to find a reason, besides a profit motive, for us as Americans to be in Vietnam if not to support a united people. It would be nice if the sacrifices and suffering on all sides was to establish unity and peace, but that doesn't seem to be the case. It seems more that each side wants what they want, and hopes to achieve their goal by forcing the other side to give it to them.

CHAPTER 49

A famous war correspondent once wrote, "What drives war is profits," and to this end there's an assemblage of wealthy people in Saigon who are either profiting from the war or hoping to. Many of them are members of Saigon's exclusive social and sporting clubs, the crown jewel of which is the venerated Cercle Sportiff Saigonais, an elitist establishment of French Indochinese elegance located in a walled compound that houses an Olympic-size swimming pool, gymnasium, tennis courts, legitimate steam room, elegant dining facilities and a cocktail lounge.

Known simply as the Cercle Sportiff, it is frequented by well-to-do men with their fashionable wives, children and girlfriends who never dare speak a word of Vietnamese while there, even though it's their native language, and even when speaking with a fellow Vietnamese, as French is the club's official language and carries with it the elitism of Vietnam's former ruling class.

Another such enclave is the Racquet Club where tennis is played as a religion and anything less than three hours practice a day is considered blasphemous. A third is the Club Nautique de Saigon, more commonly known as The Yacht Club. Its main facility is located along the tree-shaded banks of the Saigon River, half a mile or so from the Mekong Floating Restaurant, in a nautical-themed building painted blue and white that houses dining and bar facilities with a patio overlooking a private dock and boat mooring. Downstairs are the trophy and locker rooms with showers and storage for the members' motorized runabouts and, most important of all, the club's prized racing shells that are used in competition against foreign clubs. The club also owns a separate weekend facility in a rural setting located a few kilometers out of the city in a place called Ti Nghe. That facility has a swimming pool and volleyball court with outdoor restaurant and bar surrounded by a spacious lawn bordering a river canal. Like the other two clubs, these facilities are staffed by French-speaking Vietnamese who cater to its members, who are mostly wealthy businessmen, high ranking military leaders, and government officials.

Driven by the challenge and devilish desire to assault snobbery, I decide to join the Club Nautique, this being no easy task because in an effort to limit American membership, especially rank and file GIs like me, the Board of Governors, knowing that most military tours are for one year, amended the by-laws to require all prospective members be sponsored by at least two members in good standing who have been members for a minimum of two years. To accomplish this, I recruit two of my Vietnamese students who are members, one a successful businessman, the other a prominent doctor, to sponsor both me and Zoffa, the coup d'etat being more exciting to me than actual membership. When we are accepted, in celebration of the victory I order a brand new Honda motorcycle, which is highly desired in Saigon because they can only be legally imported by an American and cost a great deal of money if procured on the black market.

To my surprise, despite being low ranking GIs, we are welcomed by the club's members who look upon our Occidental bodies, especially Zoffa's, as just what they need to crew in an upcoming competition against the Royal Yacht Club of Manila. To this end, we are immediately conscripted into a training program that begins with practice rowing in a stationary shell fastened to the club's dock using perforated oars while a coxswain calls out "Attaque, un, deux, trois. Attaque, un, deux, trois" in the precise rhythm needed for crew racing.

After weeks of training we earn the privilege of going out in the Saigon River with a crew in one of the club's needle-nose racing shells, earned being the operative word because the club, its trainer and fellow crew members are fanatics when it comes to the sport and competition. As we speed past sampans, freighters and American gunboats, stroking to the coxswain's cadence, American Navy seamen taunt us and on one occasion even fire a playful round into the water nearby for amusement. Zoffa, true to his German fanaticism, takes the training and discipline more seriously than I do and works out every chance he gets in a one-man shell, so impressing the other team members they give him his own locker, which normally takes a year of seniority to get. And he, in turn, gives up the steam and cream in the belief that sex of any kind preceeding a competition is the ruin of an athlete.

As fate would have it, however, on the day before the big race against the Manila Club, Captain Staubs forbids us to participate because he fears it would expose him to negative criticism from his superiors. I'm relieved because the pressure is off, but Zoffa is so disappointed he threatens to write a letter to President Johnson. The real consequence, however, is our no-show marks the end of our popularity with the club.

CHAPTER 50

Following a cargo run up the coast, Jack and the Indo Traveler arrive back at the Port of Saigon, and notwithstanding our new persona non grata with the club, Zoffa and I take him there for lunch. Sitting at a table out on the patio, Jack and Zoffa order the fresh lapin, which means exactly that—the chef kills the rabbit when the order is placed—and me an omelette aux champignons, and for the three of us a bottle of Pouilly-Fuisse. Over lunch, Jack tells us that Graham and the Europa are in Cap St. Jacques and will be back to Saigon in a few days, but that his Uncle Juan-Carlo Choy, who lives in Hong Kong and owns both ships, has just arrived in Saigon to negotiate new cargo contracts and he wants us to meet him.

"Eees a great chap, you'll love him," Jack says, "and we can go to the baahs, because uncle loves to fool around with the popsies even though he's sixty-three years old."

He then tells us that Juan-Carlo isn't his uncle by blood, but was a good friend of his mother who was English and French, and his father who was Chinese and Portuguese and died when Jack was a young boy. When his mother couldn't afford to raise both him and his sister, Juan-Carlo, who is Chinese and Portuguese, brought Jack to live with him in Hong Kong and, given he owned a steam-ship company, it was only natural Jack took to the sea.

Predictably, when the time comes to go, Zoffa, hearing that we may end up in a club where there are girls, bows out, telling Jack he's got other things to do.

"Come on mate, you can't be serious," Jack pleads. "We'll have a good time and stick uncle with the bill. He loves to pay, he's bloody rich and is a good sport about it."

"Thank you just the same," Zoffa tells him, then gets up and leaves.

After he's gone, Jack and I take a taxi to the Caravelle Hotel where his uncle is staying, and when Jack knocks on the door of his uncle's room, a voice calls out from inside, "Entre, s'il vous plaît."

"Is it safe, uncle?" Jack calls back as he opens the door.

"Jack, Jack, come in my boy, come in," his uncle says, and when I see the two of them embrace, the love and affection they have for each other is obvious.

In the room along with his uncle is a tall, elegantly dressed Chinese man with a pencil thin moustache and slicked back hair who stands ram-rod straight and turns out to be a cargo broker by the name of Sir Robin. Having never met a multimillionaire shipping magnate before, I would have guessed Sir Robin to be the owner and Juan-Carlo, who's a short, bald, brown-skinned Oriental in loose fitting pants and shirt, to be the broker.

"I thought you'd have the blooming place filled with popsies," Jack says, teasing his uncle.

"Have a little respect for your tired old uncle," Juan-Carlo teases back.

"Don't worry, I already told Ben all about you."

"What's there to tell? You have such ideas," Juan-Carlo says, laughing at his own words. "I'm just an old man who enjoys the simple pleasures of life. Come on, let's all have a glass of scotch." He then pours four glasses from a bottle of Johnny Walker Black and all of us sit around the table listening to him tell stories about Jack when he was a little boy living in Hong Kong, how he use to stare out at the sea for hours dreaming about traveling the world and how, during breaks from school, Juan-Carlo would take him to different countries on his ships. And it's during this causal conversation I learn Sir Robin is the only Chinese person in Hong Kong to be knighted by the Queen of England. The real treat, however, is witnessing the genuine love between Jack and his uncle. It's a wonderful sight to see, two grown men whose hearts are one, having a good time trading humorous barbs and stories about one another and their treasured times together.

After an hour or so, Juan-Carlo stands up and says, "Come on, let's go upstairs to the dining room. They're waiting for us," and we take the elevator up to the Champs Elysees Restaurant on the ninth floor, which is the finest, most elegant restaurant in Saigon, where we're greeted by Monsieur Plaud, a soft spoken Frenchman who's a longtime friend of Juan-Carlo's and the managing director of the hotel, which is rumored to be owned by the Catholic Church. Juan-Carlo and Jack greet him in French, then translate his return platitudes into English for Sir Robin and me.

Here's where knowing the right people pays off because we don't have to order a thing. Great quantities of food and drink are delivered to our table, beginning with escargot along with Moet & Chandon Champagne, followed by filet mignon, lobster, creamed peas, choux de bruxelles, served with premium bottles of red and white wine, then dessert glasses of sweet sherry to go with the flaming cerise jubilee, followed by after-dinner glasses of Remy Martin Cognac. It's one of the finest meals of my life, all without having to agonize over what to choose from a menu filled with gastronomic creations, each one more tempting than the other.

When dinner's over, Sir Robin leaves to meet his girlfriend and father who live in Cholon. I learn he also has a wife who lives in Hong Kong, and the three of us are driven in the Caravel's car to a Chinese nightclub where Juan-Carlo likes to go when he's in town because he's fluent in both Mandarin and Cantonese. It's there that I discover, as Jack said, Juan-Carlo's every bit the lady's man, though more in the sense of a good natured sugar daddy than a sexual predator, meaning he likes to surround himself with beautiful Chinese girls for innocent banter and laughs rather than sex in return for generously sharing his money, which he does without batting an eye, even when the bill comes to over 10,000 Ps.

CHAPTER 51

The next morning I wake up and my head's throbbing from all the drinking and, to make matters worse, the GI in the next room has his stereo running full blast. It's then that I notice I've overslept and discover that Zoffa has left for work without waking me, which is highly unlike him, and right away I get the feeling it's going to be one of those days where nothing turns out right.

Not wanting to be late for work, I skip breakfast and go racing downstairs to the Sach, but it won't start and for several frantic minutes I spin the pedals like a mad man trying to get the engine to catch. When it doesn't, I take-out the spark plug, dry it, put it back in and resume spinning the pedals while a crowd of Vietnamese gathers around shouting advice to me in Vietnamese. Finally, the engine kicks over in a belch of exhaust. By then I'm completely sweat soaked and late for work, a serious matter during wartime, so I go speeding off into the grid-locked traffic, trying my best to weave my way through it while the exhaust from all the poorly maintained engines around me is making my already queasy stomach churn and my headache pound even worse.

On Cong Le Boulevard the traffic opens up and I twist the throttle full bore, but I'm so preoccupied about being late I run smack into the back of a taxi that abruptly stops in front of me, breaking one of its tail lights, and throwing me and the Sach onto the road.

A crowd quickly gathers around us and before I get to my feet the taxi driver is at me, pointing to the broken tail light and yelling like I just destroyed his car, though I strongly suspect it's an act to get more money from me. I deliberately hand him a couple of Ps knowing he will reject them and ask for more, which he does, and I then hand him what I would have given him in the first place, around two dollars, which makes him happy. Fortunately, when I pick up the Sachs, it starts right up and I continue on to Tan Son Nhut.

Because I'm late, Sargent Robbie comes at me big time and the guys are not happy either as there's literally tons of mail to be moved around due to the never ending increase of GIs coming in each day with no increase in help at the AMT. Despite not feeling well, I immediately begin tossing mail sacks one right after the other until the tips of my fingers are raw from gripping the canvas bags, and during lunch I can't eat a thing because my stomach's still churning and dry heaving from the salt tablets we're required to take to replenish the sodium lost through sweating. It turns out, too, that I'm not the only one having a bad day as Zoffa's upset at having received an unpleasant letter from his wife, which is the reason he neglected to wake me.

By the time the shift's over I'm barely able to ride the Sachs back to the Hung Dao. When I get there, I immediately collapse on the bed, instructing the housekeeper to wake me by eleven so I can get to school on time to teach my class. Then when I get there I'm so exhausted that, instead of giving a lesson, I instruct the students to read aloud from their essays, during which I embarrassingly fall asleep at my desk.

CHAPTER 52

After pulling an all-nighter at the AMT, I accept an invitation from Jack to join him and Graham and Juan-Carlo for the day, which Zoffa declines because he's still upset about his wife's letter, though he won't tell me exactly why. So, skipping sleep, I take a cold shower and race over to the Caravelle where Jack says, "Leave your motorbike. We're going to the horse track to win some bloody money," and the four of us climb into the hotel's long black Citroen for the ride out to the Phu-Tho section of Saigon, where the race track is located.

When we get there, little kids are running around hawking National Lottery Tickets, and throngs of poor working class Vietnamese are clustered around the multitude of food vendors and lined up at the general admission gate anxious to get in and bet their few piasters in hopes of winning.

Bypassing them, we head for the clubhouse entrance where there are no lines, then upstairs to the bar, restaurant and betting cage that caters to upper-class Vietnamese, Chinese and French out for the day with their fashionably dressed wives and girlfriends.

With no analytical data to go on, we place our bets like true gamblers, relying strictly on hunches. Graham and I play for fun, but Jack and Juan Carlo are serious gamblers. I bet 300 Ps on horse number five, Graham a 1,000 on horse number one, Jack 20,000 on horse number two and Juan-Carlo 20,000 on horse number seven. The cashier issues a paper receipt taken from a board of them, each numbered to correspond with the number on the back of a jockey's shirt in the particular race.

With our bets secured, we head to the rail and watch as the horses and riders emerge from the far end of the track, then disappear briefly in the tall grass of the infield and re-emerge at the starting line. The VN jockeys, though small themselves, tower over the pony-sized horses, their stirruped feet almost touching the ground.

When the starting gun is fired, the horses take off barely running, then quickly spread across the width of the dirt track as if afraid to get in each other's way. As they make their first pass before the Grand Stand, the air fills with shouts in several languages, the individual words amalgamated into a roar. Closer to me Jack's yelling, "Come on number two, you bloody fool!" and Juan-Carlo, "Where's my horse?" while Graham and I are more subdued, enjoying the passion of the crowd and the camaraderie more than the race itself.

On the second pass, they cross the finish line and Jack's horse wins. He's excited beyond words as he collects his winnings and celebrates by buying us all drinks.

"Listen to me mates," he says. "I'll make you all rich. Tell 'um, uncle, who's the bloody brains in the family!"

But on the next race he bets his entire winnings, not on the horse or jockey, but on his gambler's intuition that tells him it's his lucky day. When the horse loses, he rationalizes that he didn't really lose because he's even, which in gambler's logic means he's still ahead.

In the end, even though we've all lost money, nobody's down because we had a lot of fun and decide to celebrate what Graham calls "the victory of loss," starting with a meal of Spanish Paella at a Vietnamese restaurant called "The Paprika," where, along with the food, we consume liters of Sangria and have a photographer take pictures of us seated at the table arms around each other, eyes drawn into drunken slits, especially mine since I haven't slept, and mouths agape in laughter. When the bill comes Jack declares, "It's your bloody turn to pay, uncle," and Juan-Carlo faux complains saying, "Again, how can be?" as he hands the waiter a thick wad of Ps.

CHAPTER 53

With new cargo contracts signed, Juan-Carlo books his return flight to Hong Kong and Jack plans a going-away party for him, which Zoffa and I agree to host at Ti Nghe, the Club Nautique's park-like facility in the countryside outside Saigon. On the ride out in the Caravelle's car, Zoffa, having never met Juan-Carlo before, starts telling him about the recent newspaper stories of increasing confrontations between VN civilians and GIs, which lay blame for them on rampant inflation caused by foreign carpet baggers whose only interest is profiting from the war, which in turn is causing the VN people to get poorer and more desperate every day.

Besides shifting what is supposed to be a celebratory mood to a serious topic, it is particularly insensitive because Juan-Carlo's company is one of those described in the articles as profiting from the war and contributing to inflation. But Juan-Carlo, being the fun-loving, conciliatory person he is, lets it slide and even listens to Zoffa with interest and respect. It's no secret that in a free market economy there's a competitive balance between supply and demand, but in a war time economy demand quickly outpaces supply and demand will readily pay whatever supply wants, which in turn inflates the cost of goods and services down the line. Suppliers get rich and everybody else pays the bill, especially the working class and poor.

To the average Vietnamese whose income is not keeping up with inflation the comparatively well paid, free spending, and highly visible GIs are foreigners and easy scapegoats for their frustrations which sometimes result in a shouting match, and occasionally in a physical confrontation where the agitated civilian is shot dead and labeled a VC to escape consequences. From the GIs' point of view, they're risking their lives in a foreign country for an ungrateful people; although the confrontations are more the result of frustration and desperation than a lack of gratitude.

Zoffa, who loves to talk about newspaper stories, then goes on about an editorial that criticizes the US role in Vietnam, asserting that Premier Ky, who is commonly labeled the "Playboy Pilot" for his movie star looks, fighter pilot persona, and predilection for beautiful women, is a corrupt pawn of the US government.

In response to that editorial's claims of corruption, the South VN government announces they will hold free democratic elections. Pro-government newspapers publish the election framework, including who will be eligible to vote, where the balloting will take place, and what controls will be instituted to insure an honest election. But this framework assures only a very small representation of the Vietnamese people will be permitted to participate, essentially only those living in secured areas under the watchful eyes of the Saigon government and, according to the papers, opposition will only be permitted as long as it is not "too diverse," meaning any candidates posing a threat to the existing government will completely disappear or be taken into police custody on dubious charges.

This announcement prompts a GI to write a letter to the editor in which he postures that the Vietnamese are too primitive to govern themselves, comparing them to dogs because they defecate and urinate openly along the streets, notwithstanding the scarcity of public toilets. It also motivates me to write a letter to the editor wherein I question whether democracy will be served based on government restrictions that will exclude over 90 percent of the population from voting, since half are below the voting age and 80 percent live in villages that will not be permitted to vote because they are listed as "unsecured." My letter provoking the editor to respond, "As a Foreigner you should leave the question of whether Democracy will be served or not to the Vietnamese unless you adopt Vietnamese nationality." His curt reply bothering super patriot Zoffa more than me because it challenges the official basis of our being there, which is to bring democracy to the Vietnamese people. Whereas to me, it simply confirms what I already suspected, that we are really there to protect the interest of those who profit from the war.

The Club Ti Nghe's facility is reached via a narrow dirt road flanked on one side by thick jungle and on the other by a river canal used to irrigate the adjacent rice paddies. Like many American country clubs, the wives, daughters and girlfriends lie around on chaise lounges in tiny bikinis while the children splash in the pool and the men drink and play sports. The chief sports at Ti Nghe are volleyball played on the club's expansive lawn, and waterskiing in the river canal where, on occasion, a passing American helicopter gunship will swoop down to gawk at the girls in their bikinis and amuse themselves by creating a nuisance. Additionally, the facility is only open on weekends, and only during the day, because during the week the men are at their offices, and at night it's in the vicinity of deadly fighting.

Shortly after arriving we change into our bathing suits and join some men at the outdoor bar where Jack and Juan-Carlo, being gregarious and fluent in French, engage in social conversation while Zoffa the athlete goes off to the volleyball court and Graham and I head to the pool where we try to strike up a conversation with some girls in English and my limited Vietnamese, but all we can get out of them are their adopted French names, Claudia and Babette. Laying poolside, on a chaise lounge, it feels like a resort anywhere in the world, yet knowing in a few hours others will come there to kill one another and their bodies will be hauled off in time for the club to reopen in the morning, makes it surreal.

CHAPTER 54

On the day the Indo Traveler and the Europa are to sail for Qui-Nhon, Zoffa gets into one of his moods and refuses to leave the Hung Dao and go with me to say good-bye to Jack and Graham, so I end up going alone. By the time I get to the wharf, the Europa's already steaming out of the harbor and the Indo-Traveler is in the process of casting off its lines with Jack standing in the wheel house dressed in his captain's uniform complete with cap and shoulder boards. On the dock, waving good-bye next to me, is Sir Robin flanked by two sinister-looking Chinese men, and once the ship leaves he invites me for lunch at the nearby Mekong Floating Restaurant, saying he has an important business proposition he would like to discuss that will make us both a lot of money, this being one of the significant events in my journey that I spoke about earlier. After we're seated he gets right down to it.

"I need an American who can help me convert Vietnamese Piasters into U.S. dollars in exchange for a percentage of the arbitrage plus free cargo space aboard the Europa and Indo Traveler, which alone will make you a good deal of money."

He then shows me a letter from the President of the *Bank of China* in Hong Kong acknowledging a deposit in his name of three million US dollars.

"Do you know how I got this?" he asks, then continues without waiting for a response. "My father owns several small banks in Malaysia that issued letters of guarantee to the Bank of China for a loan to me at a rate lower than the cost for the letters of guarantee. Without risking a penny, I have made over two hundred thousand dollars which we can use to fund the arbitrage."

My first reaction is, going into business with him or anybody else is not something I want to do, if for no other reason I don't need the money, my tax free combat pay affording me a great lifestyle in Saigon's economy, but the challenge intrigues me so I ask him to tell me more and when I do, he interprets this response to be a definite yes.

"I hoped you'd say that," he says. "May I suggest we rent a villa where we can run the business. I'll be traveling back and forth to Hong Kong and when I'm out of town it will be all yours. I'll take care of everything." He then abruptly stands up and leaves, saying he'll be in touch.

Not knowing any of the details of what I might be getting myself into makes me uneasy, but I reassure myself since Juan-Carlo does business with him and he's been knighted by the Queen of England, he must be okay.

CHAPTER 55

A week after my lunch with Sir Robin, a message arrives at the Hung Dao asking me to meet him at the Chun King Chinese restaurant in Cholon. It's a sinister looking place in an older neighborhood where the buildings stand wall to wall on narrow streets blocking out much of the day light. When I arrive on the Sach, I see Sir Robin's long black Renault parked out front, halfway on the sidewalk. After chaining the Sach to an iron gate, I go in and find him sitting at a table with a bottle of Pernod and a pitcher of water, a glass of the murky liquid in his hand, and directly behind him at a separate table, the same two sinister looking Chinese men who were at the wharf.

"Aaah Ben, glad you could come," he greets me. "Let's get down to business. I've found a villa for us in Phu-Tho near the race track. It's one of the few in the City with a telephone. How soon can you move in?"

"I don't know. I have to work and teach school."

"The sooner we get started the better. I'll have Fatty meet you at your hotel and help you move your things. Just tell me when you would like him there." Fatty being Sir Robin's chauffer, personal assistant, and the son of Chun King's owner, which is co-owned by Sir Robin's father.

The very next day when I return from work, Fatty is outside the Hung Dao with Sir Robin's car and Zoffa helps me carry down a few things, even though he's concerned about me moving out of the secure hotel.

"Don't worry, Zoffa," I say trying to assuage both of our concerns, "remember my favorite saying 'When fear knocks on your door and you open it, nobody will be there.' Not only that, the villa's even closer to Tan Son Nhut than the Hung Dao, so you can come out and spend time with me."

When I get to the Pho-Tho villa, Sir Robin has already hired a cook, a maid and a houseboy, as well as purchased furniture, dishes, linens, water purifiers, cooking fuel, food etc. It's a beautiful villa, too, with two large bedrooms and two bathrooms upstairs, one with a regular western style flush toilet, and downstairs on the entry level, an office, living room, dining room, kitchen and servant's quarters all completely surrounded by a high concrete wall topped with shards of glass. Besides the telephone, which is a major plus because there's a two-year waiting list for one in Saigon, it has a washing machine, something almost unheard of in the City. My bedroom he tells me, is the one with the western style toilet. It opens onto a small balcony overlooking the front garden and entry, and the bed's already made up with brand new, pale green, satin sheets and pillow cases.

"How much does all this cost?" I ask Sir Robin.

"Nothing compared to what we are going to make," he says, "Let's go downstairs and talk. Quan the houseboy will put your things away."

On the table in the office he shows me a schedule of expenses, $200 for furnishings, $225 per month for rent, and $9 per month for each of the three live-in servants.

"Everything is to be split evenly between us," he says, "even though you will have the villa to yourself most of the time."

He then lays out the business plan which is a three-step arbitrage, exchange as many VN Piasters for US dollars as we can, send those US dollars to Hong Kong to be exchanged for Hong Kong dollars, exchange the Hong Kong Dollars for Vietnamese Piasters and repeat the cycle. Sir Robin will supply the piasters and I will be responsible to exchange them for dollars. Sir Robin's brother will handle the arbitrage in Hong Kong. By interjecting Hong Kong dollars, we will make seventy cents on the dollar and thus can offer a higher rate of exchange than can be gotten on the current black market.

At the end of the first week's trial run, I manage to exchange three thousand dollars' worth of piasters and by the end of the second week, more than eight thousand dollars' worth. The following week I enlist the help of VN workers at the Base by paying them a small percentage of what they exchange, and by the end of the first full month we have exchanged over fifty thousand dollars' worth of

Ps, and at the end of the second month, more than double that. But by the third month the business threatens to implode when the US Government announces it will stop paying GIs in dollars, instead replacing them with Military Payment Certificates (MPCs) that look similar to Monopoly money, and can only be exchanged for Ps at approved facilities, thus rendering them useless on the black market.

At first Sir Robin and I see this as an end to our lucrative business, but a few days later I come up with a plan I believe will not only allow us to continue, but greatly grow the business due to less competition. This plan involves having GIs use the MPCs to buy US Postal Money Orders at the military post offices, then exchange the money orders with us for piasters. Sir Robin will then send the money orders to his brother in Hong Kong to buy Hong Kong dollars, and subsequently exchange the HK dollars for Vietnamese piasters as before.

After the first MPC payroll, I do a test run that yields seventeen thousand dollars' worth of postal money orders. After sending them to Hong Kong, we receive back a one word encrypted telegram from Sir Robin's brother reading, "Mokay," meaning "money orders okay, send more." To celebrate this success we have a special dinner at the Villa that includes Sir Robin's father who looks every bit the part of a rich patriarch and Sir Robin's girlfriend Nancy, an attractive, half Chinese, half Japanese model-thin girl in her late twenties. When we're through eating, Sir Robin's father brings out a large package, wrapped in newspaper, containing stacks of piasters equating to thirty thousand

U.S. dollars, which he turns over to me and I immediately take upstairs to lock in my armoire.

When I return, Sir Robin's father is gone and sitting on the sofa is a VN man with a young Oriental girl who looks like she could be his daughter.

"I want you to meet Mr. Van," Sir Robin says, introducing us. "He's with the Ministry of Commerce and a good friend of ours. He's brought you a gift. Her name's Tin and she's yours to enjoy for the night."

When I look at the girl she's like a wax figure, her eyes staring blankly out.

"It is customary in business," Sir Robin goes on, "when someone brings you a gift, you give a gift in return and Mr. Van is a good person to have on our side."

"What do you suggest?" I ask.

"A carton of American cigarettes would be fine."

With that I go back upstairs and return with a carton of Camels which I give to Mr. Van who thanks us then departs, leaving Tin behind. Sir Robin then goes to his room with Nancy leaving me alone with Tin and the realization hits me that I've just traded a carton of cigarettes for a human being.

I also realize that unlike bargirls who choose to be sex workers to feed their families, Tin is most likely the unfortunate victim of yellow slavery, a chain of events that often begins when a man or woman from the city approaches a poor rural family burdened with too many children to feed and offers the parents a few Piasters for their daughter, promising them that she will have a better life working as a servant for a wealthy family in the city and getting to live in a nice house with plenty to eat, with the possibility of sending money back to help out the family. But once they drive away with the girl, they throw her in the trunk then take her back to the city where she's beaten into submission and sometimes drugged, then turned out into the sex trade.

Not wanting to contribute to this evil business yet not wanting Tin to get in trouble, I take her upstairs and let her spend the night, but without sex, even when she tries out of fear to initiate it, and in the morning, when the curfew is lifted, I have the cook feed her, give her a thousand Ps and Quan put her in a taxi.

After she leaves I join Sir Robin and Nancy for breakfast and Sir Robin says to me, "Quan told me you offered to help the girl. You should know if you try to help her, she'll be killed. It's much easier for them to get a new girl than deal with problems. You can take comfort in knowing she's better off than most who are forced to work in a brothel and serve dozens of clients each day."

CHAPTER 56

Living at the Villa away from the company of others and the hustle of downtown is lonely so I ask Zoffa to come out and stay with me for a few days, but he doesn't feel safe without an MP standing guard and a barricade between him and a carload of explosives.

In an effort to persuade him, I argue that the VC know the Hung Dao is filled with GIs, that's why the MP is there, but nobody expects to find any Americans way out here, and even if they did, they wouldn't care about one or two when they can kill a dozen.

Sound or not, my argument works and he agrees to give it try, but after one night he's back at the Hung Dao saying he can't sleep without hearing the military jeeps and trucks patrolling the streets at night.

CHAPTER 57

I n a letter from home, my mother writes about riots in the Watts neighborhood of Los Angeles, primarily a Negro community where people have taken to the streets looting and destroying property after a white policeman tried to arrest a Negro man for reckless driving. It seems things are not that much better at home.

In a letter from an old girlfriend she writes that she's living in a commune, getting high and living off the land. Her letter reminds me, as Einstein said, how we see life depends on who we are, as everything is filtered through the seer's unique conditioning. If the war has taught me anything, it is that we cannot rely on the Government's, or anybody else's, concept of right or wrong to guide our behavior because they are culturally, politically and experientially biased, which leaves us only to weigh the consequences of our actions in making a decision.

CHAPTER 58

When I meet Mark for lunch at the Cercle Sportif, he tells me he's depressed because he's close to rotating, which means the end of his bachelor life in Saigon and a return to the routine of being a workaday husband and father back in the States. This depression has caused him to drink even more and talk poorly about the Vietnamese who have loyally worked for him during his tenure at the Embassy. Whereas before he praised them as patriots and friends, he now blames them for tricking the US into fighting THEIR war.

When I change the subject and tell him about Sir Robin and our business he warns me, "You better be careful of those Chinese characters. Interpol is on to them." Which is similar to what Jack said when I told him which was, "You best be careful. You can't trust these bloody

Chinese chaps, especially Sir Robin. I've told uncle many times to discharge him," and Jack being part Chinese. That's two warnings and I begin to worry about how to end my involvement.

CHAPTER 59

W hen I invite Jack out to the villa for a visit Sir Robin greets him like he's family and insists he make it his home whenever he is in port saying, "Ben did the right thing bringing you here. My bedroom is your bedroom. Nancy and I will stay at my father's house."

Jack protests, but Sir Robin cuts him short and won't take no for an answer, then quickly shifts the conversation to business asking him how the recent trip to Qui-Nhon went.

"Not so bloody good, I'm afraid. Graham's stuck up there. The Europa still draws too much for the harbor and he's got to hire lighters to discharge some of the cargo before she can be floated up to the wharf, and the bloody crews on both ships are worried about the escalating war and want to be repatriated back to Hong Kong."

"They have a contract," Sir Robin says. "I'll send some people to talk to them."

With that Sir Robin and Nancy have Fatty drive them to his fathers' and Jack moves into the Villa, leaving his first mate Bull MacGregor in command of the Indo Traveler. He also sends Quan to pick up his clothes and the ship's cook, a Chinese man from Hong Kong who Jack calls "Boy," which to me sounds demeaning, but I'm told is the proper way of addressing a Chinese male servant, and he being an exceptionally good cook.

In the morning Sir Robin returns to meet with Jack on the issue of the crews wanting to be repatriated, and after much discussion they determine the matter cannot be settled without a visit to the British Embassy which has jurisdiction over Hong Kong as a Crown Colony. They also want me to go with them since my cargo arrangement makes me an interested party and my being an American might add weight to their argument.

When we arrive at the Embassy I'm amazed to see Gurkhas in full uniform guarding the place and stuffed-shirt British officials bowing to Sir Robin because he's a "Knight of the Garter." But even with this status we end up leaving with orders to repatriate the crews back to Hong Kong on the earliest plane. What this means is the ships will be idle until Jack and Graham can find Vietnamese crews, but to me, it's more time for us to spend together.

CHAPTER 60

S ir Robin is so pleased with the new MPC arbitrage he decides to fly to Hong Kong and pick up the next batch of piasters. Before leaving he invites Jack and me to dinner at a Chinese club owned by his father, to include a Chinese girl for the evening, which is a special treat since Chinese sex workers are less abundant in Saigon than Vietnamese ones.

That evening, Fatty drives us to the Club, which is hidden behind some tenements on one of Cholon's narrow streets with nothing on the exterior that would indicate it is even there. Before we enter, Sir Robin tells us we are in for a real treat because the Chinese girls who work there are trained like Japanese geishas in the art of pleasing men beyond just having sex. From the moment we enter the momason and her staff treat us like royalty, ushering us to

Sir Robin's special table in an alcove off to the side of the main room separated by privacy curtains, then send over copious amount of food without us having to order a thing, along with several girls from which to make our selection. Although disarmingly beautiful, none of the girls interest me sexually because they're on the chubby side, which I am told is highly desirable to many Chinese men because to them it symbolizes wealth, which I find interesting since Sir Robin's girlfriend Nancy is model thin. After my rejecting one after the other, the momason is visibly irritated and alleges that I do not like Chinese girls.

"I like Chinese girls very much," I tell her. "It's chubby girls who don't turn me on," and to make my case I tell her I like the girl who's singing in the main room.

"She no Chinese," the momason tells me. "She Vietnamese."

"I no care, I like her," I tell her.

"She no for customer, she singer."

Clearly upset, the momason says something to Sir Robin in Chinese and he interprets it to me. "She's insulted that you do not like Chinese girls."

"I like Chinese girls a lot, but I like the singer more," I tell him. He then says something to the momason and when the singer finishes her next song, she's escorted to our table and introduced to me as Loan, which is pronounced Lo-anh, a beautiful name to go with her petite body and angelic face framed by long black hair draped over one shoulder.

"I like your singing, "I tell her.

"Thanks, you very kind," she answers.

"Would you like something to drink?"

"No thanks you."

"I would like to spend more time with you."

"I'm sorry, buts I cannot. I must sing."

And before she returns to the stage, I learn she is 22 years old, the daughter of a government mapmaker and has 13 brothers and sisters. By then I am so captivated by her that when she resumes singing, I go and sit in the main room where her voice draws me to her like a siren's call. Then, when her set ends, I ask if I can give her a ride home.

"Sir, I cannot," she says softly. "My father comes for me on his bicycle."

"Perhaps another night?"

"I am sorry sir, buts my father would never let me be with an American."

"Then I will come here to see you again,"

My meeting her turns out to be another important part of my journey to come.

CHAPTER 61

Afrer Sir Robin leaves for Hong Kong, I talk Jack into returning with me to the Chinese Club so I can see Loan, and when she joins us at the table, I ask if I can talk to her father about our seeing each other, only her answer is the same.

"I sorry my father will never allow it." And when I persist, she finally says, "You must forget me and no come see me again."

With that she leaves the table and seems so distressed I tell myself, "Maybe she's right," and for the next two weeks stay away from the Chinese club even though I can't get her out of my mind. Neither the escalation of VC attacks in the City nor the increasing risk on our sorties distract me from thinking about her for more than a few minutes at a time. For example, when the VC detonate a bomb in front of the Metropole Hotel BEQ killing and injuring 160 people, I'm shaken to the core, but minutes later find myself thinking about Loan. And when I see the ever increasing number of aluminum caskets stacked up at Tan Son Nhut, knowing the tremendous suffering they will cause so many families exacerbated by an increasingly ungrateful country, it saddens me to tears, but my mind drifts back thinking of Loan. Even reasoning doesn't help when I remind myself there are thousands of beautiful girls available to me at any given moment.

The only respite comes when the Honda motorcycle I ordered arrives and provides me with a temporary distraction. It's a beautiful shiny blue and silver machine that can easily carry both me and Zoffa, and the next day I sell the Sachs to Map from the AMT for only five dollars, which makes him very happy, and Zoffa and I start cruising around the city together. But after a few days I find myself stopping by the Chinese club to see Loan only to find out she's no longer working there, and no one will tell me where I can find her.

The thought of not seeing her again causes me to race back to the villa to get Quan, who's Chinese, and take him back to the Club thinking, "A Chinese will talk to another Chinese," but on the way back I'm so distracted by my thoughts of Loan, I lean too far into a turn and the Honda goes out from under us, sending Quan flying across the road and me sliding along under it. I'm okay, my pants are ripped and my arms are bleeding, but Quan's not moving. When I rush over to him, I'm relieved to find he's okay, just winded from the fall, and otherwise no worse off than I am.

"Maybe Quan drive Honda," he says, and I nod in agreement.

When we get to the Chinese club I wait outside while Quan goes in to inquire about Loan then returns to tell me she is now working at the Tour d' Ivoire, and when we get there, Quan waits outside while I run upstairs to the main lounge where her sweet voice calls to me like it did the first time I heard it.

Taking a seat where she can plainly see me, I order a beer, never taking my eyes off her beautiful face while thinking, "if Buddhism had angels they would look like her."

When her set's over she comes to my table. "You hurt?" she says noticing my torn clothes and bloodied arm.

"Accident with new Honda," I say.

"Why you come here?"

"I no can forget you."

"I no forgets you, buts you no can come here."

"But I must see you."

"I no can see you. If I see you, I no can sing."

"But I want see you."

"Okay, maybe I come you house, buts you no can come here okay?"

"You come my house?"

"You give me where house, maybe I come."

I then write the address of the villa 2/2 Lu Gia, Phu-Tho on a napkin along with the times I will be there, and back downstairs to Quan, consumed with the thought of seeing her.

CHAPTER 62

On my next day off I don't want to leave the villa for fear of missing Loan. Even when Sir Robin returns from Hong Kong with a new batch of Ps, I quickly distribute them to my network of exchangers, then rush back and check with Quan who has strict instructions to have her wait for me should she show up.

It's during this time that Sir Robin approaches me with an additional business opportunity that he says will make us even more money than the arbitrage and with a lot less work. Because I have unrestricted access to the flight line at Tan Son Nhut, which also serves international airline flights, he wants me to carry packages to and from these flights, bypassing customs, and for this simple act he tells me I could earn hundreds of thousands of dollars. From a logistical standpoint, it's something I can easily do, and with little risk, but it doesn't take much analysis to know it's something I do not want to get involved in, and when I decline he ends the discussion by asking me just to think about it.

When the villa gate bell rings, the maid goes out to open it then escorts Loan into the living room. Seeing my beautiful Buddha angel standing before me dressed in a striking white Ao Dai, her long silken hair draped over one shoulder, puts me into space where I'm so mesmerized nothing else exists.

"Please, sit down. Can I get you something to eat or drink?" I ask her.

She shakes her head gently as if too shy or uncomfortable to speak. It's then that I sense Sir Robin's presence is making her nervous and say, "Let's go upstairs to my room," and immediately worry how she might respond when she sees it's a bedroom. But when we get there, she goes over and stands next to the bed as if expecting that's where we would end up. The sun is at her back, streaming through the open balcony doors and rendering her Ao Dai translucent revealing the shadow of her form, and I can't help but take her into my arms and press my lips to hers. It's the first time I'm kissing a girl since coming to the Nam and her hand on my back is telling me, it's what she wants too. As if fulfilling destiny, we undress and lie on the bed, caressing and kissing, followed by love making sex and the feeling that I never want her to leave my side.

"You please stay here tonight," I whisper.

"I no can stay," she says softly, "buts I come tomorrow."

"I want you live here with me."

"I want too, buts my father never okay me be withs American."

"I will talk to him and change his mind."

"Okay maybe, buts I talk sister Muoi first and she talk to father before you come."

"What will she say?"

"She say Loan want happy in short life."

CHAPTER 63

When Jack returns to Saigon, he moves back into the villa and brings with him his new VN girlfriend named Le, which only intensifies my longing for Loan so I ask him to help me talk to Loan's father.

"He works for the government," I say, "so he must speak French and my Vietnamese is just not good enough."

"Come on mate, you can't be serious. I'm no Maurice Chevalier."

"Please, Jack. I really want to be with her." And seeing how desperate I am, he agrees to do what he can.

A few days later, after Loan tells me her sister has prepared her father for my visit, Jack and I head out on the Honda armed with the address she wrote on a piece of paper. But there's no consistency in the house numbers and in many cases no numbers at all, so we end up driving up and down the street, stopping everybody we see to show them the address, and by the time we find the house we're late and Loan's out front nervously waiting.

"I think you no come," she says, before leading us inside where her older sister Muoi tells us their father has already agreed to let Loan live with me. Hearing this, both Jack and I are relieved, but Muoi then tells me I must still ask him for his permission.

While I wait nervously for him to come into the room, Muoi turns her attention to Jack, asking him if he has a girl-friend and when he tells her he has, she ignores this and says she does not have a boyfriend, then goes on to tell him about her deceased husband who was an ARVN officer and got killed in action, leaving her a widow with four small children.

"Before him die," Muoi says, "he go America." She then brings out a photo album and shows us pictures of him standing in front of the US Capitol, the Lincoln Memorial and the White House, followed by photos of him in his ARVN uniform lying in a casket. "Him killed from V.C. I sad too much, children sad too much," she says, her eyes now filled with tears.

When Loan's father appears, he's a humble looking man dressed in business trousers with a white shirt and necktie. After we exchange nods and greetings, Jack takes over, mor-phing into the role of a captain standing in for one of his crew and speaking to Loan's father in beautiful-sounding French while I try to read his face, but it gives up nothing.

"What did he say?" I ask Jack when they're through.

"He said you got yourself a popsie. If that's what Loan wants, he will not be angry but he will not be happy either."

CHAPTER 64

The next day Loan moves into the villa and when I tell
Zoffa he surprises me by saying, he envies me, only
"not for da beautiful girl or da sex, but da freedom to be
spontaneous," and telling me he feels imprisoned by guilt
and responsibility, then abruptly walks away and starts tossing heavy mail sacks into the bins as if they didn't weigh
anything.

Later the same day, he confesses to me that he's been
going to the steam and cream regularly and feeling really
bad about it. In an effort to ease his guilt I tell him, "Zoff,
in normal times the temptations of easy pleasure would be
challenging enough, but in this land of body bags, sex is
not sex, but a refuge from the insanity of war so there's no
need to feel bad about it." Then ask him not to respond,
but to just consider what I said.

CHAPTER 65

As the fighting escalates, so do our sorties and they take us to a greater number of remote camps where our conversations with the GIs stationed there is increasingly about torture and mutilation of the enemy. It's not something they want to talk about, but seemed compelled to do in an effort to unload a terrible burden, knowing as fellow GIs we won't judge them and that we may never each other again. It's interesting too, that in these stories they see themselves as the victims and the military as the perpetrator.

There are stories about cutting off VC and NVA body parts, mostly scalps and ears, and trading them for beer under pressure from the chain of command to verify proof of enemy kills. And others about tossing men, women and children out of choppers because they are suspected of aiding the VC. And others of incinerating entire villages for the same reason, and doing so with such frequency they jokingly referring to them as zippo raids after the popular cigarette lighter which is used to ignite the thatched roofs, even doing so with families still inside. And still others of randomly killing farm animals needed to work the land, and destroying food supplies so the enemy can't get them, leaving entire villages to starve.

It's no secret to these GIs that such actions constitute war crimes and crimes against humanity, as defined by international agreement and the Geneva Conventions, which have been ratified by the US and every member of the United Nations, but the mindset of unbridled power is so manipulative it can rationalize any action as necessary to serving a greater good and avoid consequence by classifying those killed as the enemy, even though they may be toddlers and infants or poor apolitical subsistence farmers caught between the ruthless VC who hate the South Vietnamese government; and the ruthless NVA who hate all southerners; and the ARVN who are willing to kill their own people to serve their cause; and the American and free world forces who are conditioned to believe they are serving a noble cause in saving the world from the scourge of Communism.

It can be said of this that worse than being ignorant, is the certainty of being right. And for the unfortunate recipients of this carnage, the end result is the same, only the perpetrators differ. And for the perpetrators, that they too have lost because as in the law of physics, the consequences of every action are inescapably imbedded within the action itself.

I remember reading that the soldiers in ancient armies were not paid, their compensation was the right to rape and pillage the enemy, which gave them great incentive to fight and win. To some extent this culture still prevails, because as GIs in war we are not held accountable to local laws and our dollars go so far in the local economy we can take what we want, and what cannot be bought can be taken by force with little or no consequence. It's not a far stretch to foresee that once consumed with such power, there will be those, who when they return home, will seek positions with authority over others so they can perpetuate it, and those whose who will suffer because from the guilt of abusing it. Subliminal signs of both of these syndromes can be gleaned in the messages embroidered on the custom-tailored jackets many GIs choose to wear such as, "If you kill for pleasure you're a saddest, if you kill for money you're a mercenary, if you kill for both you're a Ranger" and "In memory of when I gave a shit," and "That's Mr. Asshole to You."

CHAPTER 66

Having Loan in my life not only makes the war more bearable, but gives me a sense of normalcy. Our relationship is not just about sex, but kindness, mutual respect and fun. She has her job as a singer and I have mine as a GI, teacher and entrepreneur. Together we share a comfortable home, go to movies and parks and dine out. And thanks to my business, we have more money than we can possibly spend. The shelves of my armoire are stacked so full of piasters it resembles a bank vault more than a closet, in part because of the parity between the dollar and the P and that Ps don't come in large denominations.

On a whim, I lease a 1957 Ford Fairlane four-door sedan and have Quan drive us around in it like we're royalty. It's even more of a thrill whenever I see Premier Nguyen Cao Key in his official government car, a much smaller

Ford Falcon, although replete with flags flying from its front fenders. As a result of this ostentatiousness, when my fellow GIs see Quan drop me off for work at the Tan Son Nhut gate, they start referring to me as the Mayor of Saigon.

With all this attention, it's not long before Sgt. Robbie takes me aside and says, "Look here, Kovner. How about cutting your old sergeant in on this business?"

His question is not entirely unexpected as others have similarly approached me and my answer's always the same. "There's lots of money to be made if you want to work," and most of the time they don't, they're too content hanging out at the bars drinking and having sex, or hanging out at the hotel drinking and playing the slot machines. For me, recruiting others to change money is the only way I can grow the business and when I tell this to Sgt. Robbie, he quickly says, "Count me and the general in." the general being Robert E. Lee White who is Sgt. Robbie's closest friend.

"Why don't you both come out to the villa after work and I'll get you started," I tell him. "You can ride with me in the Fairlane."

"If it's just the same with you," he says, "we'll take a taxi and follow you. I don't want the others to know."

When the shift is over he and the general follow me down Plantation Road, past the French cemetery with its 17,000 neatly arranged white crosses that serves as a reminder of the price they paid when they tried to defeat Ho Chi Minh, and on to the villa where I give them a quick tour, intentionally including a peek into my bedroom so they can see my beautiful Buddha angel Loan sleeping naked with her legs wrapped around our satin-covered Dutch wife pillow, before heading back downstairs to talk business.

"You sure know how to live, Kovner," the general says, "but you're a crazy fuck staying out here in VC territory."

"It's safer here because I'm the only one," I counter wanting to assure them, then get down to business. "I need guys to purchase money orders with MPCs, then exchange the money orders for Ps. I supply the Ps and pay a ten percent commission so for every hundred dollars in money orders you give me, I give you a hundred and ten dollars' worth of Ps which at today's rate is about 20,900. And you are free to negotiate a better exchange with your customers which will make you even more money, and should be easy, given what they are getting for MPCs now."

Hearing this, the general's ready to commit, but Sgt. Robbie, who is career military, has some concerns. "Ain't that illegal?" he asks me.

"Well Sarg, when you used to exchange dollars for Ps on the black market, wasn't that illegal? And it's not illegal to buy money orders."

"I guess you're right about that, Kovner." He then looks at the general and says, "You got yourself a deal! Just two things. When do we start, and how the fuck do we get a taxi back to the Hung Dao from way out here?"

"You can start anytime you want and I'll have Quan get you a taxi."

CHAPTER 67

With their new French and English speaking Vietnamese crews, Jack and Graham are back to making regular runs between Qui Nhon and Saigon, and Sir Robin and Nancy have moved to another villa so they can have more privacy, and Loan and I can have the villa all to ourselves.

With their new found wealth, Sgt. Robbie and the General have taken to dressing in custom-tailored clothes like those worn by the celebrities they see in magazines and to buying dresses, hairspray and jewelry as gifts for their bargirl girlfriends; even though they are both married.

The only hint of trouble comes when clerks at the post offices start getting suspicious about the volume of money orders being purchased, but I quickly quell this by advising everyone to say since they can't get a good rate of exchange on Ps anymore, they're sending their money back home.

When Loan and I go out to dinner at Saigon's finer restaurants, we occasionally see Premier Ky sitting at a table nearby, always in the company of a pretty girl even though his wife, a former Air Vietnam stewardess is as beautiful as they come. His brazen style of public displays however, fuel the Saigon press that never stop attacking him for being morally corrupt, saying he'd sell his soul to the VC if they offered him enough money, and questioning how he manages to live like a millionaire on his modest official salary. Whatever the truth, Ky is always the dashing icon in his black flight suit, thin moustache and baseball cap, usually with a cigarette dangling from his mouth.

When they come to class my students take to bringing me gifts, inviting me to their homes for meals and sending me notes of appreciation always addressed to, "Dear Kovner, my American teacher."

The monthly paychecks I receive from the school are written in French and drawn on a local Japanese Bank for Vietnamese currency and getting them cashed takes hours due to antiquated banking procedures that are further burdened by VN employees who seem to feel every transaction, which they refer to as "sorties," will be the only transaction they will have to process for the entire day.

Life in the Nam for most GIs is centered on complaints, and one of the major ones at the AMT is about ROK mail, more specifically, packages sent from families in the Republic of Korea to their sons in VN who are part of the Free World Forces fighting alongside the U.S. All too often this mail contains glass jars of kimchi, a fermented cabbage dish that is a staple for Koreans in the way a hamburger is to Americans and salsa to Mexicans, only the glass containers often break during shipment and the odor of kimchi, especially when exposed to the heat and humidity of Saigon, is even worse than Nuc Mam. While the ROK troops are particularly well liked and highly respected for their discipline, never goofing off or going to bars, and one hundred percent hardcore fighting machines, the smell of kimchi is more than American olfactory senses can take and whenever a jar of it breaks the guys curse the ROKs and threaten to kill them.

Other Free World Forces fighting alongside us come from Thailand, Taiwan, Australia, New Zealand and the Philippines, and rumor has it that others are from India, Canada, Spain and Poland under the banner of something called the International Controls Commission, although neither I, nor anyone I have met, has encountered them.

At this stage of the war, each enemy attack seems to give rise to a new American strategy for defeating them. One of these strategies is psychological and involves dropping aspirins in containers by the thousands from aircraft flying over VC/NVA territory. The idea is to demoralize the enemy who are largely without medicine by showing them we are so well off we can afford to give it away, thus enticing them to come over to our side. This program is short lived when it fails to produce any measurable results.

Another strategy is carried out in a program called Chieu Hoi, which loosely translates to Open Arms, and involves the dropping of leaflets over enemy territory offering to pay each VC or NVA money to surrender, plus an additional sum for each weapon they turn in, no questions asked. This program though is mired in controversy when it is discovered that some of those surrendering are doing so multiple times, at least on paper, and may not even be VC or NVA. Notwithstanding this, both the US and VN governments declare the program a success, claiming approximately 15,000 enemy surrenders at an average cost of $125 apiece versus $300,000 apiece, the official cost of each enemy killed in combat; though I suspect the statistics are being manipulated to keep financial support for the program coming in and that most of the money is flowing directly to the pockets of those running the program.

GI moral in the Nam is in the hands of a Navy Captain who is in charge of all military support activities for the entire country. He is frequently seen being driven around Saigon in his jeep, the only one in the country with white wall tires, seeking photo opportunities like a celebrity. To boost moral he makes sure the BX is stocked with items highly desired by many VN girls who will gladly exchange sexual favors for them, in particular hair spray so they can stylize their hair like the American girls they see in magazines, and sanitary napkins which are superior to whatever they can get locally. With very few American women in the Nam, rumor has it the Captain explains this inventory to his superiors by claiming the hairspray is an effective fire starter, and the sanitary napkins are used to clean weapons. In addition to these BX items, he organizes beauty contests where GIs get to vote for the most beautiful VN girls among those who work in his command. All this endearing him to the GIs, but bringing down harsh criticism from those in Washington.

Thanks to our Australian allies, who are considered skilled jungle fighters, Aussie bush hats are highly desired by American GIs who get them embroidered with patches that read "Fuck you" and "Go to hell," to go with the tailor-made jackets previously mentioned.

CHAPTER 68

The movie "My Fair Lady" comes to a theater in Saigon and Loan and I go to see it. A third of the screen is taken up by subtitles in Vietnamese, Chinese and French. The second feature is "The Story of Buddha," which is in Korean and subtitled in English, Vietnamese, Chinese and French, resulting in most of the picture being behind writing. Both of us sit in the dark theater nervously aware that at any minute a VC bomb could blow the place up, but life requires a balance between normalcy and risk.

With war time opportunity being what it is, it doesn't take long before some resourceful Vietnamese have figured out a way to exchange MPCs the way they did dollars, and I suspect somewhere in their scheme is an American profiteer like me. This competition causes me to step up my marketing efforts and I get Quan the houseboy to recruit money changers through his VN contacts who work for the military, who in turn, recruit others thus building a network similar to the Nutrilite and Avon models in the States. And it doesn't take long before Quan has made more money from his share of the enterprise than he has ever seen in his life and buys himself a Lambretta motor scooter which, to the average VN in Saigon, is the equivalent of a Chrysler or Buick in the States.

While the arbitrage business is making a lot of money for me, the Vietnamese economy is inflating faster than local wages. Food items that months ago cost pennies now cost nickels and dimes, and more beggars crowd the sidewalks desperately pleading for anything they can get. In response, the VN government issues a statement asking that we do not give them anything, saying it's an insult to those who work for their money. But how do you turn away from someone who's hungry, especially when they are with little children or holding babies and pleading "babyson hungry," even when you know a fair percentage of them are opportunistic cons who burn the babies with cigarettes or prick them with needles to get them to cry on cue?

CHAPTER 69

Graham's back in Saigon, having solved the problem of getting into Qui-Nhon harbor by loading the Europa with less cargo, thus making it light enough to float over the shallows to the wharf and he can do this and still turn a profit because cargo rates, like everything else, have shot through the roof making small freighters capable of navigating the rivers, and crews willing to man them, in high demand.

With Jack gone, I invite Graham to stay at the villa, but he does not want to leave his ship in the hands of his crew, in particular his first mate, a Filipino he distrusts. In return, he invites me to stay on the Europa and I accept giving Loan a chance to spend the night with her family.

We begin the evening with dinner at La Cigale French Restaurant where we have a first-class meal of escargot, followed by Dalat salad and bowls of Bouillabaisse Marseilles, and end with a nightcap of Cognac before heading back to the Europa where he has a Vietnamese girl waiting for him in his stateroom. Before joining her for the night, he tells me he's looking forward to a 'morning glory,' meaning sex the first thing after opening his eyes, saying it's his all-time favorite way to wake up and start a new day. Only before that opportunity arrives he becomes sick as a dog and sends the first mate to get me in my cabin. And when I enter his stateroom, he's lying on his back holding his belly, begging me to get him to a doctor fast and blaming his illness on the bouillabaisse, saying it was tainted.

With the help of his First Mate, we get his 240-pound body down the gangway into a taxi and over to a French doctor on Phan Thanh Gian Street who injects a large needle into Graham's stomach, providing him with enough relief that he's more upset about missing the morning glory than the pain and suffering he endured; though he's still blaming the bouillabaisse even though I tell him I ate it too and I'm alright.

CHAPTER 70

Whenever we can, Loan and I picnic at a park in Saigon like romantic couples do everywhere in the world, and occasionally go to the zoo where little rag-tag kids wander around with baskets of peanuts or sugar-cane on their heads, soliciting everybody to buy some and feed the elephants. Like many zoos, the air reeks of animal smells, especially urine and feces. But as unpleasant as these odors are, they are much less offensive than those in Saigon's streets where mounds of garbage and toilet waste sit decaying in the sun, prompting me to comment in letters to my family and friends back home that the Saigon zoo is the only zoo I've ever been to that smells better than the city.

Another place Loan and I go to escape the war is the expansive lawn across from the Xa Loi Buddhist Pagoda where its spiritual presence makes us appreciate the destiny that brought us together. Notwithstanding this, Loan makes it perfectly clear she will never go with me when I leave Vietnam because Vietnam's her home, and she can only eat Vietnamese food, honestly believing she would starve to death without it.

Sometimes times we drive out to Ti Nghe with her riding side saddle on the Honda dressed in her white silk Ao Dai and looking like both an elegant woman and a little girl at the same time. Once there we lie around the pool on chaise lounges, her in a tiny bikini, her beauty outshining that of the privileged girls who have nothing else to do, this because it's not just physical, but emanates from her unpretentious soul.

Other days we ride out to the town of Bien Hoa, twenty miles north of Saigon on Highway One, a dangerous thing to do because there are VC all along the route. I am dressed in civilian clothes, hoping the VC will think I'm French whom they no longer care about, and if they do stop us, thanks to Graham, I carry Panamanian Merchant Seaman's papers for added protection. From Bien Hoa we usually make the return trip on the old road that runs through unspoiled landscapes, rice paddies and simple villages where the pace is slow and each community is known for a particular gastronomic specialty. In Tuc Duc, for example, we always stop for their cha gio, which are egg rolls made of paper thin rice dough filled with crabmeat, pork and chopped vegetables, fried and served with fresh watercress and noc mam. They're widely considered the best in Vietnam and we always buy some for Loan's family and watch as they devour them with delight.

Another place we like to go is the Ho Tam Noc Thuy swimming pool, which is very popular with the Vietnamese military and local girls who go there not only to swim, but also in hopes of meeting a boy. I'm always the only Occidental there and once, in the locker room, a nineteen-year-old ARVN soldier confides to me he's planning to desert because he is scared of the war and wants to get back to his village and care for his family. "America number one, Vietnam number ten," he tells me, and I feel compelled to respond that America and Vietnam are the same, because people are the same. Before we part, he gives me his ARVN military ID card to remember him by, saying he won't need it anymore and I give him a couple of thousand Ps to help him on his journey, not caring that his deserting leaves us to pick up the slack in fighting for his country, because I know the war has nothing to do with rural subsistence farmers like him and his family.

CHAPTER 71

At the villa, the maid and the new cook, who fills in when Jack's cook is back on the Indo Traveler, tell me they dislike Loan because she insists on doing the cooking, cleaning and washing for me, which are their jobs. And Sir Robin's chauffer/assistant Fatty complains because Quan gets to drive the Fairlane that I paid for, while he has to drive the Citroen. Who knew having servants could be so much trouble?

Yet there are more serious issues to be concerned with. VC attacks in and around Saigon have become so frequent that living out in Phu-Tho is getting increasingly dangerous. One night while driving the Honda back on Plantation Road, where there are no lights and it's pitch black, a shot rings out and whistles past my ear, rapidly followed by another, then another. I immediately duck down and shut off the headlamp, knowing it's making me an easy target. The road is straight, but driving in pitch blackness is scary so I switch on the headlamp for a second to make sure I'm still going straight. And when I do, I see a truck, that turns out to be deserted, parked across the road just a few yards ahead and immediately lock up the brakes, sending the Honda skidding out from under me. Bleeding from superficial wounds, I crawl under the truck as a barrier between me and the sniper, my 38 in hand, knowing it's useless against a distant and unseen shooter and lie there for almost an hour before an Army convoy comes along and informs me the treat has been neutralized.

In the weeks ahead, several more of these sniper incidents are reported in and around the Phu-Tho neighborhood not far from the villa, and I know it is time to leave, but decide to wait until after the coming holidays before doing so.

CHAPTER 72

With Christmas approaching, cards, letters and packages pour into the AMT from all over the world, overflowing the building and forcing us to store some outside under tarps. Besides family and friends, churches, school children, and nonprofits like "Operation Christmas Vietnam" and "Operation Star Lift" send countless thousands of cards and gift boxes, enough for every GI in the Nam two or three times over, many filled with soap, deodorant, razors, candy, canned soups, combs, brushes, Kool Aid, handkerchiefs, and a few with more expensive things like transistor radios and watches.

In addition to these, there are boxes of home baked cookies crushed into crumbs from thousands of miles of transit under the weight of other cargo, and they quickly become contaminated with rats and insects. We laugh, too, at the mothers who send overcoats, scarfs and wool caps to their boys, not realizing that while it's winter at home, it's over 100 degrees and humid in Vietnam, these items quickly succumbing to mildew.

Among the many thousands of greeting cards and letters there are those from grade school kids across the country written in shaky cursive as class projects, some with snap shots of their authors, many reading like these:

Dear Soldier,
I want you to have a nice Christmas because you are helping me to have a Merry Christmas. I live in Las Vegas.
Sincerely,
Aaron Russel
PS: I hope you get home

Dear Soldier,
This little letter is to thank you for your kindness. Merry Christmas, I love you and you are my friend. I watch Batman every night. It is a good show. I like it very much. Smile your (sic) on Candid Camera.
Your friend, Jeffrey

Dear G.I.
Merry Christmas. I no (sic) what it is like because my brother was in the army and he tells me all about the games. I no (sic) that you give (sic) on doing your best to help us. I hope you could right

(sic) me back. We pray to our Lady that all of you
will get home safe. Well I better get going if I don't
I will get hit by my teacher.
Jeff

Besides grammar and spelling, I can't help but think how
much better it would be if, instead of discussing the war in
righteous terms or praying to their Lady just for our safe return, they taught these young minds to celebrate the Prince
of Peace's birth by making themselves an example of his
teachings, and how to resist the impulse to have their own
way at the expense of others, which is what ultimately leads
to war.

CHAPTER 73

T he Holiday season also exposes a sentimental side to Sir Robin and he asks me to help him arrange for a Christmas party at the villa.

"I will have Quan get us a tree, and the cook make a turkey," he says, "and I'll cable Manila for an ice cream cake. They do a splendid job of packing it in dry ice and flying it here in only a few hours. Will you please get some ornaments and carol records from the BX?"

"I'll do what I can, but who will we invite?" I ask.

"Jack and Le and Graham and a girlfriend if he wishes, and your Loan and my father and Nancy and maybe a few of your GI buddies, and maybe some people from the school where you teach. We'll have a gran, old fashioned English-American Christmas with trimming the tree and singing carols."

The following day I invite the guys from the AMT, but only Zoffa says he'll come, the rest preferring to stay in town where they feel safe and celebrate the Holiday with the special Christmas dinner planned by HEDSUPAC. I invite Mark Breslin too, but he tells me he will be in Singapore for Christmas with his family on his last visit before leaving Saigon. In return, he invites me for a pre-holiday lunch at the Cercle Sportif.

On the morning of that lunch I have Quan drive me in the Fairlane over to the Tax Building and wait outside while I go upstairs to Jacklyn's Barber Shop for her deluxe treatment, which includes a haircut followed by shampoo, hot towel shave, ear cleaning, nose hair clipping, manicure, pedicure, shoe shine, steam bath, body massage with sexual release optional, a hot bath in a tub given by a beautiful girl using a luffa, then towel-off and help getting dressed in my freshly pressed clothes. All this while Jacklyn, the owner, a Vietnamese woman who is rumored to have financed the business with money earned from being a prostitute, walks around serving drinks and making sure your every need is being satisfied. The total cost for this being only ten US dollars, and everybody from high ranking government officials and military officers to the wealthy elite make sure to get groomed there as often as possible because it's hands down the best salon in Saigon.

When I come back down, Quan drives me to the Cercle Sportif where Mark's waiting with a martini in hand. The first words out of his mouth when he sees me in my brand new, freshly pressed Guayabera imported from the Philippines are, "You look like the goddam Mayor of

Saigon," not knowing it's the same nickname the guys at the AMT gave me when they saw Quan driving me around in the Fairlane.

"That's because I just came from Jacklyn's," I tell him, then order a citron soda and listen to him go on about how, because of his relationship with my aunt, he feels responsible for me and is worried about me being mixed up with "those Chinese characters" and living in Phu Tho where the VC are increasingly active at night.

"I don't know what you're doing," he says, "but whatever it is, you better end it and move back to town before it's too late. Interpol is on to those guys. I'm telling you this for your own good."

While I believe his concern is genuine, I can't help but feel the stress and worry I see on his face are due more to his impending rotation and personal issues with his family, something he's expressed to me so many times; he's not an easy going person to begin with. Knowing he'll be gone in a few days, I promise to take his advice and dissolve my relationship with the Chinese and move back to the Hung Dao by the end of the month when the rent is due on the villa.

CHAPTER 74

A message arrives for me at the Hung Dao, reading, "Telephone call from Jill Cohen New York City. Connection will be 0900 local, 24 December at Transcontinental Phone Office, U.S.O. Building 119, Nguyen Hue Street, Saigon."

Telephone calls from the States to GIs are far and few between due to the difficulty of making the connection to Vietnam and the high cost, but Jill, who's an old girlfriend, comes from a super wealthy New York family. When news of the call gets out, some of the guys at the AMT are envious and resentful, associating the call to the privileged lifestyle they perceive I am living. And when I try to down play it by reminding them anybody can call, it doesn't help because they realize their wives and girlfriends could do so if they really wanted to, though I suspect they'd be pissed off if they did, because of the money.

One of the guys taking this position is the General and it surprises me because he and Sgt. Robbie have been not only making a good deal of money but spending it lavishly on high living. When I take him aside to call him out on this, he apologizes and explains that while they appreciate the opportunity, they no longer feel comfortable being involved and we let it go at that.

CHAPTER 75

Twenty minutes before the scheduled call from Jill, I present myself at the U.S.O. Despite the rarity of such calls the place is crowded with GIs like me. On one side of the room is a bank of numbered phone booths, on the other, a counter behind which an American USO worker is routing the calls via a switchboard, while another worker announces the name of the person receiving the call, and the booth to which it is being routed. Alongside them is third USO worker taking reservations for outgoing calls and above her a large clock with a sign reading, "All calls limited to 3 minutes."

After presenting my call notice, I take a seat on the bench waiting to be called and passing the time by staring through the glass doors of the booths at the faces of those talking trying to guess what they're saying and what is being said back to them, especially when the three minutes are up and everyone knows it may be the last time they ever hear from one another. The profoundness of this is evident when the doors to the booths open and they hesitate in a moment of reflection before leaving.

When I hear "Los Angeles calling for Ben Kovner in booth number two," I enter the booth and wait for the ring. Then when it comes, I have no idea of what to say in three minutes.

"Hello?"

"Go ahead New York," from the operator.

"Hello, hello." Only all I hear is thousands of miles of undersea cable noise similar to what you receive when you hold a sea shell up to your ear. Then finally a faint and distant, "Hello, hello can you hear me?" and it's Jill's voice reverberating in an echo.

"Jill, is that you? It sounds like you're in a tunnel. Can you hear me? Where are you? How are you?"

"I'm good. I'm back in New York. Can you hear me? Where are YOU, how are YOU?"

"I'm in Saigon. I'm okay."

"Ben, this is crazy, what time is it there?"

"A little past 9 A.M. What time is it where you are?"

"I don't know, I just got up."

"What day is it there?"

"I think it's Thursday. What day is it there?"

"It's Friday.

"So tell me, what's Friday going to be like?"

"Depends, what do you have planned?"

"Too much to tell. What's the war like?"

"Crazy. I think we're going to lose."

"What makes you say that?"

"Our government's lying to us. Don't believe what you read in the papers. I can see with my own eyes that our casualties are a lot greater than what they're saying. And the South Vietnamese people don't trust Thieu and Ky. Many of their soldiers are fighting because they're forced to, and because they fear the North more than they hate Thieu and Ky. From what I can tell, this is a civil war between the North and the South, and Catholics and Buddhists, and historic cultural animosities with each side distrusting the other. And when it ends, it won't be over. One side will eventually dominate the other, and like the American civil war, the losing side will suffer until memories fade."

"That's heavy. I don't know what to say."

"It's the government's war and the people are being sucked into it. The North bates their people with the fear and hatred for colonialism, and dreams of a Vietnam governed by Vietnamese. And the South bates their side using fear and hatred for the North and Chinese Communism, but anybody who looks at the history of Vietnam can see that both North and South hate and distrust the Chinese communists more than we do, and the North is only accepting their help because they need them to sustain the war against the South. Supposedly we're here to prevent the spread of Communism, but if we were to pull out today and the South were to fall, both the North and South would unite in their hatred and distrust of the Chinese. Not only that…"

"I'm sorry, your three minutes are up," The operator cuts in.

"Listen, Jill, thanks for calling. Take care of yourself, I miss you."

"I miss you too."

CHAPTER 76

The Christmas party at the villa comes to life with Sir Robin and Nancy, having already emptied a bottle of Champagne, singing carols in harmony with a recording of Bing Crosby on the phonograph. Nancy, who's half Japanese, is wearing a kimono with nobe, and Sir Robin a long sarong that he tells me is the real national dress for men in his ancestral home of Indonesia. When they sing "Rudolph the Red Nose Reindeer" it comes off sounding like "ludoph the lead nose lane-deer," but it doesn't matter because the music is joyous and the expressions on their faces euphoric.

Jack and his VN girlfriend Le are sitting in one chair, she on his lap wearing a short revealing skirt, and next to them the Japanese pine tree Sir Robin had flown in from Tokyo, even though there are plenty of pine trees available from the mountains in Vietnam. The tree is decorated in the American tradition with colorful bulbs and tinsel that Sir Robin and Jack call "Al-u-minium hair," along with an angel on top that I got through the BX. Above the door to the dining room is a banner reading, "Merry Christmas," and on the floor a cardboard cutout of Santa Claus, both "borrowed" from the Christmas decorations in the Hung Dao dining room.

Zoffa's on the sofa next to me and Loan, offering a toast "To a good looking tenebaum," and Graham, across from him on a chair, dressed in his formal Captain's uniform along with his not so pretty but nice VN girlfriend Hue in an elegant black silk Ao Dai, seconds Zoffa's toast with, "Here's to good mates, good grog and a good shivoo."

Hue doesn't understand much "In-grish," but that doesn't stop Graham from speaking to her as if she is fluent, saying things like, "Hue darling, would you care for some more Champagne?" and "Hue darling, can I get you something to eat?" Hue always responding with a puzzled expression on her face, which Graham translates into whatever he wants it to mean. Then there's Sir Robin's father along with his entourage, which includes some sinister-looking Chinese men and Fatty, who watch expressionless from across the room and don't participate.

On the dining table are platters of prawns, whole cooked fish, lobsters, and a ham I bartered from a Navy cook in exchange for the location of a cheap brothel and along-side them, a roasted turkey with its head still on, caviar with chopped egg, rice, vegetables, mounds of ripe fruits and the ice cream cake Sir Robin had flown in from Manila, still packed in dry ice.

When we sit down to eat, Sir Robin insists on carving the turkey, severing the head and serving it to me, explaining that in his culture it is considered the best part and given to the most special guest. Not wanting to be ungrateful, I pick it up with my chopsticks and bit down, its potato chip thin skull crunching in my mouth then leaking its warm liquid brain down my throat. Zoffa winces at this and I remind him how Germans eat blood sausage and pickled pig's feet, and he laughs, then digs in, filling his plate with ham, shrimp and lobster.

After dinner, aided by alcohol, we all sing along to a Bing Crosby record that includes the Holiday favorites of "Chestnuts Roasting on an Open Fire," "White Christmas," "Silent Night" and "O Come All Ye Faithful." Then, just before curfew, Quan drives Graham and Hue back to the Europa, Jack and Le go upstairs to their bedroom, Sir Robin's father leaves with his entourage and Sir Robin passes out on the sofa, his mouth agape, with a drunk Nancy dancing all by herself even though the record is no longer playing. When Zoffa can't keep his eyes off of her, Fatty steps in and takes her out to the car, then returns for Sir Robin.

With the party over, Loan and I go upstairs to our bedroom and Zoffa bunks down on the sofa. It is then, with the music gone and laying on the bed, that I notice something's amiss. It's way too quiet in an eerie unnerving way, like something terrible is about to happen and it sends a shiver through my body until I discover what it is.

In recognition of Christmas, President Johnson ordered a twenty-four hour cease fire, and for the first time since coming to the Nam there're no bombs booming in the distance. It's so quiet it's spooky and I can't sleep. With my little Buddha angel Loan lying beside me already in dreamland, random thoughts start drifting through my head, one of them about the famous Christmas Truce of World War 1 where British, French and German enemies crawled out of their foxholes and mingled like friends, singing Christmas carols, playing sports and exchanging souvenirs until the truce ended and they went back to killing each other. And another about General Westmoreland's strategy of killing more of the enemy than they kill of us that results in only a few hundred Vietnamese left before we declare victory and go home.

CHAPTER 77

After being up most of the night I get ready to leave for at the AMT and go downstairs only to see the servants are still asleep and the leftover food from the party is still on the table—the meats, the fish, the caviar, all of it spoiled from the heat and covered with flies, left to waste in a land of starving people only because the servants failed to put it in the refrigerator. I expected poor people to have more respect for food.

CHAPTER 78

Graham's decided he's in love with plain-looking Hue proving two of my observational theories—the first being there's somebody for everybody, and the second that beauty is entirely subjective. Out of thousands of available girls, she is the one he wants. He's serious, too, lovesick with an eighteen-year-old (so she says) bargirl, and he a thirty-eight-year old man with two children and an ex-wife back in Australia.

"I'm going to marry her," he declares. "I'm not getting any younger and a bloke's got to know he's got a Sheila waiting for him when he's at sea."

"But Graham, ole cobber," I say, using the Aussie vernacular he taught me meaning a good friend, "Don't you think you should wait until you know her just a little bit better?"

"I've waited too long already. I'm tired of running loose."

Hearing this, I don't need to be clairvoyant to know the odds are Graham would be making a terrible mistake. He and Hue are very different people, different cultures, different religions, different life experiences, different languages. They can't even talk to one another, and even in bed the odds are they're each having sex with someone other than who they think they are. The only thing they have in common is the need for one another, but likely for different reasons. Even though it's easier to describe color to a blind man than reason with a closed mind, I feel as Graham's cobber it's my duty to try.

"What are you going to do when you leave Vietnam for good?" I ask him. "Can you picture Hue living in Australia?"

"These sheilas come from the tough side of the tracks," he says. "They can adjust to anything."

Okay, but as a favor to me, why don't you wait a month or two to see how things go before getting married?" I ask.

"That's fair dinkum mate, I wasn't planning on getting married for a few months anyway."

CHAPTER 79

More problems arise with the local charterers, and Sir Robin wires Hong Kong for Juan-Carlo to fly back down to Saigon. The principal issue is the charterers claim it's the owner's responsibility to pay for repatriation of the Hong Kong crew, while Juan-Carlo claims under the contract it's the charterer's responsibility, and this brings everything to a halt.

To break the stalemate, Juan-Carlo returns to Saigon and brings with him the remarkable ability to separate Juan-Carlo the sharp, powerful businessman from Juan-Carlo, the fun-loving guy and after a full day of tough negotiations with the charterers, he manages to turn the evening into a good time. He not only knows how to laugh, but how to make everybody else laugh too. Even more amazing to me, he can tell a joke in four languages, seamlessly without a break in continuity as demonstrated during our dinner at the Caravelle when he speaks French to Masseur Plaud and Jack, English to me and Graham, Chinese to the charterers, and Japanese to the female hotel guest he invited to join us. It's an extraordinary talent that leaves me in awe.

CHAPTER 80

After several days of negotiating, it is agreed that Jack will return to Hong Kong with Juan-Carlo to give testimony before a special maritime court that will make the final decision on who is responsible for the cost of repatriation. But before he goes, Jack decides to throw a farewell dinner aboard the Indo Traveler to be prepared by his new Vietnamese cook who apprenticed with a classically trained French chef. The menu includes Champagne from the Caravelle's cellar and continues with escargot, oysters, foie gras, smoked salmon and duck rillettes.

At the table are Juan-Carlo, Sir Robin, Jack, Graham, Jack's first mate Bull MacGregger and me; Zoffa having declined once again without giving a reason. Bull, a native of Scotland, has been a merchant seaman most of his sixty plus years and he's seen the world many times over, at one point living in South Africa. Most notably, he's an irascible character, a stereotypical image of an old salt and the only one at the table not fully dressed, refusing to wear anything other than his everyday uniform of baggy faded blue shorts with no shirt to cover his chest of bushy white hair and no underwear to keep his saggy old balls from hanging out the bottom of his shorts whenever he lifts his leg. He's crude and belligerent, and when he drinks too much, directs this behavior toward people he perceives to be below his station, which includes most other nationalities, especially the VN crew and dockworkers who need their jobs and can't fight back.

This side of him comes out during dinner after he's drunk too much and starts verbally attacking Sir Robin who's Chinese and therefore, in his eyes, not his equal, Knight of the Garter or not, and Juan-Carlo, the ship's owner, and Jack who are both part Chinese, blaming them for the trouble with the charterers and following this with a thinly disguised innuendo about Juan-Carlo not being man enough to clear up the problem, and Jack being too young and inexperienced to be a captain. But Jack, knowing it's the alcohol talking and needing Bull's experience as first mate, ignores the slights and tries to change the situation by asking me about the well-publicized VC attack at Tan Son Nhut the night before.

"It really didn't amount to much," I tell him, "only a few minutes of small arms fire, all of it on our side. What happened was word got out the VC were planning to attack the Base thinking we'd be off guard celebrating New Year's Eve so everybody was on pins and needles, and around mid-night some GIs decided to shoot off a few tracer rounds to simulate fireworks, and when they did, others thought it was the expected attack and started shooting back, and when others heard them, they started shooting too, and within minutes it was a full-on fire fight, only without any opposition. I was more scared of being shot in the back by some panicked GI than the VC. Thankfully it ended when somebody realized nobody was returning fire."

I further tell how the entire incident is only symptomatic of everybody being on edge because of the escalating attacks in and around the City and the second time in as many days I came close to being killed because of it. The other being when I stopped in at the BX to buy a replacement for my thermos and the glass vacuum bottle fell out of the bottom of the box as I lifted it off the shelf, exploding on the floor and causing the GI standing next to me to whip out his gun. If not for the requirement that all weapons be cleared before entering the BX, he might have shot me.

With the main course over, Jack brings out tins of English Christmas pudding he's been saving for a special occasion. Even though Christmas has passed, I can tell from the look on his face they represent more than a good eating to him.

"Ahhh mates," he says, "this pudding reminds me of my grandparent's home in St. Albans, all of us sitting around the warm fire topping off a grand meal with bowls of Christmas pudding. There's nothing finer and it makes me homesick just thinking about it."

Along with the pudding, he serves a sweet dessert wine and the conversation gets nostalgic with everybody except Bull, sharing stories of family holiday traditions and expressions of optimism for the New Year. It's during this time that Bull loudly complains that the wine is "rank" and he's going up to his cabin and get some scotch. Nobody pays much attention to this until we hear him out on deck yelling, "I'm going to kill you bloody kanakas!" and go racing out to find him standing at the rail with a flare aimed down at some poor VNs who are alongside the ship in a sampan.

"Hold on mate," Jack yells. "What the hell's going on?"

"The bloody bastards stole me sextant, captain, the rotten Kanakers."

"Who Bull?"

"Those bloody kanakers in the sampan," he says, pointing at the Vietnamese who are looking up their faces frozen in fear. "They've been crawling all over this tub ever since we tied up. I'll just pop a few of em off an teach em a lesson."

"I don't see anything in their sampan," Jack says,."The thief could be long gone." He then calmly orders Bull to surrender the flare gun and confine himself to his cabin.

"Aye Captain," Bull says reluctantly, but before going lifts the leg of his shorts and pees on the people in the sampan.

CHAPTER 81

With Juan-Carlo and Jack in Hong Kong where they finalized the settlement allowing Graham and the Europa to sail for Qui Nhon, and Sir Robin in Kuala lumpur on business, and Mark Breslin already rotated back to stateside, and the school term at Hoi Viet My over, I decide it's a good time for me to put in a request for an R & R, military speak for rest and recuperation.

It's a routine request because every GI in the Nam is eligible for a five or seven day R & R to their choice of Hawaii, Sydney, Bangkok, Kuala Lumpur, Manila, Singapore, Taipei or Tokyo. Sydney being popular with GIs wanting a safe place where English is spoken, Hawaii with those whose families can fly there to meet them, and Bangkok, Kuala Lumpur and Manila by those wanting an exotic place where they can sight see and have inexpensive sex. In fact, upon arrival in Bangkok, you can actually sign a legally enforceable contract with a girl to be a tour guide and sex partner for the week. Singapore, Taipei and Tokyo are also chosen for sex, but are more upscale and expensive. For me it's Hong Kong because it's an exotic and intriguing place where an important part of my arbitrage business is located, and because Jack is there and has decided not return to Vietnam due to the escalating danger.

After my request is approved, I stop by the Indo-Traveler to ask Bull for Jack's address so I can surprise him when I get to Hong Kong, and find him sitting outside his cabin with his feet propped up against the rail, his chest bare, and balls hanging out the bottom of his signature faded blue shorts. Having little to do before the new captain arrives, he's bored and won't give me Jack's address until I listen to his stories about all the cities and bars he's been to, and the woman he's been with, and his advice on how to prevent VD by taking a piss right after having sex and washing your cock with a disinfectant like hydrogen peroxide. "In sixty-three years I never once got the clap, and I've been with some boggin women," he tells me. Then when he finally gives me Jack's address at Hong Kong's Capital Hotel, he also gives me the names of two friends he wants me to look up and say hello for him, telling me they'll be happy to hear from him and will treat me right.

Before boarding the R&R-chartered Pan American Clipper Dusseldorf aka "the little freedom bird," I turn in my weapon. It's raining cats and dogs on the tarmac, but two minutes after takeoff we're above the weather in a world of blue skies and sunshine, the horrors of the war concealed below the clouds, and all around me the captivated faces of my fellow GIs staring at the round-eyed stewardesses as if they've never seen one before.

Three hours later we deplane at Hong Kong's Kai Tac peninsular airport and are greeted by an American army captain dressed in a handsomely tailored civilian suit who turns out to be the local R&R director. At his side is a drop-dead gorgeous young Chinese girl, who looks like a teen fashion model straight out of Vogue magazine.

He starts off by telling us that it's his job to insure our five days in Hong Kong will be safe and enjoyable and the informational pamphlets we received on the plane should answer most of our questions, then continues on with his briefing.

"The US government cannot recommend any specific hotel, but in the pamphlet we've listed several hotels that are moderately priced and able to accommodate the influx of R&R troops. When you leave the terminal, buses will be waiting outside to take you to these hotels. They will stop at each hotel beginning with the closest one first, simply get out at whichever one you choose. But before you leave here, there are two things I want to impress upon you. The first is about girls." And when he says that, all heads turn to the Chinese girl at his side as if he brought her to demonstrate what a Hong Kong girl looks like.

"I don't want any of you to show up here in five days with some girl and tell me you want to get married." Everybody laughs. "I know it will be tempting, but let me tell you a story. Last week a GI called me just before boarding his return flight to the Nam and says he and his girlfriend, who he met only two days before, want to get married and when I arrive at the airport there are tears flowing from her eyes and he's so messed up he says he won't leave unless they can get married and tells me he doesn't care about the disciplinary consequences or anything, just the girl. Fortunately, I was able to talk him out of it before the flight left, but not before he gave the girl every penny he had in his possession, along with the promise to send her more and make arrangements through proper channels for them to get married. After his plane takes off I watch the girl go into the Ladies room and come out with fresh make-up, then head over to meet the incoming flight of GIs." After everybody laughs, he continues.

"The next thing I want to talk about is desertion." More laughter and a few cheers. "Don't even think about it. You're here to have a good time, not to take up residency and ruin your lives forever. Believe me, no matter what you do, wherever you go, you'll be caught. If you need me for anything during your stay, feel free to call. And one last thing, for god's sake use a rubber!" More laughter. "VD could get you court-martialed for making yourself unavailable for duty. Now go and have a great R&R, Hong Kong awaits you."

He then leaves with the Chinese girl, and all eyes on the backside of her form-fitting chung sam as if it's a promise of what's to come.

CHAPTER 82

I get off the bus at the Grand Hotel on Humphreys Road, and after checking in call Jack at the Capital Hotel, which was not one of the hotels offered to us, only to find he's out of town and not expected back for two more days. I next try to find Juan-Carlo's number, only there are countless thousands of Choys listed in the Hong Kong phone directory, none with the name Juan-Carlo and far too many with the first initial "J" to think of calling. Then, after showering and dressing, I'm left with a mild sense of despair of what to do because I had counted on seeing Jack and had not given much thought beyond that.

While staring out the window I see a pair of panties blow off a clothes pole on the multistory apartment tenement across the street and watch as it floats down several stories before getting snagged on the clothes pole of an apartment below, and this makes me laugh when I imagine how finding a strange woman's panties might affect the lives of the people living in the other apartment; and this snaps me out of my funk so that I'm now ready to go out and see what Hong Kong has in store for me.

After exiting the hotel the first thing that overwhelms my senses are all the neon signs with Hanzi characters, then all the double decker buses and Mercedes Benz taxis, which in the States are rich people's cars, and seeing Rolls Royces driving alongside primitive rickshaws pulled by skinny Chinamen wearing sneakers. Though not nearly as bad as Saigon, Hong Kong's air is hot and humid, filled with unfamiliar scents of different foods cooking and the all too familiar scents of engine exhaust and beeping horns. All of this unfamiliarity feeding my spirit for adventure and I head out, armed with a map of the city and the addresses of Bull MacGregor's mates that he asked me to look up and say hello for him.

Hailing one of the Mercedes Benz taxis for my first ride in one ever, I head over to the August Moon Hotel where Bull's friend Brodie is supposed to be the bar manager. Along the way it occurs to me, in a city where I am unknown, I don't have to be a GI on R&R. I could be anybody I want and when I get to the August Moon and ask for Brodie and the bartender says "Who wants to know?" I give him my name and tell him I'm a principal of the East West Shipping Company, which is only a slight exaggeration since my arbitrage deal gives me cargo rights on two of the company's freighters.

As it turns out, this new identity fits in perfectly with the August Moon's bar scene, which is decidedly upscale and not the kind of place I would expect to find a crude old salt like Bull MacGregor. While waiting for Brodie to show up I order a Pernod with water, a gentleman's drink I picked up from Sir Robin who after all, is a British Hong Kong Knight of the Garter, then sit listening to the voices around me trying to identify the different languages they're speaking, and watching in amazement as they pay for drinks in francs, pounds, dollars and marks, the Chinese bartender, having apparently memorized the daily rates of exchange, effortlessly figuring out the correct amounts to charge and give back as change, using an abacus. It's all so mater-of-fact I can't help but think how incensed people in the States get when they discover a Canadian penny inadvertently mixed in with change from a purchase.

After several minutes the bartender directs me to a bald-headed man sitting at a corner table with an Oriental girl. At first when I go over and introduce myself, mentioning the hello from Bull, the man seems bewildered.

"Bull MacGregor, first mate on the Indio-traveler," I tell him again. "Are you Brodie?"

"I am him, but I don't recall any Bull MacGregor."

"An irascible Scotsman with white hair who works on freighters."

He ponders for a moment then says, "Oh that guy. Where did you say he is?"

"Vietnam."

"Well, if you see him again, tell him I'm still waiting for him to pay back the money he owes me." And with that he turns his attention back to the girl he's with and I walk away deciding not to pursue Bull's other friend.

CHAPTER 83

Determined to spend the day exploring the City, I ask the bartender at the August Moon to teach me how to say a few key phrases in Cantonese like "Hello" and "please" and "thank you", and "take me to the Star Ferry," carefully writing down his pronunciation phonetically so I can correctly repeat them even though I know being a British Dependent Territory many people speak and understand English, and all I have to do is say the words "Star Ferry" and every taxi driver in the City will know where I want to go.

Intent on keeping up with my new persona of being a shipping magnate, when I get to the famous Star Ferry I pay the full fare rather than present my military ID for a discount, the difference being only pennies, then ride across the bay from Hong Kong Island to Kowloon on what has to be one of the greatest ferries rides in the world, packed with commuters and tourists alike and lots of signs in English and Chinese saying "No Spitting," the Chinese being notorious spitters. Riding the ferry with me are lots of American Navy sailors in uniform and on shore leave, their arms around young Chinese girls and likely crossing the harbor for a day of sightseeing followed by lunch, a commemorative tattoo and some souvenir sex before having to go back to their ships.

As for me, I'm most interested in seeing Kowloon, because of its intriguing name which I'm told comes from the Chinese words "gow lung," meaning nine dragons and because it's only kilometers away from the border with the Peoples Republic of China, propagandized in American as the Red Devil, a land of mystery and secrets and millions of oppressed people who would suffer a terrible fate if they dare speak out against their leader, the powerful Chairman Mao whose infamous "Little Red Book" contains such quotes as, "War is the highest form of struggle for resolving contradictions" and "We the Chinese nation have the spirit to fight the enemy to the last drop of our blood." Red China also being home to the mysterious Forbidden City of Peking where it is said, no one in the entire Western world knows what goes on in there.

It's this lifetime of conditioning that makes being in its proximity so exciting along with the fact that Hong Kong in general was once the epicenter of the world's opium trade and is now recognized as the number one home of international infiltrators and a black market where you can buy anything from drugs to diamonds, including books, records and brand-named goods without regard for copyright or law at a fraction of the cost of those sold legally. For example, a Beatles record, which in the States sells for six dollars, can be purchased in Hong Kong for only fifty cents, and that same price disparity goes for everything else.

Surprisingly, for such a nefarious place, walking down Nathan Road, Kowloon's main drag, I marvel at how immaculately clean and orderly it is. From the streets to the sidewalks to the policemen's white uniforms, everything is spotlessly clean and there's symphonic command in the way the police direct the substantial traffic of double decker buses, cars, rickshaws, push carts, motor scooters and bicycles using a baton like an orchestra conductor. And it's the same on every street, even those where ancient trolleys clang by in the middle of the road. I've been assured, too, by my hotel clerk that these are the safest streets in the world. The police don't even carry guns, and this according to him, is because any Chinese not toeing the line knows he or she will be deported to dreaded Red China. It's so safe he says, I can even walk down the darkest alley in the city at any hour day or night without fear of harm, and this alone makes it different from every other big city in the world.

But there are similarities to other big cities too, and before I've gone a couple of blocks a rickshaw driver runs alongside me calling out, "Hey American, I take you fuck best Chinese girl in Hong Kong only twenty dollars," meaning twenty Hong Kong dollars, which is the equivalent of three dollars thirty cents U.S.

Even though I'm more interested in seeing the sights than having sex, I can't help but meet his offer with a counter by saying, "I won't pay more than five Hong Kong dollars," in the foolish belief that the low price will blow him off, forgetting that the Chinese are among the world's most determined business people, well known for never passing up any deal if there is profit to be made no matter how small. He then counters with, "Okay, fifteen dollars."

"No, six dollars." I tell him.

"Okay, ten dollars, I take you now fuck best Chinese girl you see."

"No, seven dollars."

"Seven dollars, okay you get in rickshaw I take you."

And before I know it, I'm taking my very first rickshaw ride sitting high up behind a skinny Chinaman who's trotting down the busy street surrounded by speeding cars, buses and trucks crisscrossing in front of us and making me feel like I'm riding in a baby carriage in the middle of a highway. I'm embarrassed too when we stop at a red light and people in cars stare up at me, probably thinking there goes another low life GI tourist from Vietnam on his way to fuck some cheap prostitute, and this feeling making the green light take forever.

When the light finally changes, the rickshaw driver holds out his arm to signal a right turn then trots down a side street and stops at the end of a cul-de-sac flanked by high rise apartments resembling a massive public housing project. He then calls out in Chinese and a minute later a woman sticks her head out of an upper story window and calls down to him. After they exchange words, the driver shakes his head then turns back toward the main street. When I question him, he tells me the girl was busy, but not to worry he has another "best Chinese girl in Hong Kong." When the same thing happens at the next stop, it occurs to me with all the GIs on R&R and conventions in town, the sex workers must be busy. I'm about to tell him to forget it when he meets with success and leads me up a staircase and down a narrow, dimly lit hallway packed with Chinese men and women smoking and socializing, me having to brush against them as I squeeze by, and they eyeing me like the fuck wallet tourist they know I am. Worse than embarrassing, I begin to wonder if I'll make it out of there alive and have to keep reassuring myself of how safe the city is supposed to be. At the end of the hallway there's a Chinese woman standing in the open doorway of an apartment, with her hand held out for me to pay.

Nothing in this scene feeds my libido and I want to turn around and leave, but the potential for argument and having to push my way back through the hallway packed with strangers where I could be assaulted and robbed with impunity does not seem like a good alternative, especially over what amounts to pennies, so I hand over the money and when I do, the rickshaw driver insists I give him three HK dollars for the ride, but I stand firm on our deal and he backs down. The woman then leads me inside and to a small bedroom where a young Chinese girl is sitting on a bed dressed in pajamas. It's a tiny apartment and I sense the girl is the woman's daughter and not the least bit interested in what she knows she has to do, but when the woman closes the bedroom door the girl gets undressed, then lays down without saying a word.

CHAPTER 84

The next morning I'm up early, ready to explore Hong Kong Island, starting with a brisk walk to the Peak Tram for a bird's eye view of the harbor which is as busy as the city's traffic-congested streets only with junks, sampans, freighters, ferries and lots of battleship grey American Navy boats. From there I go to the tourist spots of Tai Hang and Tiger Balm Gardens to see the colorful figurines, gardens and flowers that attract even the locals, and from there on to the Stanley market, beautiful Repulse Bay and window shopping where I strike up a conversation with a American Jeweler just in from Beverly Hills, California, who speaks fluent Chinese and is in town to buy pearls. Even more amazing we find out we have a mutual friend and ask him to say hello for me when he gets back, knowing my friend will wonder what the hell I was doing in Hong Kong. This happenstance reminding me of the old cliché of what a small world it is, but in thinking about it, I realize the cliché works because even with the world's vast population, there are comparative few who can afford to travel.

For dinner I go to a Chinese restaurant highly recommended by the hotel clerk as a place where the locals go to eat and am overwhelmed by the excellent service, actually having my own exclusive waiter whose only job is to stand behind me the entire time and cater to my every need and then some. If I pull out a cigarette, he's there to light it. If I tap an ash into the ashtray, he immediately replaces it with a clean one. If I set down an empty tea cup, he slips in to fill it. And all this service, along with an outstanding multicourse meal, only comes to twelve HK dollars, about two American dollars. And as if that isn't enough, when I hand the waiter a fifty-cent tip he's overwhelmed with appreciation and gratitude.

Following dinner I walk back to the hotel, but before going up to the room decide to hang out on the corner for a few minutes and smoke a cigarette. It's then that a rickshaw driver pulls up and propositions me saying if I give him one Hong Kong dollar he will return with the most beautiful girl in all Hong Kong who will be mine for the entire night.

Despite my experience the night before, curiosity gets the best of me and I hand him the dollar and he immediately leaves the rickshaw on the sidewalk and jumps into a taxi, returning minutes later with a girl in tow. She's teenage cute and like the previous night's girl, dressed in pajamas and not at all looking enthusiastic about being there.

He then asks me for an additional five Hong Kong dollars for her to spend the night with me in my hotel room.

"I don't think she wants to," I tell him.

"No, no. She like fucky, fucky," he assures me.

"She no look too happy," I tell him.

You give five dollars she happy."

He then says something to the girl in Chinese and she forces a smile, so I say "Okay." But when we get to my room, the girl, who apparently doesn't speak English, wants me to place a call for her indicated by handing me a piece of paper with the number on it and pointing to the telephone. After the hotel operator makes the connection, I hand the phone to the girl and wait while she chatters away in Chinese, wondering who she's talking to and what she's saying, musing to myself that she's probably telling her mother "after this idiot foreigner fucks me, I'll stop by the market and pick up some noodles for dinner."

After she hangs up, she sits on the bed and undresses, then takes leave of her body, abandoning me to take any pleasure alone. But I'm not inclined to engage in yet another night of solo sex with a mannequin so I ask her to leave, but she won't go. Instead she goes down on my cock, generating just enough stimulation for us to get it over with.

More exhausted from the day's outing than the night's sex, I drift off to sleep and when I wake up it's three A.M. and I'm surprised to see the girl is sound asleep next to me. So I go back to sleep and when I wake up again it's seven A.M. and she's gone. Happy to be rid of her, I jump out of bed, remembering what a politician said when he was caught paying prostitutes for sex, "I don't pay them for sex, I pay them to leave."

It's then that I instinctively check my wallet only to find it empty, approximately fifty American dollars gone. Angry, I race to the door irrationally hoping to catch her, but when I open it all I see is the floor porter staring back at me with a telltale smirk on his face. It's obvious he knows what happened since it's his job to stand outside my room 24/7 in case I need something.

Embarrassed at being suckered like a stupid tourist, I surmise he likely got a cut for letting her go then rush back inside to check under the mattress where I hid over a thousand dollars, and am relieved to find it still there.

But my ego is bruised and I won't let go of being suckered and later that day when I connect with Jack who was in Macao gambling with Juan-Carlo, I tell him the story and ask him to help me get the stolen money back."

"What can I do?" he says. "There are thousands of hookers in this City. You're lucky it was only fifty dollars."

"I've got her phone number," I tell him. "She wrote it down when she called from the room. You speak Chinese, just call the number and tell who ever answers you're with the police and if she doesn't give the money back you're coming after her."

But when he calls, the person on the other end just laughs and hangs up and my only consolation is to rationalize the poor girl and her family probably need the money more than I do.

CHAPTER 85

When Jack was in Macao he ran into some bad luck and lost the equivalent of twenty-five hundred American dollars, but he believes my unexpected visit is a sign his luck has changed and wants me to go back to Macao with him right then and there, even though he hasn't slept in two days and has dark puffy bags under his eyes, a stubby beard and yellow-stained hands and teeth from nonstop smoking.

Why don't you rest up a bit and we'll go tomorrow," I say?

"I can't stop now that my luck's changed," he answers. "We'll go by the bank on the way to the hydrofoil and get some fresh money."

"But won't you do better after a little rest?"

"Never rest when luck's on your side."

It's then I remember GIs aren't allowed to go to Macao because even though it's Portuguese territory, it's on the mainland of Red China, but when I tell him this he just says, "Don't worry I can get you a tourist visa."

There's no arguing with a gambler who feels luck's on his side and without even stopping to get a change of clothes, the two of us head over to the bank where he withdraws several thousand dollars and I change some US dollars into Hong Kong dollars, receiving back a couple of those ridiculously large HK five hundred dollar bills, each the size of a magazine page that need to be folded over six times before they're small enough to fit in a wallet. From there it's down to the wharf to board one of the modern, sleek-hulled hydrofoil boats for the trip to Macao. And during the crossing I have a genuine visceral experience seeing ships flying the scary Red Chinese flag and knowing that I'm headed to the Chinese mainland where I'm not supposed to be in the first place.

In Macao, which is only a few acres of land packed wall to wall with hotels and casinos, the Portuguese Customs and Immigration officers sell us three-day visas for only a few dollars and no questions asked. From there we head into the town where I expect to see Portuguese people, but find only Chinese and the yellowest Chinese I've ever seen. Jack tells me they are from the northern provinces of China and run the hotels, restaurants and gambling enterprises whose primary purpose is to infuse the isolated Chinese economy with foreign exchange.

After checking into the Estoril Hotel and Casino, we immediately go to the gambling tables where Jack starts putting his money to work, pushing it forward and pulling it back, depending on what his gambler's intuition tells him to do in the moment; moving real wads of money on the roll of the dice with nerves of steel, totally absorbed, the expression on his face never changing, win or lose. In between watching him, I gamble with what can only be called spare change, a few HK dollars on roulette and a few on black-jack, but mostly on the dollar slot machines that can be played progressively so at any one time, if you want, a significant amount of money can be riding on a single spin of wheel. For the most part, however, I stand behind Jack with a bottomless glass of Pernod in hand, studying his gambler's instinct and watching the others playing alongside him. Having been to Las Vegas and observed gamblers before, the Chinese seem to be much more focused and not the least bit interested in being distracted by free drinks, pretty girls or any other perks. They're true gamblers and dead serious about it.

Several hours into it, Jack's ahead and insists we spend the night, but not in the hotel room we paid for, but at the tables, and by the time we leave in the morning he's been awake for several days, including his previous trip, with little more than a cat nap here and there. But he's not only made up his loses, he's ahead over three thousand American dollars, while I'm down a little over thirty, thus proving his gambler's instinct correct, that my being there changed his luck.

On the return trip when the Hydrofoil enters Hong Kong harbor, I get another lesson in just how serious and impatient Chinese gamblers can be when, due to heavy ship traffic, the harbor master orders the Hydrofoil captain to hold off docking for fifteen minutes. Outraged at the delay, most of the passengers undo their seat belts and confront the captain, shaking their fists and threatening him in a near riot and keeping this up until the Hydrofoil's cleared to go forward.

CHAPTER 86

With only one day left on my R&R, there's little time to sleep and Jack decides it's his responsibility as my friend to make sure I see everything there is to see in Hong Kong before returning to the Nam.

To accomplish this, he rents a small Datsun and we drive out to the countryside in the New Territories section of the City, stopping first at a place where busloads of tourists are standing around staring across duck ponds and rice fields, snapping away with their cameras. A large sign reads, "DANGER. DO NOT GO BEYOND THIS POINT. BORDER OF CHINA AND HONG KONG." Jack then tells me it's not really the border, but a replica to fool the tourists so the bus and taxi drivers don't have to spend their time and gas driving all the way out to the real one. He then takes me to the real border that looks just like the fake one only is less crowded, and where there are Chinese women dressed in traditional costumes hustling souvenir postcards and wanting money to pose for pictures.

From there we drive to an ancient stone-walled city where, according to Jack, fifty thousand people live, and even though located on Hong Kong soil, through a special treaty it's governed by Red China and off limits to the British government.

"The place is full of spies," Jack tells me, "and the British government knows it, but there's nothing they can do about it."

For lunch we take a boat across the harbor to the world famous Tai Pak Floating Restaurant where we can enjoy great Cantonese food while watching the ships, ferries, sampans and junks crisscrossing the bay. Then afterwards get back into the Datsun and switch seats with Jack navigating, and me taking a shot at driving. Only with the steering wheel on the right, and having to keep to the left side of the road, it's a strange sensation for me, contrary to everything I've been conditioned to do about driving since starting out as a teenager. At any given moment I feel we're going to have a head-on collision and this doubly so when we get to the roundabouts.

With me at the helm, we drive around New Territories, passing multitudes of checkerboard ponds filled with millions of ducks where women and children wearing lamp shade hats are stooped over ninety degrees to the ground, working calf deep in the muck of the rice paddies, while the men steer primitive wooden plows behind huge water buffalos. Even in the age of diesel tractors and supermarkets, this is the essence of Asia, millions upon millions of simple people laboring every day just to feed themselves and their families, and procreating so they can continue the same in perpetuity. Watching them I can't help but wonder if the concept of war originated when someone got tired of this cycle and thought that preying upon another was a lot easier than hard labor, perhaps coming to the conclusion, as a philosopher once noted, "When the game is over the king and the pawn go back into the same box", so what the hell; although this revelation cuts both ways.

Hong Kong being the bargain basement of the world we go shopping and I buy gifts for Loan and her family, Zoffa and myself. Wristwatches and transistor radios for them and a brand new Nikon SLR camera with telephoto and wide angle lenses for me, the bargain basement prices being just too great to resist.

At Lee Kee's, the world famous bespoke cobbler who advertises he will hand make any style boot or shoe to your personal foot measurement for less than half the price of an off the shelf pair bought in the States, I order dress shoes that amazingly will be ready in only a few hours and hand delivered to my hotel. Not only that, they make a plaster cast of both my feet so I can order boots or shoes anytime, by just mailing them a photograph of what I want, the salesman showing me their collection of foot molds stacked floor to ceiling in cubby holes with customer's names on them, many of whom are movie stars and dignitaries.

From there we take the Star ferry back to Hong Kong Island and visit Jack's long-time tailor, Woo Fat, who measures me for a suit, and being the honest man he is, won't make promises about the fit because, as he explains, without a minimum of two fittings a custom suit isn't a custom suit at all and I'll be leaving before that can be done. But that's why Jack took me there in the first place instead of one of the more famous tailors in Kowloon that display autographed photos of Hollywood movie stars who supposedly get their clothes tailored there, and where tourists order custom suits from measurements alone, with minimal or no fittings, and think they're getting a real bespoke suit. According to Woo Fat, what they're really getting is a forty dollar suit sold to them for eighty and they're happy as pie because they believe it to be worth two hundred. After my suit's finished he is going to send it to my parent's home in Pasadena, and it'll be the best suit that can be made under the circumstances.

According to Jack, it's not just bespoke shoes and suits that buyers must beware of in HK, but just about everything else. That five hundred dollar Rolex watch at seventy or eighty percent off may really be a Mickey Mouse watch on the inside with a Rolex face on the outside, and that 24 karat gold might be 18 karat, or simply gold plated, or not gold at all, and that designer dress may be a knock-off of such low quality it will fall apart after the first cleaning and the same goes for cameras, transistor radios, peals, etc. Hong Kong is truly a shopper's paradise, but it's also a place where imitation and trickery are the names of the game and they are masters of it.

CHAPTER 87

Over drinks, Jack and I make plans for my last night in HK and he calls up a retired sex worker turned madam he knows by the name of Wanda, and asks her to send over two of her best girls to help make my last night a memorable one. The plan is for the four of us to go to dinner at an upscale restaurant, then a night club for some entertainment, then our respective hotel rooms to cap off the night with some good sex.

At 7:30 we meet the girls at Jack's hotel. One of them, JoJo, is a real beauty. She looks like the famous Chinese actress Susie Wong and chosen by Wanda especially for Jack. The other girl Mona has a pretty face, but is on the fat side and doesn't appeal to me in a sexual way, and when I tell Jack, he immediately calls Wanda to see if she can arrange for another girl, but Wanda tells him with all the Navy ships in port, conventions in town and GIs on R & R, no other girls are available and not only that, Mona is one of her top girls because she's also a ballroom girl.

"What's a ballroom girl?" I ask Jack, after he tells me the unfortunate news. "They work in high class dance halls and can make over $150 US a night dancing with lonely guys. It's bloody outrageous, but the Olympics spoiled everything."

"When were the Olympics in Hong Kong?" I ask.

"The Tokyo Olympics," he says. "People figured as long as they're going to Japan they might as well stopover in Hong Kong, and when they did they threw their money around, inflating prices and ruining it for everybody."

While this explains the situation it does nothing for my libido, which is conditioned to believe that sexy means movie star and model thin; and Jack doesn't offer to switch girls.

For dinner, we go to the Ho Fook restaurant, which is a local favorite, a big place with countless tables and waitresses who walk around carrying trays loaded with a particular food specialty displayed in a uniquely shaped bowl or plate. When you see something you like, you simply point at the waitress and she brings the dish over to your table. At the end of the meal your bill is determined by the number and shapes of the plates on your table.

From there we go to the Kings Night club where there's a big neon sign outside blinking on and off like a beacon and under the marquee announcing his appearance in the weeks ahead, a photograph of Ricky Nelson who I haven't seen or heard of since his "Ozzy and Harriet" days. It's a beautiful club with a large ballroom and good music, a place where waiters mix the drinks at your table so you can see the exact bottle and label they're pouring from, though who knows what they put into them, after all it is Hong Kong and the fact that they even do this, is in itself telling.

Fortunately, Mona has a good sense of humor and the four of us have a great time laughing and dancing, though I'm not much into dancing and she's a professional. Then when it's time for us to leave we say our good-byes and Jack and JoJo hail a taxi to his hotel, but Mona insists we to go to her apartment instead of my hotel, saying we'll be much more comfortable.

To my surprise, her apartment is very upscale, impeccably furnished with high end furnishings, original oil paintings, crystal ware, and fine china on display in an expensive looking hutch, she even has a full time live-in servant who serves us tea before we move from the living room into her bedroom, where she opens the double doors of a wall-to-wall closet to show me her collection of fashionable clothes, then strips naked and puts on some expensive looking lingerie before lying down on the bed. While the lingerie is nice, it only emphasizes her rolls of fat and this, along with the pressure to perform, puts me in a state of flight or fight. All I want to do is get out of there, but I don't know how to do so without ruining what was up to then a great evening. Glancing at my watch I say, "I've got to be at the airport in a few hours. I better get back to my hotel and pack."

But she ignores this and undoes her bra, releasing her large sagging breasts with their saucer-like areolas, then slips out of her panties and pulls me to her leaving me little choice but to reach over, kill the light and try hard to pretend she's JoJo and for the first time in my life I'm proud of how quickly I can finish. Then before leaving I thank her for a wonderful evening, and when I do, she hands me her business card and says, "If you know anybody coming to Hong Kong, please give this to them."

CHAPTER 88

When my flight from Hong Kong lands back at Tan Son Nhut, I feel like I've descended into a toxic rabbit hole. The few days away had reminded me what a normal life was like and the sight of all the military equipment on the Base makes me sick, not only because they're symbols of death and destruction, but of the horrible corrupt war itself.

From the tarmac I catch a military shuttle to the front gate, then hail a taxi out to the villa, passing the familiar sights along Plantation Road that remind me I'll soon be seeing my sweet Buddha angel Loan, and the closer I get to the villa the more I'm looking forward to being with her. But when I arrive, instead of her leaping into my arms, I find her entire family in the dining room eating and looking like they've moved in while I was away. This disappointment coming after the built up anticipation turns into passive aggression and I flip them a tepid "Hello," then immediately head up to my bedroom with Loan running up behind me.

"I think you no happy I have family at house," Loan says when we get to the bedroom.

"That has nothing to do with it, but since you brought it up, how long have they been here?"

"When you go Hong Kong maid go no come back, Quan go no come back, only cook Ba Sam stay and I afraid people take from house and I afraid stay house withs self."

"Where did everybody go?"

"I no, no, they no say me, and Ba Sam no speak Vietnamese, only Chinese."

She then opens the door to the armoire, which is still filled with stacks of cash and takes out an envelope. "You friend Graham come house say I give this for you."

Inside the envelope's a letter that reads, "Ben, by now you know about Sir Robin, but more importantly, Hue is pregnant with my child and I need your help. Please see to it that she gets the best of care and everything she needs, doctors, medicine, food, clothing and I will send you the money as soon as I can. She lives at 5/2 Pham Dang Hung. Thank you for doing this for me. Your cobber, Graham"

I have no idea what he means about Sir Robin, but Loan's explanation makes me feel like a heel and I decide to go downstairs and apologize to her family and tell them how grateful I am for their taking care of her and the villa in my absence. But when I get there they're all gone and I feel terrible. All I can do now is to tell Loan how sorry I am for behaving so poorly toward her and her family and ask for forgiveness. In the process of doing so, I give her the gifts I bought for and her family in Hong Kong, but being the Buddha angel she is, she refuses to take them, saying all she wants is to make me happy and then blames herself for disappointing me. She's so upset she tells me she is going to move back with her family at least for now, and there is nothing I can say or do to convince her otherwise.

CHAPTER 89

With Loan gone, the villa's empty except for Ba Sam and not knowing what happened to Sir Robin, I'm at a loss about what to do next. Being away from the war those few days in Hong Kong has made a world of difference to my psyche and I don't feel I can actively support the suffering of others any longer. It then crosses my mind that the Honda's chained up outside in the courtyard and I could be in Cambodia in seven or eight hours and from there to Thailand or Burma, or even Pakistan and India where nobody will ever find me, and with the money I have in the armoire I can live in obscurity and peace for a long time before deciding what to do next. The VC will never expect to see an American riding solo on the road to Cambodia, they'll assume I'm French, and as a backup, I still have the Panamanian seamen's papers Graham gave me.

This fantasy fuels my imagination, and while I'm running through the various scenarios of how well I could live in those countries with their low cost of living, I hear the front door close and the sound of someone coming up the stairs. At first I think it must be Sir Robin or Quan, but when the bedroom door opens it's Loan, and she's dressed like I've never seen her before in bargirl tight slacks, and a low cut blouse and high heels.

"Anh oi, I live withs you buts I no madam, Ben" she says, "I same, same bargirl."

"No. You girlfriend Ben, no same, same bargirl," I tell her.

"Maybe I be withs you, but I no can lives withs you," she says, then bursts into tears and runs out of the villa into a waiting taxi, leaving me to wonder what I can do to remedy the situation and putting my plan to escape on the back burner for the moment.

From what she said and the way she was dressed, I guess she's going through a period of confusing emotions, as I am. On one hand she was the one who said our relationship can never be more than what we have in the moment, because she could never leave Vietnam and doesn't expect me to stay there, especially with the war. On the other hand, she now seems to want it to be something more.

With these emotions dominating my thoughts I realize I have genuine feelings for Buddha Angel Loan, and while going to Thailand would be a great escape and adventure, the attendant consequences would be just too high a price to pay. It would mean giving up much that is dear to me, including family and country, perhaps forever, so the next day I report back to work at the AMT where the situation can best be described by the popular GI acronym SNAFU, which stands for "situation normal, all fucked up."

With the escalating war there are now over 300,000 GIs stationed in the Nam, a huge increase from only a few months ago, and the volume of mail has outgrown both our facility and capacity to deal with it. It's even worse than it was during the Christmas holidays and much of the mail remains piled up outside languishing on pallets covered with tarps to protect it from the monsoon rains, and in steel Conexes waiting to be processed, and every day MATS charters are bringing in more GIs and with them comes more mail. The only relief comes when Congress votes to extend the Franking Privilege to GIs in Vietnam, which allows us to forgo the laborious process of selling and affixing postage simply by writing the word "Free" in place of a stamp, although for some unknown reason, we still have to hand cancel the word "free" as if it were stamp.

When I give Zoffa the watch I bought for him in Hong Kong, he thanks me, then goes on about how much worse things have gotten in the week since I've been gone. "Da Good Times Bar vas blown up and two GIs vas killed, and a whole bunch more injured, and da floating restaurant vas blown up again, and dhere is more shooting in da streets every day. You better move back to da Hung Dao right avay."

"I will Zoff, just as soon as I settle things with Sir Robin and I don't know where he is."

When I return to the villa, Ba Sam has prepared a meal for me but I'm more interested in finding out what happened with Sir Robin so I can settle things and move back to the Hung Dao. I shower and change into civilian clothes, then drive to the Saigon River looking for Bull MacGregor, hoping he can enlighten me, but the Indo-Traveler is nowhere to be seen. A dock worker tells me it left about a week before, which coincides with Loan's account of Sir Robin's disappearance.

My next stop is the Harbor Master's office where I learn the Indo-Traveler has been confiscated by the VN government for transporting drugs and other contraband, and is now tied up at the ship yard under twenty-four hour military guard. They also tell me they have no knowledge of what's become of Bull other than he was arrested at the time of the seizure.

From there I head to the VN charterer's office only to find it vacated and padlocked. Not knowing what else to do, I go to the Post, Telephone and Telegraph building on John F. Kennedy Square to telegraph Jack at the Capitol Hotel in HK. The PT&T is the most grandiose building in the city, reminding me of Grand Central Station in New York with its high ceiling, ornate architecture and great hall. It's the very epicenter of Saigon's communication with the outside world where street vendors sell stationary and collectable stamps, and public scribes write letters for the illiterate, and you can buy regular postage, and arrange to make and receive telephone calls and telegraphs.

I send the following telegraph to Jack, "Sir Robin, Bull, Indo-Traveler gone STOP. Please enlighten me STOP," and then go over to La Pagode to wait for his response while lingering over a cup of their strong French coffee sweetened with condensed milk.

Sitting there I notice a new tailor shop across the street with the name "007" which makes me realize how much influence America is having on Saigon culture, reminding me too of a cartoon that recently appeared in the Saigon Daily News depicting the Vietnamese people on their knees worshipping a Buddha in the shape of a dollar sign. In the same way Saigon was once a French city, it has become an American one, prompting me to speculate that in the future there will be one dominate culture in the entire world and how sad it will be because every culture has so much to offer to the fabric and enjoyment of life. It will be a sad day when you travel the world only to see a McDonald's restaurant on every corner.

Two hours later I check back at the PT&T, but no response has come. Feeling restless and alone I drive over to see my Buddha angel Loan. Fortunately she's home and happy to see me. After apologizing to her family for my rude, ungrateful behavior at the villa, she and I take off on the Honda, with her sitting side saddle behind me in a beautiful Ao Dai instead of the bargirl clothes, and head out to the countryside, past the rice paddies and water buffalos that are symbols to me of the real Vietnam, arriving a short time later at the Club Nautique's facility in Ti Nghe. It being a week-day, the place is locked down and deserted except for a watchman and even though I show him my membership card, he refuses to let us pass until I bribe him with couple of hundred Ps.

After parking the Honda, Loan and I walk to the pool out of the watchman's view and take off our clothes, then slip into the water, but after only a few minutes of peace and quiet our privacy is interrupted by the ear-splitting sound of a passing Huey gunship, that hovers overhead just long enough for the door gunner to flash us his middle finger and for me to angrily reflect how the government put a multimillion dollar killing machine in the hands of children.

CHAPTER 90

A reply telegram finally arrives from Jack. "Sir Robin arrested for drug smuggling STOP. A phony, bought title STOP. Indo-Traveler lost in seizure STOP. Bull released/repatriated to HK STOP. Europa/Graham in HK worried about Hue STOP. Be careful STOP." Jack.

That same day Loan spends the night at the villa helping me to move out for good and during the night we're awakened by the sound of small arms fire coming from just outside the villa wall. Grabbing my pistol, I jump out of bed and crawl on my stomach out to the balcony, telling Loan to stay down on the floor, but she's too scared and follows behind me. With the light from the entry I see several black pajama-clad men on the other side of the wall returning fire behind them, and moments later they breach the front gate and enter the garden. Feeling threatened, I discharge a few rounds and watch as one of the men falls to the ground, causing the others to look up at me. But before they can react, several ARVN soldiers burst into the garden, guns blazing, and all the men are dead. Loan and I are left shaking, trying to process the experience. Propped up, with my back against the balcony railing, I reach out to her and take her into my arms, and when I feel her naked flesh against mine, and her heart beating wildly in her chest, I get overpoweringly aroused and lift her up onto to my lap with her legs around me, then enter her with a primal desperation to unite with one another.

The next thing I know, the ARVN are pounding on the front door. Barely able to stand, we hurriedly dress and run downstairs to let them in before they break it down. It's then that we learn the dead VC in the garden had attacked a Canh Sat substation a few blocks away, killing one of the white mice. After searching the villa and grounds and finding only Ba Sam, the ARVN try to question her, but she doesn't understand Vietnamese and nobody speaks her specific dialect of Chinese so the ARVN trung uy, the equivalent of a lieutenant in American ranks, wants to take her in for questioning, but I assure him she's not a VC sympathizer and he agrees to let her stay.

We then watch the ARVN toss the dead VC into their truck and leave, then go back upstairs but there's no sleep for me, the near-death experience forcing me to confront my own mortality and the powerful primal response that followed. In doing so I recall having read that one of the French terms for an orgasm is "la petite mort," meaning the little death, because in the moment of orgasm our individual identity disappears into undifferentiated unity, this helping to explain the need I felt to unite with my Buddha angel Loan.

When daylight comes, I immediately go downstairs and give Ba Sam several thousand Ps and try to get her to leave, but she won't go. Nonetheless, I'm determined to move out and after giving Loan all the furnishings, water purifiers and food included, who has them loaded into a truck for delivery to her home, I move back into room 415 at the Hung Dao.

CHAPTER 91

Riot troops behind coils of barbwire with wicker shields, and armed with automatic weapons are now stationed on streets throughout the city lobbing tear gas at anti-government protestors. Another Buddhist monk sets himself on fire in a demonstration against premier Ky and president Thieu and the next day there's a story in The Saigon Daily News claiming that a large cache of guns was found hidden in the floor of a Buddhist pagoda.

Thousands of Buddhists continue to march in protest. Even though Ky's a Buddhist, he's from the North and they say he can't be trusted, and even though Thieu's from the South they say he can't be trusted because he's a Catholic. Everyone distrusts President Johnson because he's a foreigner and represents a country that first backed the North against colonial France, then switched sides and backed the

French against the North, then installed President Diem who had been living in the United States, then backed the coup that deposed and assassinated him, then sent in military advisors followed by thousands of combat troops without first seeking South Vietnamese government approval to do so.

Cars are vandalized, windows are broken, and buildings are burned down and blown up. Innocent children are fitted with explosives by the VC and sent into gatherings of GIs, ARVN soldiers and innocent civilians. A prominent monk stops eating and declares he will not resume until Ky, Thieu and Johnson get out of Vietnam. Thousands openly pray for the monk's life while the newspapers report he's living comfortably on dextrose and sugared tea in the finest private maternity hospital in Saigon.

Other stories report how Americans are burning their Draft Cards by the thousands and running to Canada, and those already drafted are refusing to go to war despite facing courts martial. General Thao Ma, a Laotian Air Force Commander, claims 100 supply trucks a month are passing along the Shihanouk Trail in Northern Cambodia to supply the Viet Cong gorillas in South Vietnam. Families are deeply and tragically divided, some members sympathetic to the South, others to the North, and others confused about what it is they're fighting for. Vu Van Thai, South Vietnam's Ambassador to the United States, declares the friction between political factions in Saigon will likely continue until a well-defined political program can be developed. Vietnam's Foreign Minister calls all suggestions to neutralize Vietnam nonsense, stating, "Just as nobody can think of neutralizing

North Korea and East Germany." General Maxwell Taylor, former ambassador to the Republic of Vietnam, asks the American People to give money to help feed the estimated 600,000 Vietnamese people who have reportedly fled the communists. Other reports claim far more civilian by-standers are being killed and wounded than rebel and government troops combined. Communist Chinese Premier Chou En Lai repeats his warning that if the United States continues the war in Vietnam, Red China and the Vietnamese Communists will drive the U.S. out of South-East Asia. His Holiness Pope Paul VI calls for peace through example in the name of Christ.

A news story claims more journalists are covering the Cannes film festival than the war in Vietnam and in that same vein, a front page story appears in the Saigon Daily News about a chance meeting between Mrs. John F. Kennedy and the Duchess of Windsor at the Penthouse of French and Co. where they were busy buying expensive jewelry, followed by another story about a U.S. News and World Report on how the U.S. now has 90,000 millionaires, seven for every millionaire there was in 1918. Buried on page three of that same paper is a short story about a senior Whitehouse official declaring he is confident of victory in Vietnam.

CHAPTER 92

Each day I wake up to the snowballing call of "Gooood Morning Vietnam" being howled by DJ Ira Cook, cheerfully narrowing the gap between home and hooch via the Armed Forces Radio and Television Service (AFRTS), which brings music, the New York Knicks and news of the world to thousands of GIs from the Delta to the DMZ.

Popular as he is, Hanoi Hanna, North Vietnam's version of WWII's Tokyo Rose, is even more popular because of her sexy velvety voice and because she spins the discs the GIs like best. Her broadcasts going something like this: "Hello boys. While the imperialistic aggressors in Washington are using you to do their dirty work, they're sitting in their big comfortable homes getting rich from your blood. So go home, boys, and refuse to be their pawns. And now, the latest back home hits, the ones your wives and girlfriends are dancing to right now, here's "Buffalo Springfield."

Then there's Tom Tiede, an honorable journalist who publishes an Ernie Pyle-type book about our men fighting in Vietnam, a chronicle of stories about GIs performing extraordinary acts of bravery like jumping on a grenade to save their buddies or stepping out from cover to charge the enemy with M16 blazing. Not to take anything away from these ultimate sacrifices, I can't help but wonder if such acts, executed in split seconds, have more to do with conditioned reflexes driven by exposure to television and movie heroes like John Wayne, than a reasoned decision and, by glorifying them, diminishing those who understandably don't want to sacrifice their lives in such a manner yet continue to fight.

CHAPTER 93

Television is introduced to the Nam via two specially equipped Lockheed Super Constellation aircraft that fly in an elliptical orbit over Saigon for a few hours each day broadcasting to some 500 television sets installed on poles in outdoor public areas where ordinary Vietnamese citizens can watch the miracle of American life. It's both a psychological demonstration of our superiority over the enemy and instrument of propaganda.

One hour of each broadcast is in Vietnamese, the rest in English. Improbable as it may seem because of the suffering caused by the war, the most popular program among the Vietnamese is the fictional series "Combat," a WWII drama depicting Americans vanquishing their enemy.

Even more bizarre, the television repair store that existed for months before there was TV has now completely disappeared, and I wake up to find my copy of Camus' "The Plague" on the floor next to my bed riddled with rat bites.

CHAPTER 94

Following Graham's request, Zoffa and I visit his girl-friend Hue to help her with rent, food and prenatal medical attention. When we arrive she proudly shows us her distended belly, though it looks more like a condition common to many VN girls that is the result of a diet too rich in rice starch rather than a pregnancy.

"When Graham come Saigon?" she asks us, quickly followed by, "When he give more money for babyson? I no can work bar, GI no like girlfriend ba bao (pregnant). I need money for house, need money for eat."

"Don't worry, Hue. Graham's going to stick by you. When babyson come?" I ask her.

"Babyson come sau months," she says holding up six fingers.

"Sau months, fa sure sau months?" I ask.

"Fa sure."

"Well, if sau months, babyson no can be from Graham."

"No, no. Babyson from Graham fa sure. You say Graham send money."

Suddenly it is a totally different situation and I sense my cobber Graham is being suckered. It then occurs to me he's no fool and must know the truth, but for reasons unknown to me, he's accepted Hue's pregnancy, real or fake, as his responsibility and has decided to support her. Either way, as his cobber, I decide to report the facts as I see them just in case.

So I note Hue's claimed financial needs, which interestingly come to seventy US dollars a month, the average going price for keeping a bargirl girlfriend and several times higher than the actual cost of living for a working class Vietnamese, and telegraph this information to Graham along with my thoughts. The next day I receive his reply.

"Absolutely certain baby is mine. STOP. Sending you money STOP. Please see that Hue gets everything she needs STOP. Grateful for your help STOP. Your cobber, Graham."

When his bank draft for one hundred dollars arrives, I cash it, then deliver the money in Ps to Hue and when I do, discover she's still working at the Trami Bar though she tries to convince me she only stopped by to see her girlfriends. Nonetheless, I honor Graham's request and give her the money.

CHAPTER 95

The tempo of fighting continues to escalate as more and more GIs are deployed in-country. Air Force B52s accelerate the bombing of strategic targets, especially the NVA supply trails from the north to the south, including secret bombings in neighboring Laos with or without Laotian approval, and in the process turning virgin jungle into lifeless craters. Navy boats blockade the coast and lob lethal artillery shells miles inland. Swarms of Huey gunships strafe village after village, and infantry troops search out and destroy everything and anything, all in a country half the size of Texas.

The "Free World Forces," a political smattering of allied support that includes token numbers of Thais, Filipinos, Koreans, Australians and New Zealanders, fight alongside American GIs while ARVN troops, whose country we're supposedly fighting for, are seen, perhaps undeservedly so, to take a backseat and are resented for it by American GIs. Collectively, ARVN resolve seems low and their desertion rate high, perhaps because many don't trust their government and are conscripted rather than volunteer, kidnapped off the streets of cities and villages by roaming trucks on the prowl for eligible males, then given little training and no term limit to their service. It's no secret too, that some ARVN soldiers assign their military pay to their commanding officers who then pockets the money in exchange for counting them present when in fact they've deserted and gone back home. Of those who stay, they have a reputation among GIs, though not universally deserved, for sleeping on guard duty and running at the first sign of trouble, which further engenders animosity and distrust of them as a whole.

Unlike other wars where the strategy is to seize and occupy enemy territory, the strategy in the Nam is simply to kill more of the enemy than they kill of us. Thus progress is measured by statistics known to be exaggerated and lacking in credibility. American casualties are deliberately underreported or mischaracterized to deceive the public and promote continued support of the war. Such mischaracterizations are accomplished through false tallies, delayed reporting and classifications such as "Missing in Action," "Injured" and "Deaths due to non-hostile causes" instead of "Killed in Action." And on the enemy side, the numbers are grossly exaggerated by including innocent civilian dead, by far the highest number of casualties, and intentional double counting, one enemy scalp is proof of one kill, but two ears are proof of two.

As pressure from Washington mounts, a 'shoot any-thing that moves' policy is implemented and posits if a vil-lager runs it's not because they're frightened when they see soldiers with guns, but because they are the enemy or support the enemy. This scorched earth policy results in entire villages being torched and burned to the ground with impunity and its inhabitants—including infants, chil-dren, the elderly and their animals—slaughtered. GIs who back home wouldn't hurt a fly find themselves compelled, through band of brothers conditioning and deliberate por-trayals of the enemy as gooks, slopes, Charlies and targets rather than human beings, to reach inside themselves to a place so dark they can slit the throats of the elderly and children, and rape and torture others with the certainty that god and right are on their side.

It's no secret that these atrocities are war crimes as de-fined by international accords, and prosecuted or not the consequences are inescapable. They will haunt us for gen-erations to come, because like the laws of physics, which are devoid of judgment, every action carries within it, an ines-capable consequence. The Hindus and Buddhists call this the law of karma while Jewish and Christians say, "As you do unto others it shall be done unto you." And international law at The Nuremberg trials of WWII rejected the defense "I was just following orders." Thus leaving the only path to follow, that which Gandhi advised, "To make of ourselves, life as we want it to be."

CHAPTER 96

Each day Buddhists and Catholic mobs burn the city and throw rocks in the name of peace while the Viet Cong continue to toss bombs and shoot at people from motorcycles, hoping to achieve the same goal. Looters, thieves and war profiteers prey on citizens while the South Vietnamese government erects signs honoring those who have died for their country. Rampart inflation continues to reduce the poor to desperate and the working class to poor. American pacifists, labeled "peaceniks" by the Press, arrive in Saigon and march down Tran Hung Dao Boulevard protesting the war and shouting "Peace" and "America go Home," which confuses the Vietnamese people and angers many GIs who pelt them with eggs and fruit while calling them "Communist pigs" and yelling "Death to the Commies."

As the anger escalates, a few GIs mount a physical attack, beating the Peaceniks viciously until MPs and Kinh-sats intervene and bodily carry the Peaceniks off to jail, charging them with civil disruption and, in doing so, save their lives.

The following morning I'm at Tan Son Nhut airport when the Peaceniks are forcefully carried by their arms and legs from the back of green and white Kinh Sat vans, up the steps of a US-bound Pan American Jet while tossing anti-war leaflets into the air, and the Kinh-sats are running around trying to pick them up before they can subvert anybody. Hundreds of GIs, along with news reporters, witness the spectacle from behind police barricades, with the GIs screaming "Kill the bastards," "Kill the peaceniks," "Shoot them, don't let them get away." And when an American journalist muscles past the Kinh-sats to take a photo, he is beaten with clubs and his camera smashed to pieces.

CHAPTER 97

With the increase in GI deaths, civilian morticians at Tan Son Nhut are working three, eight-hour shifts of embalming, and the sewer leading out of the mortuary never ceases its crimson run.

Body bags go in and aluminum caskets go out in assembly-line fashion, each one stenciled "Contents: One Cadaver. When Empty Return to TSN Mortuary, Republic South Vietnam", and on one end the word "Head."

Forklifts then stack the caskets onto flatbed trucks parked along the ramp to await transport back to the States aboard Military Air Transport Service (MATS) or Air National Guard (ANG) C-141 Star lifters, the cargo bay of each plane the size of a football field. When the planes arrive, the caskets are forklifted from the flatbed trucks up to the aircraft's massive cargo doors where they're off loaded by hand and stacked inside by reserve airman or guards-men fulfilling their two weeks a year obligation, who before departing, stop by the BX to buy radios, cameras and ste-reos at greatly discounted, duty free prices, to take back to the States.

One day, I say to one of the guardsman, "Don't believe the government. Casualties are a lot higher than they're reporting."

And he comes back with, "Are you saying the govern-ment's lying?"

"I can count as well as you can and I also see the re-ports." I tell him.

To which he responds, "Well, I'm an American and I believe our government."

CHAPTER 98

News comes from Jack in Hong Kong. Sir Robin is out on bail awaiting trial for drug trafficking and fraudulent misrepresentation of shipping contracts, but luckily for him he's out of reach of the Vietnamese authorities. No more telegraphs come from Graham and I suspect he's either out at sea again or reason has caught up with him and the $100 he sent for Hue was a one-time conscience payment or gift.

Zoffa and I regularly ride around the city on the Honda, aghast at the increasing destruction we see. "It's da beginning of da end," he says every time we pass a newly destroyed building. On one such trip we're behind a long black Renault when it suddenly blows up and the concussion knocks us to the ground. We escape with only a few scrapes and bruises, but the South

Vietnamese government official in the car and his driver are killed.

Another day we're less than a block from the Hung Dao when an explosion rocks the building across the street, sending smoke and debris flying all around us, followed by a second more powerful explosion that shakes the ground like an earthquake. Except for billows of dust, windows blown out, and doors off their hinges, the Hung Dao is otherwise intact, but out in the street are multiple dead and wounded, and amid the debris, an arm here and a leg there, and a car covered with blood and flesh.

"Curiosity killed that cat," an MP tells us, pointing to the mutilated remains of a VN man. "Whaddaya mean?" I ask.

"After the first blast he came out to see what happened and the second explosion got him."

Days later we learn the bomb was a plastic charge placed in the building's elevator shaft by a trusted Vietnamese employee, a reminder that in this war the distinction between friend and enemy cannot easily be discerned and may even change from one moment to the next.

CHAPTER 99

Amid the chaos that has descended upon Saigon, Premier Ky, perhaps as a distraction, announces he will clean out the prisons through public executions of all persons convicted of serious crimes. The first five men are to be executed the following day, one of them a boy in his early twenties whom, according to the Saigon Daily News, was accused of raping a girl six years earlier, but never reliably identified or properly convicted, yet he has languished in prison all those years.

The newspaper further notes: "After years in a Vietnamese prison with rats, cockroaches, mosquitos, little or no medical treatment, a single bowl of maggot-infested rice and one cup of water a day, execution must certainly be looked upon as a reprieve."

Those words and images bringing to my mind William Blake's metaphoric poem about an imprisoned bird.

"A robin red breast in a cage, mother nature in a rage
A dove house fill'ed with doves and pigeons
Shudders Hell thro' all it regions
A Dog starv'd at his Master Gate
Predicts the ruin of the State."

Zoffa and I debate going to see the executions. I'm hesitant because I envision an emotionally disturbing scene where the condemned men, legs wobbly, unable to stand, are dragged out in front of a firing squad, tied to a post and made to hear their fate read aloud before ARVN soldiers pull the trigger. Zoffa's hesitant, because he's concerned about residual, recurrent nightmares. But in the end, base curiosity prevails and we decide to go.

The executions take place in front of a sandbag wall at the side of the police headquarters building in downtown Saigon where major streets converge onto a large traffic circle that doubles as a park. In the center of the circle is the marble bust of a seventeen-year-old girl who was fatally shot by the former Chief of Saigon Police during a protest against the old Diem government and subsequently made into a martyr, fueling the coup that toppled Diem from power and ended with his execution. Adjacent to the circle is the large central market where, in a city with little or no refrigeration, countless thousands shop for food daily, essentially making the circle and its environs the closest thing to a public square.

The sandbags are stacked in a semi-circle almost eight feet high, and in front of them, five wooden posts set into the ground. With the executions set for dawn, Zoffa and I arrive early and are surprised to see thousands of people, mostly the poor, already there to witness the spectacle. Rather than somber the mood is festive, many of them squatted on their haunches shoveling bowls of pho into their mouths while engaging in lively conversation and laughter.

At the appointed time, four ARVN jeeps arrive, machine guns mounted on their hoods and park two on each side of the sandbags, guns pointed toward the crowd. And for a brief moment I wonder if it is we who are to be executed; it's an uncomfortable feeling having soldiers in a third world country at war, pointing guns at you. Next, a tanker truck backs in beside the jeeps and when it's in place all headlights are turned on, presumably to prevent unauthorized photography. Then a green and white Canh-sat van arrives and the five condemned men are led out by helmeted ARVN troops and tied to the posts, their heads bowed. I scan them for telltale signs of fear, but they seem more inanimate than alive as if, as the newspaper said, they have already died in prison. The ARVN soldiers take up positions not more than ten feet away, each one facing a prisoner, their rifles raised awaiting the command to fire. And it's this moment before life disappears into death that holds everyone's attention in silence. Then five rounds crack the air in unison like a single clap of thunder and the bodies' slump against the ropes; whatever held them up now gone in an unseen flash, like a magician's sleight of hand; and it's so anticlimactic there's no reaction from the crowd. Working in teams of two, the ARVN soldiers untie each body from its post, carry it to the van and toss it inside like Zoffa and I toss mail sacks into the bins at the AMT. When they're finished, the tanker truck releases a surge of water washing away the blood and the crowd disperses, most of them into the central market to shop for the day. After all, the living must eat.

CHAPTER 100

O n the way back from execution square Zoffa says, "I want to go the Annex."

"Are you sure?" I ask him, his words taking me by surprise.

"Life is too short." He replys.

"Why don't you wait a day just to make sure this is what you want to do?" I suggest.

But his mind is made up and he wants me to take him to the Annex right then before further reflection might cause him to change it. So we head down the alley alongside the Hung Dao to the Annex gate where I call out for the moma-son who shuffles over in her plastic sandals and asks us the standard question, "You short time or all night?" And when Zoffa looks to me for guidance, I say "all night," thinking if he's enjoying himself he can stay as long as he wants and if not he can leave and the extra cost is not that significant.

After we each hand her a thousand Ps, the going rate of just a few weeks ago, she wants another five hundred apiece, explaining as best she could, with hyperinflation and the government crackdown on brothels she has to pay the Canh-sats more money to stay in business. This amounting to a fifty percent increase in less than a month.

Once we give her the money she instructs the girls to line up in front of us so we can take our pick. With Zoffa being a "cherry boy," I let him choose first then wait as the girl leads him off to her bedroom before making my selection.

Half an hour later I leave the girl I'm with for a few minutes to check on Zoffa and when he comes to the door I can tell he's totally consumed by the experience to a point where nothing else matters.

In the morning, as soon as curfew's over, we go back to the hotel, shower and change into our uniforms, then ride out to Tan Son Nut on the Honda, and the whole time Zoffa doesn't say a word about the Annex. That doesn't come until later when we're sitting on mail sacks in one of the bins taking a break, and he says, "I can't stop thinking about her. I'm going back tonight and if I still feel the same way tomorrow I'm going to move in with her."

"Don't you think you're rushing things?"

"You said it yourself Ben. Time doesn't exist here and by not jumping from girl to girl I von't feel so guilty."

"I would think it's the opposite. By staying with one girl it's more like a relationship than sex."

"Vell maybe, but dhere's less of a chance of getting VD. Oh, dhere's one more thing. I vould like you to go vith me just one more time. I treat you."

So when our shift ends we shower, change into our civilian clothes and head back to the Annex where, in addition to paying momason her fee, Zoffa gives his girl a can of hair spray from the BX, instantly making him, her number one boyfriend.

Unlike Zoffa, I chose a different girl to avoid any hint of wanting a relationship and when the girl takes me back to her room and slips out of her pajamas, I can see she's pregnant. Noticing me staring at her belly she gets upset and says, "Troi oi you think I no want babyson? I want American babyson too much, have pretty eye, pretty nose, no same, same Vietnamese nose. Later I sell babyson, rich Vietnamee pay beaucoup money for American babyson."

Harsh as this may seem to our Western culture where such an act is both unthinkable and illegal, it's not that uncommon among sex workers in war-torn VN who, having known insecurity most of their lives view everything as a commodity for survival, often converting excess Ps into gold, pearls and diamonds and in the case at hand, even monetizing Amerasian babies. She knows too, whoever buys her baby will provide it with a far better life than she could, which is the hope of every mother who has ever given up a child for adoption. For me, it's the first time I have sex with someone who is pregnant, and as it turns out too, the first time while actively engaged in sex, that the girl's mother comes in and instead of getting upset, nonchalantly carries on a conversation with her daughter as if I am not even there, except to ask if I would like some tea.

CHAPTER 101

Our last sortie together as a team with Snover will take us to Camp Holloway, an Army Huey assault unit just east of Pleiku. Upon our return, Snover will officially be a short-timer, meaning he will have less than a month to go before rotating back to the States and will spend the rest of those days doing relatively safe things around the AMT and not taking any chances that might send him home in pieces or in an aluminum casket. For this reason he's got short-timer-itis and determined to play it extra safe.

After checking out our weapons we drive Ole Grey over to Flight Operations this time at a respectable 25 miles per hour, arriving with plenty of time to spare before boarding the Caribou while it's parked at the ramp, instead of running after it while it's taxiing. Once aboard, Snover straps himself into the seat harness instead of forgoing it like he's done so many times in the past. And when the crew briefs us about VC activities in the sector, instead of being his cocky self he gets real worried, taking it to be a bad omen.

Despite all this concern, everything goes off without a hitch until we're ready to return and learn that our ride back to Tan Son Nhut will be delayed for a couple of hours. Instead of hanging out at the camp, we catch a ride into town and go to a local bar where Snover gets into a pissing contest with a GI who tells him how we have it made living in Saigon compared to the boonies with Snover arguing back how it's really much more dangerous in the city with all the shootings and bombings. While they're going at it, I go into the bathroom and seconds later there's an explosion that blows the bathroom door off its hinges and knocks me to the ground. When I get up the bar's in shambles and everybody's on the floor. Concerned about a secondary explosion, I hesitate for a minute then run over to Zoffa and Snover and I can tell they're gone.

. At the same moment I hear small arms fire coming from outside and GIs are rushing into to the bar to triage the wounded. When they notice I'm having a hard time, one of them leads me outside where the bodies of four VCs are lying in the street. I'm told they're the ones who tossed the explosives into the bar, but I can't attach anything to this, the words just pass right through me. An ARVN soldier starts kicking the bodies and stripping them of their possessions, a few photos, ID cards, not a single P, and strangely the saying, "It is easier for a camel to go through the eye of a needle than for a rich man to enter the kingdom of god" passes through my mind. It then hits me I will never see

Zoffa and Snover again and I don't know how to process this. Should I be dead too? Did I do something wrong? I know I'm supposed to hate the VC but don't, they're soldiers just like me with families who will never see them again and grieve. In training we're told not to dwell on such death, to be thankful we're alive and to use our emotions against the enemy. I want to blame someone, the military, the government, the carpet bagging profiteers, but know that blame changes nothing, it only shifts attention from what is. Maybe Einstein was right about a parallel universe and I just came out of the bathroom through the wrong door and if I go back, and come out the right one, everything will be the way it was.

CHAPTER 102

Back at Tan Son Nhut, the body bags containing Zoffa and Snover are taken to the mortuary and I'm instructed to report to the field hospital to be checked out by a doctor. And when I get there and see all the GIs with missing limbs and wired jaws and bandaged heads and hear the sounds of their agony, the full impact of Zoffa and Snover's deaths hits me and tears pour uncontrollably from my eyes and nausea forms in the pit of my stomach. All this suffering, I think, just so a few people who already have too much can have more. Then the unthinkable crosses my mind and I wonder if any of these poor souls have lost their manhood, the one thing all GIs fear and the one thing the labels of patriot and hero cannot come close to healing.

CHAPTER 103

The next day when I pass the Tan Son Nut mortuary on my way to the AMT, I can't help but wonder if any of the blood flowing out of the open sewer belongs to Zoffa or Snover, or if any of the caskets being forklifted onto the flatbeds for shipment back to the States contain their bodies. Then when I arrive at the AMT everybody stares at me, not knowing what to say, I'm wondering if they're thinking why am I still alive and Zoffa and Snover are dead, and if somehow I'm responsible.

Captain Staub calls me into his office and on his desk is a file euphemistically labeled "Incident Report."

"It's my job to caution you not to discuss the particulars of this incident with anyone, he tells me. "That information should be disseminated only through the appropriate offices."

I see his mouth moving but his words fly past my ears. I know he's reading from a script and if he hasn't done so already, he will just requisition two new replacements. Ignoring him I decide I will write letters to Zoffa and Snover's families, telling them how wonderful they were and offering to do anything I can to help then going over the wording of these in my mind.

I then hear the captain say he's sending me to Vung Tao for a five day in-country R & R to aid in my recovery from the trauma and I tell him I don't want to go because it will only make me feel worse knowing my buddies lost their lives and I get a vacation out of it, and it will also distance me more from the guys at the AMT, but he tells me I don't have a choice.

CHAPTER 104

Vung Tau is Miami Beach to Saigon's New York City. Situated some 50 miles southeast, it was once a chic French resort known as Cap Saint Jacques with impressive hillside villas overlooking beautiful white sand beaches. Only now, it's filled with sleazy girly bars like those in Saigon, the main difference being it's small and laid back, a town where you can smell clean sea air instead of odorous piles of garbage, and there's none of Saigon's hustle and bustle or fume-choking traffic, they even use horse draw carriages for taxis, making it a good place to wind down and attempt to put the war behind you.

Walking past Vung Tao's China Doll Bar, I recall Snover bragging about his girlfriend Lan who works there telling everybody she's a legend among GIs in the Nam because she's built like an American girl, tall with big breasts and real curves, unlike most Oriental girls who are petite, small breasted and slim like adolescents. According to Snover, after they had sex she followed him to Saigon and begged to be his girlfriend. Curious to see this legend I go in.

"Where Lan?" I ask one of the bargirls.

"Lan no here. Lan come soon, you wait okay." And unlike the bargirls in Saigon, she walks away without trying to hustle me.

When Lan arrives there's no mistaking her. She has Raquel Welch's body but a face that's more plain than pretty, though I doubt many GIs even notice it.

"How you know my name?" Lan asks me.

"You no remember me?" I say guessing she has been with so many GIs she can't possibly remember them all.

"I no see you before."

"I see you in Saigon when you come see Snover."

"You friend Snover? Snover dinky dao, (meaning crazy) where Snover?"

"Snover go back America."

"Why you come see Lan?"

"In Saigon you say me when I come Vung Tao I be with you."

She laughs, "Okay, buts you no can be withs Lan tonight."

"But I come from Saigon to be with you."

She laughs again. "Okay, maybe next day you be withs Lan, tonight you stay house friend Lan."

She then calls over one of the other bargirls. "This Xu," Lan says introducing her to me. "Tonight you stay house Xu. Xu take you house now."

I then follow Xu down a narrow street behind the bar to a small shanty where she shows me to a platform bed. "This bed you. You give Xu five hundred Ps, I give you food for same, same money."

After I give her the money she introduces me to her son Bill, whose American father she tells me, lived in VN long before the war. Bill's a diminutive sweet-looking kid who appears to be eleven or twelve years old and stares at me like he's never seen an American before although Vung Tao is full of them.

"You change clothes," Xu says to me. "We go beach now see Lan."

After the three of us change into bathing suits, we hail a horse-drawn carriage and ride along the frontage road flanked on one side by bars and restaurants and on the other by white sandy beaches leading out to the blue waters of the South China Sea. Looming above the town are two verdant mountains, their slopes dotted with palm trees interspersed with the red-roofed villas formally belonging to prominent French families and now owned by wealthy Vietnamese. The natural beauty and leisurely pace of the horse providing me with just the escape from the outside world that I need, this tranquil moment broken when little Bill reaches over and takes my hand into his. At first I'm uncomfortable, but then remember it's common for male friends in the Nam to hold hands, ARVN soldiers often walk hand in hand, so I shoot him a smile then get back to enjoying the tranquility.

When the carriage stops at a two-story restaurant on a near deserted beach sheltered in the lee of one of the mountains, we get off and go upstairs to an outdoor patio with tables and chairs and an unobstructed view of the bay.

Little Bill sits with me while Xu goes to the counter and returns with Coca Colas for her and Bill, and a ba mou ba for me.

"Lan come soon, you no worry," she tells me.

"I no worried," I say, and hand her money for the drinks.

"You no pay. I say you I give food with house, beer same, same food."

"In Saigon, the girls always want money."

"I no same same Saigon girl" she says, then tells little Bill to leave me alone and go sit by himself.

"It Duoc roi," I say, meaning he's not bothering me.

"You speak Vietnamese?"

"Tee Tee," I respond, meaning very little.

"Ah ver-ly good. No too much GI speak Vietnamese. Maybe you talk Bill Vietnamese, he talk you English."

"Little Bill, ong noi tieng anh duoc?" I say, hoping he understands my pronunciation.

"Yes, I speak English," he answers, laughing.

"Anh manh gior cho?"

"I am good thank you."

He then points to the sea, takes my hand and pulls me after him. Xu yells for him to leave me alone, but we're already at the stairs heading for the sand and from there into the water where he swims out and signals for me to follow him and when I do, he swims further out until I reach him and the two of us bob in the incoming swells with me blissing out in the cool water, surrounded by the blue sky, white sand and verdant mountains.

When we return to the patio Lan's there, her volup-
tuous body exploding out of a tiny black bikini. While
she's not my type, more caricature than real, she's a legend and there's no doubt in my mind she knows why I
came to see her.

"We go play in water," she says waving bye-bye for me to
follow her as she heads for the stairs then across the sand
and into the bay where she swims out. When I catch up to
her she undoes her bikini top and loops it over my head
then uses it to pull me against her breasts. Then laughing,
she wraps her legs around my waist and slips her hand inside
my trunks to tease me and when I reciprocate by slipping
my hand into her bikini bottom, she breaks away playfully
and we head back to the patio.

"Fa-sure Snover go home?" she asks me when we're back
sitting at a table.

"Fa-sure," I say.

"You no sau?"

"I no sau."

"You no Snover he no likes girl. He come Vung Tao no
see Lan, he come see Bill. He pay Lan go Saigon say other
GI Lan girlfriend him."

Hearing this, I first question my understanding of what
she's saying, then quickly search my memory trying to recall
any of Snover's behavior that might corroborate it. Nothing
comes to mind other than he often talked about brothels
and bargirls, but never seemed to participate in them. I
then look at little Bill trying to imagine the two of them
together and wonder if little Bill's handholding gesture was
more than friendship. If what Lan says is true I reason, it

makes perfect sense Snover would reach out to the most notorious bargirl in the Nam to aid in his subterfuge.

You no sau?" I ask Lan.

"I no sau," she says.

And while I'm struggling to process this, I recall reading that ancient Greek and Roman soldiers routinely engaged in homosexuality with boys the same age as little Bill, and that there are societies, particularly in the mid-east, where men still do. To them it is not an aberration, but the norm.

For lunch we order cracked crab with spicy sauce along with beer and colas, which I insist on paying for, then sit out on the patio eating and drinking until it's time for Lan and Xu to get ready for work.

"You no come China Doll tonight." Lan tells me, "I fini work I come house Xu be withs you."

"Okay, I wait for you." I say.

Then when they leave for the China Doll I head over to the Chicago Bar where I meet two Aussie soldiers, a Caucasian named Peter and an aboriginal named Denis who is the first aboriginal I've ever met and the blackest person I've ever met too. When I innocently ask Denis if he's an aborigine, Peter immediately jumps in and corrects me saying, "Denis is an aboriginal!" I apologize for my ignorance, but neither of them are offended, understanding it's a common mistake for people outside Australia to make and nothing more, and going forward we quickly bond over beer as friends and soldiers.

A few beers later we leave to make the rounds of other Vung Tao bars, stopping next at the Las Vegas Bar where we slip into a conversation about the war.

"You Yanks are bloody good, but don't know a hang about jungle fighting," Denis says to me. "Trouble is you're loaded down with sixty to eighty pounds of equipment and can't out maneuver the enemy." With Peter adding, "You want all the comforts of home wherever you go."

"I'm not a jungle fighter so I can't speak to that," tell them, "but if it's all the same, I'd rather talk about something other than the war."

"That's fair, dinkum mate, but it's tough not to, even here in Vung Tao," Peter says. "Last week half a block from here on the beach road some ARVN blokes got pissed at some Yanks and tossed a grenade into the lot of em, killing them all."

"The ARVNs are angry," Denis adds. "They don't have the money you Yanks do and even if they did, the local sheilas prefer you Yanks and that doesn't sit well with them."

Hearing about a grenade being toss starts me down the dark hole of remembering what happened to Zoffa and Snover, and I quickly change the subject, saying the first thing that comes to mind.

"Whenever my cobber Graham was in port he always raised the Aussie flag so that any countrymen like you two would stop by for some Foster's piss, which he made sure to tell me is not the best piss in Australia, only the best he can get in South East Asia," ending this with a toast to Aussie piss, then another to the sheilas in Vung Tao followed by another to good cobbers, and it's just enough to change my mood.

From the Las Vegas Bar we head for the Paradise Bar and on the way encounter a GI having a heated argument with a bargirl, the girl claiming the GI owes her money for sex and the GI claiming she wasn't worth it. Hearing this, Peter runs right over and grabs the GI by his shirt and pins him up against a wall, telling him he's a disgrace to the American uniform and ordering him to pay the girl what he owes her. After the GI pays and runs off, Peter tells me, even though he's an Aussie, he holds America in high esteem and can't stand to see anybody make it look bad, especially a fellow soldier.

However gallant, the very act of violence triggers an emotional response in me and all I want to do is be by myself so I tell them I forgot that I have to meet Lan, but before I go Peter gives me his Aussie bush hat as a souvenir to remember him and Denis by, and without giving it a thought, I hand him my Zippo lighter engraved "Spain 1969," the one Graham and I exchanged when we made plans to reunite in Spain, genuine Zippos being highly prized in the Nam.

CHAPTER 105

Back at Xu's house I lay on the platform bed under the mosquito netting trying to forget the violence I witnessed by counting the rats scurrying across the metal roof and waiting for Lan to show up, only she never does and in the morning having had little sleep and too much to drink the night before I'm feeling completely spent.

In contrast after hustling drinks and GIs all the night at the China Doll, Xu's up early preparing breakfast for the three of us setting it out on a straw mat atop the floor. Squatting alongside the two of them, I slurp broth and noodles from a bowl of hot Pho, they getting a kick out of me using chopsticks with my left hand to shovel in the vegetables, hot chilies and pork, and me being careful not to say a word about my disappointment that Lan never showed up not wanting her or Xu to know that I care, though my caring has more to do more with Lan being a legend than the actual sex, and only because someday when I'm an old and sitting around trading war stories with fellow VN vets and Lan's name comes up I can truthfully say, "me too."

After breakfast the three of us head to the beach for a repeat of the day before and when Lan joins us I feign not caring that she didn't come, though I sense she knows the truth, and when she says to me, "Tonight I come fa-sure." I nonchalantly acknowledge her with a casual "okay" then turn back to Xu and Bill and the fun we're having taking pictures with Xu's pride and joy, a Kodak Instamatic that a GI boyfriend got her from the BX.

On the way back to town the four of us stop for an early dinner of spaghetti eaten with chopsticks, after which Xu and Lan get ready for work and little Bill and I take a walk along French Beach stopping to count the ships laying at anchor in the Bay, twenty eight in all, and all of them waiting for dock space up the river in Saigon to unload their greatly inflated cargos of war supplies. It's on this walk that little Bill again reaches over and takes my hand only now, knowing about him and Snover, I wonder if I should send him a signal that I'm not same, same Snover wondering too if he's really homosexual or just an affectionate kid who regards people as gender neutral or gender fluid and with this decide to take his handholding at face value, a sign of friendship and nothing more.

After the China Doll closes Xu comes back to the house and not knowing I'm still awake, quietly changes out of her bargirl clothes into pajamas, and then lays down atop her straw mat bed on the floor, not far from me.

"Where Lan" I whisper to her.

"Lan no can come. Boyfriend Lan come Vung Tao. Tomorrow he go Song Be, you go house Lan."

"Can I sleep with you?" I ask Xu who I find much more attractive than Lan.

"You boyfriend Lan."

"I boyfriend Xu too."

"You no say Lan?"

"I no say." I assure her, and with that she slips into bed beside me.

CHAPTER 106

Following breakfast instead of going to the beach, Xu goes off shopping and I go with little Bill who leads me up one of the mountains overlooking the town so we can take in beautiful scenery and enjoying the serenity of hearing only the breeze whispering past our ears. Then on the way back, after hours of vigorous hiking, we stop at a juice vendor cart for fresh Papaya juice which made me nostalgic, because it's what I did as a boy his age, after long walks with my grandfather.

That night I move into Lan's house and when she returns from work at the China Doll we have sex with the passion of a production worker knocking off one more widget before punching out for the day, but it doesn't matter because it secures my place in history which was my goal in doing so.

CHAPTER 107

With one day left to my R&R, little Bill asks me to climb the mountain with him again so he can show me something really special and I jump at the opportunity to spend more time in nature before going back to city hustle of desperate Saigon.

Dressed in his everyday outfit of short shorts and plastic sandals he takes my hand and we ride part way up the mountain in a horse drawn carriage then get out and continue on by foot climbing up a dirt trail until the town shrinks and mirrored ponds of the rice paddies along the banks of the Saigon river look like squares on a checker board; the river itself a muddy snake slithering through the Mekong delta into the South China Sea. Further on we pause to watch an American gunboat chugging up the Mekong, one of the killing machines I was hoping to forget and seeing it reminds me that I've left the relative safety of town and am now in VC territory.

After cresting a steep slope little Bill leads me to a wooden arch carved with oriental symbols, half hidden behind some thick foliage and behind it steps up leading up to a Zen Monastery where he leaves his sandals, and I take off my jungle boots, at the base of an enormous five or six story high white marble effigy of Gautama Buddha seated on a lotus flower with the world visible in front of it for fifty or sixty miles. The magnificence of towering symbol set against the blue sky in the stillness of nature instantly infuses me with profound sense of peace and which consumes me until little Bill takes me by the hand to an alter where we light incense which is said to calm our souls even more and purge them of all negativity, after which we sit gazing at the tranquility in Buddha's face before little Bill once again takes off this time to run around flapping his arms like he's a bird, and demonstrating to me one of the wonderful tenants of Buddhism, that it's not sacrilegious to express one's inner soul in the presence of divinity. Later we descend the mountain and catch a Lambretta jitney back to town stopping at the juice vendor on the way.

In the morning before catching my plane back to Saigon, Xu gives me a small ivory and gold pendant of Buddha and I give little Bill the Aussie bush hat I got from Peter, it's far too big for him, but I know he really wants it. Xu refuses to take any money from me for her hospitality, and Lan, the most famous bargirl in the Nam, is nowhere to be found though I guess she's at home resting up from her work as a legend.

CHAPTER 108

Without Zoffa, Snover, Mark Breslin, Jack, Graham, Sir Robin and the others, Saigon no longer feels familiar to me and it's not just because I miss them, but the City's hostile like its soul has become infected with the plague of anarchy.

When I hail a taxi the driver wants two hundred Ps for a ride that was only twenty Ps a few weeks ago, and when get out and slam the door in protest, the driver tries to run me over not once, but several times, eyes bulging with the same malignancy that has infected so many others who are trying to deal with the increasing uncertainty of rampant inflation. The price of a fish that was the equivalent of ten cents less than a year ago, now costs a dollar or more with incomes nowhere near keeping up and because of this the city's become a dog eat dog arena reminding me of a story I once read in the New York Daily News about a man who was taking his wife and children to a museum on a Sunday afternoon. After driving around the block several times looking for a parking space, the man suddenly spots one, but it's up a one way street so he tells his wife to drive around the block while he stands in the vacant spot to hold it. After his wife drives off, another man with his wife and children looking for a parking spot and similarly frustrated, pulls up and demands the first man step aside. The man refuses and a fight ensues and by the time the first man's wife and children arrive he's lying dead in the street, having hit his head in the scuffle.

CHAPTER 109

O n my first day back to work at the AMT after returning from Vung Tao, Sgt. Robbie assigns me to ride
shot gun for Vinh who drives the big rig tractor trailer that
carries the big steel conexes of boat mail between the AMT
and the port at Khanh Hoi, this because of my familiarity
with the city and the VN language and that I was once a
teamster in civilian life.

On the way to the port we get stuck in gridlock traffic
surrounded by an angry mob of Buddhist monks protesting against the Saigon government. Boxed in and unable
to move we're hit with a barrage of tomatoes that comes
sailing through the windows of the cab, our military truck
being an easy target for their anger. When the mob starts
climbing on the truck and pounding on the hood, Vinh
fearing for his life opens the door, jumps down and runs

off. Even though I'm armed with an M-16 and 45 automatic I know it would be suicide to use them. I consider running too, but unlike Vinh who's Vietnamese, I fear I'll not get past the mob. While I wait for them to pull me from the cab, the only thing that comes to mind is, I can get a few of them before they get me.

Just as the windshield is smashed a monk with a bullhorn redirects the mob to the intersection where another monk is seated in the lotus position. From my position high in the cab I watch as another monk carries a Gerry can from the adjacent Esso Gas Station and pours its contents over the seated monk then tosses a match instantly setting off a loud wooosh of combustion that engulfs the seated monk in a fiery cocoon. Unmoved, the burning monk is clearly visible inside the cocoon of flames and within minutes his black-ened silhouette topples over as the putrid stench of burned flesh permeates the air. The mob then begins to disperse and Canh Sats move in to break up the grid lock. When they do, I inch the big rig forward past the monk's remains where other Cinh-sats, their noses covered with bandanas, are maneuvering the charred remains onto a litter using long poles, so they can haul it away. The next morning, the front page of every Saigon newspaper carries a photograph of the burning monk clearly visible inside the cocoon of flames; the war continues as before, and I'm assigned duty as driver for port runs.

On the same front page with the photo of the burning monk, is a story about LeRoy Turkus, owner of the Pleasure Palace and latest victim of the Saigon government's crack-down on American owned businesses which is purely symbolic because it is a well-accepted rumor the countless bars, night-clubs and brothels have ties to them, and that the slot machines in the BEQs, and BOQs are run by an Army Sargent with ties to high ranking military officers, US government officials and Las Vegas casino owners.

According to the story, LeRoy was arrested, jailed and fined every penny he ever made. But a follow-up story that appears weeks later claims when he was released he still had seventy-five thousand dollars that he managed to hide from authorities which he invested in monkeys and sold to zoos around the world, quadrupling his investment and wiring the profits to a bank in New York before anyone found out. And the day after that story appears the Saigon government counters it with a story that claims when the government got wind of the deal they wouldn't let the monkeys out of the country and a flat broke LeRoy had to be repatriated by the American Embassy. The last line in the story quoted a Vietnamese government official as saying, "if LeRoy had been a Vietnamese, we would have shot him." Whatever the truth there is no doubt LeRoy was only a scapegoat for countless others who are profiting from the war and paying the South VN government to look the other way.

CHAPTER 110

Waiting for me at the Hung Dao are two letters and a notice from the BX. One of the letters is from my parents telling me how anti-war protests across the Country have gotten violent and the other from a military buddy stationed in Okinawa saying he's getting married to a local Japanese girl. The notice from the BX informs me the Mixmaster I ordered has arrived.

After picking up the Mixmaster I take it to the Paris Tailor Shop. Mai immediately sends her oldest son via cyclo, to fetch her sister so she can come by and get it, and when Madam Binh arrives, she's beside herself with joy and wants to pay me for it, and then some, but I refuse to accept any money out of my friendship with Mai. In return for this Madam Binh invites me along with Mai's entire family for a dinner at her villa which will not only be a treat for me, but Mai who rarely leaves the shop.

When I get to Madam Binh's luxurious villa I'm greeted like an honored guest with full attention given to my comfort and desires in an unpretentious way, not by their numerous servants, but by Madam Binh and her husband Mr. Khai themselves. She is elegantly dressed in a white silk Ao dai and her slightly rotund husband in a white Palm Beach suit.

Right off I can tell her husband, who's impressively fluent in English, is a gracious gentle soul when he hands me an aperitif then takes the time to explain he doesn't drink alcohol because his religion forbids it, but does not judge others for doing so and tells me this just so I won't feel uncomfortable. And as the evening progresses I also learn that even though he's a multimillionaire, he humbly celebrates life with a host of strict disciplines and is not the least bit tempted by the material or social privileges afforded a man of his wealth.

Dinner begins with those golf ball size snails Saigon is famous for, neatly prepared in garlic butter, each shell imbedded with a reed of grass so one easy pull removes the meat, this followed by roasted chicken, and baked fish with rice, both served on my behalf western style with plates instead of bowls and knives and forks instead of chopsticks. These sumptuous dishes however are for the rest of us with Mr. Khai getting one solitary plate upon which, almost lost in the middle, are a few slices of raw carrots, onions, cauliflower and celery. He explains it to me this way.

"I am a Buddhist. My religion forbids that I eat meat after a certain age. For nearly thirty years I have not tasted meat, fish, or poultry. Three times a day I eat one plate of these same vegetables. My sons as they get older will eat less and less meat until one day they too will not eat flesh, only vegetables. Now my eldest son is allowed only one meal of meat a day and soon he will be completely vegetarian."

I can tell too, from the way he speaks, he does not see this religious edict as an imposition or sacrifice, but as an honor, yet I can't help but look at his wife whose plate is full of chicken and wonder how she and their religion reconcile this. As if reading my mind, her husband explains it to me. "My wife does not have to be a vegetarian. It is only for the men." Though this explanation does little to reveal the rationale behind the canon.

When we're finished with the entrées one of the servants carries in a beautiful heart-shaped cake inscribed with the words, "Thank you friend Kovner" and sets it down in front of me.

I made it with the Mixmaster to show our appreciation" Madam Binh tells me, and all eyes turn to watch my face light up with gratitude for the effort they made, to make me feel special and at home with their family.

"Thank you," I tell them. "It is I who am deeply moved and appreciative for this wonderful meal and the warmth of your hospitality."

With the meal over one, of their sons plays Chopin on their concert size piano, the language of music expertly communicated through his years of disciplined practice. The recital is followed by a game of ping pong between me and their younger son who is so good my longer reach is of no advantage; though he's more humble in victory than I am in defeat.

Another treat comes when I have the opportunity to sit alone with Mr. Khai and learn about life and the war from his prospective as a Vietnamese and practicing Buddhist. My first inquiry to him is aimed at helping me understand the Buddhist sacrifice of self-immolation.

"Buddhism does not teach death and destruction," he says. "There are many who would hide behind it for political advantage, but they give Buddhism an unfair reputation. Such displays are merely tragic theater for public influence."

I then ask him about former President Diem, explaining how I heard he was considered a puppet of the United States government and had been living in the U.S. for many years when Washington officials "installed" him as president, and how Michigan State University under a federal grant, worked with the CIA to help train and equip his police force to keep him in power until our government turned against him and supported the coup."

"It was different when President Diem was here," he tells me. "We could travel freely and there was less killing, yet many injustices were put against the people of South Vietnam mostly by Madam Nhu President Diem's sister-in-law who forbid the people to dance, and ignored their requests for better living, and it was for this the people overthrew his government. Diem as a man was not hated except I am ashamed to say by some Buddhists, but only because he was a strong Catholic. His weakness was he permitted wicked Madam Nhu to rule injustice against the Vietnamese people. For this the people sadly killed him while today Madam Nhu the one who was most hated, is still at large. President Diem was a man who loved his country, but he was a weak man."

What about Ho Chi Minh?" I ask him. "I read that he liked and admired the United States and even lived in New York City and Boston where he worked as a baker at the famous Parker House Hotel. And that politically he was a nationalist committed to unifying Vietnam as one country under a constitution similar to that of the US, but that the US, which originally agreed to help him expel the colonial French, like we did the colonial British, reneged and backed the French, deciding its ties to the French were more important, leaving Ho no choice but to search for any government that would help him unify the country, eventually turning to the Chinese who he vehemently disliked."

"It is not that simple," Mr. Khai answers. "Ho's good intentions became corrupted by power and politics and he was forced to cede power to those who are driven by their hatred of the South and desire to dominate it. The Buddhist South fears if the country is unified, the Catholic North with its greater population will rule harshly over us. After centuries of foreign dominance, Ho along with General Giap, inspired many for self-rule after they demonstrated at Dien Bien Phu that little Vietnam could defeat a mighty power like France. For this Ho became a national hero, but General Giap, a military hard liner, seized this power and uses Ho as a symbol to brutally crush any opposition to his desire to rule over the South."

"I'm not a religious person," I tell him, "but I'm intrigued by the Biblical saying, 'If thine eye be single, thine whole body shall be full of light,' which I interpret to mean when we understand that everything is an indivisible part of the same whole, we intuitively know harming another is harming ourselves. To me it's basic physics, everything is interconnected and within every action is an equal and opposite reaction. Given this, we are fighting against ourselves and one side will eventually prevail, but both have already lost."

In Buddhism," Mr. Khai tells me, "there is a saying, 'The way is not in the head, but in the heart.'"

CHAPTER 111

If the newspapers are correct, in terms of money the Vietnam War is costing the US taxpayers a million dollars an hour, but I suspect being war money the accounting is manipulated to hide the true numbers. For example, if a GI in Vietnam signs the receipt for a shipment of trucks, or a tanker full of oil, or a container of C-Rations, all of them already sold to the American people at highly inflated prices, and less is delivered or disappears after delivery, no questions are asked, everything's just written off as the cost of war.

I get a taste of this when sent to the flight line to sign for the last shipment of payroll cash before implementation of MPCs, millions of dollars stacked up on pallets and strapped down under tarps. When the loadmaster hands me the receipt to sign, I ask "How am I supposed to know how much money is there?" And he says, "It's on the receipt, just sign it." And of course I did, and so did the paymaster after me.

Each day the newspapers are filled with stories of profiteers and politicians who travel to Vietnam on official "fact-finding missions" making up to $80,000 per week on inside deals. One such group is caught at Tan Son Nhut customs with nearly a million dollars' worth of gold and it's rumored that fifty to seventy-five percent of all ship's cargos never reach their official destination. Of those that do, some are filled with broken furniture and useless items like millions of IBM punch cards that are moved directly from the ships to private warehouses for resale on the international market.

Despite the Vietnam government's symbolic crackdown on foreign-owned businesses, more continue to open under hidden ownership. When the corrupt government taxes them up to $10,000 per month, they still manage to operate profitably, the brunt of the tax being picked up by higher prices without any increase in wages. One well publicized example of this is the great Saigon Tea revolt that begins when the price of a Saigon tea served in city's countless bars sky rockets from thirty-five Ps to three hundred Ps almost overnight. In response, the GIs organize a boycott and refuse to buy any for the girls, only buying beers for themselves, greatly affecting the girls' income that they need to feed their families. When the local papers get wind of this they label it "The Great Saigon Tea Revolt" and the tea prices are eventually lowered, but it's the girls who lose because the bar owners still have to pay the tax and do so by taking a larger percentage from the girls' share. When some of the girls walk out in protest, they're forced back due to a surplus of girls willing to take their place.

Adding an element of absurd comedy to this event, stories in the Saigon papers report that when word of "The Great Saigon Tea Revolt" found its way back to Capitol Hill in Washington, carried there by politicians on a fact finding mission, the context was distorted and entered into the Congressional Record that our boys in Vietnam are not getting enough tea. Shortly thereafter, American news crews started showing up in Saigon bars to interview GIs and film "The Great Saigon Tea Revolt" for TV viewers back home. The farce temporarily upstaging stories on the war itself.

CHAPTER 112

Desperation follows inflation as sure as inflation follows greed and soon more and more of the poor go from passively begging to aggressively fighting for a few extra Ps, crowding the sidewalks and pushing their starving limbs into your face. Children run wild snatching wristwatches, wallets, fountain pens, anything that can easily be carried away and sold. Ten, eleven, twelve-year old boys and girls with infants on their hips chase after GIs grabbing onto their shirts and pants, begging them to come home and fuck their sisters who are not much older than they are. Money changers pray on GIs, promising a high rate of exchange then shorting them with a fast count before disappearing down an alley.

While sitting on the patio of the Club Nautique, I watch a young boy perhaps ten years old, grab a Frenchman's wristwatch, pop it into a bag, then make his escape by jumping into the water and holding onto a piling with the bagged watch above his head. The irate Frenchman who's in a business suit won't jump in, instead he goes and gets a Canh-sat who comes over and stares down at the boy, but refuses to jump in himself. Eventually they both leave and the boy swims ashore with the reward for his efforts. While I find humor in how the little boy defeated both the businessman and cop, it's tragically emblematic of the increasing struggle to survive in the war torn economy.

Two local newspapers print the names of well-connected persons supposedly smuggling drugs into and out of VN, one claiming to have proof Premiere Ky is involved, and the next day both papers are seized and the owners disappear.

Males of fighting age from poor families continue to be conscripted, snatched right off the street to give their lives so that the rich can profit from the war while their own fighting age sons lounge at outdoor cafés like one at the Hotel Continental, dressed in fashionable clothes and sipping expressos over lunch.

CHAPTER 113

On the front page of both The Saigon Post and The Saigon Daily News it is announced, "Any person found guilty of an act detrimental to the cause against the Communists will be executed." Behind the edict is a government desperate to vanquish their critics and do so with impunity under the guise of law rather than have them covertly disappear.

A special "War Crimes Court" is established to mete out this justice and its first victim is a Vietnamese of Chinese descent. He's in his mid-thirties, the father of eight, husband to an attractive woman and the multimillionaire owner of an Import/Export business who also owns a Mercedes Benz and several homes. The charge against him is hoarding logistical materials by storing them in warehouses to create a shortage then selling them at a huge profit. After a one day trial he is convicted and sentenced to public execution by firing squad. That he is of Chinese decent makes him a perfect scapegoat to counter the growing protests against corruption as he is less likely to engender sympathy or criticism from the ethnic Vietnamese majority.

With no time for appeal and his wealth seized by the government, he is tied to a stake at the side of police headquarters building and in front of a large crowd of mostly poor, with his wife and children off to his side begging for mercy, bullets from two police carbines put an end to his life.

The next day a newspaper reports, "Justice was served a few hundred feet from the very Import/Export office where the corrupt Chinese businessman perpetrated his crime against the poor people of South Vietnam."

A few days later the next victim is announced. He's the former Mayor of Dalat, a resort city in the mountains, who was arrested for corruption. The court finds him guilty and sentences him to mandatory death, but after reviewing the case, Premier Ky reduces the sentence to a short jail term. The official reason, "the former Mayor is an old man who is needed by his family and his life should be spared by a merciful state." The unofficial reason, he is Vietnamese, not Chinese or Indian like the merchant who was previously executed for possessing foreign checks, and has friends who are friends of Ky's and no doubt paid a hefty ransom on his behalf.

The third victim in the anticorruption war crimes purge is another ethnic Vietnamese, a harbor official who unwisely deposited seven hundred thousand dollars in a personal bank account and upon investigation was found to have nearly three million dollars' worth of skimmed United States war supplies hidden away in warehouses he owns. He's tried, convicted and sentenced to death, only when the sentence is reviewed by the Ky/Thieu government his assets are confiscated and he's given a reduced jail term.

As Americans, every injustice has our names attached to it.

CHAPTER 114

With little less than a month to go before becoming a short-timer, I feel a need for closure and stop by the Playboy Bar for the first time since ending my relationship with Thuy many months before. As soon as I come through the door Dung runs up to me and says, "Troi oi, long time you no come Playboy" then without hesitation, "you buy me one Saigon Tea?" Somethings never change.

"Where Thuy?" I ask.

Thuy no work here, Thuy withs babyson."

"Babyson, who give Thuy babyson, me?"

She laughs, "No you. Thuy have beaucoup GI boyfriend when you fini her. Father babyson go back America, buts Thuy ver-ly happy, Thuy want America babyson too much." Reaching down she picks up the hem of her Ao

Dai and blows her nose in it before continuing. "You have girlfriend?"

"No have girlfriend. I go America soon."

"Okay, you buy me one Saigon tea?"

I nod and she signals the barboy to bring her a Saigon Tea then solicits me to go short time, but I decline. Besides having no interest in her it's too close to my PCD which is GI speak for "pussy cutoff date," the date marked on every GI's calendar thirty days prior to rotating so as not to return home a victim of the Nam's eighty five percent VD rate, and even more important, a reminder to curtail risky behavior that might get you killed or injured.

From the Playboy I head over to the Van Canh night club on Calmette Street where I heard my Buddha angel Loan is still singing. It's been almost two months since we last saw each other, right after Zoffa and Snover were killed, and the moment I do all I want is to be with her again like we were before. After her set ends, she comes over to my table.

"Anh oi I happy to see you, buts I sad too," she says, "I miss you too much." I then learn she is pregnant with our baby.

"I no sad for ba bao," she tells me,"I want babyson, buts I sad you go home America and babyson no have papason."

Unprepared for this news I don't know what to say and blurt out the first thing that comes to mind, "Why you no fini babyson? I no can go America knowing you and babyson are here in this war."

"I sorry anh oi I want babyson you, I no care." She says her tears escaping from her eyes.

"But babyson no for remember Ben, Vietnam number ten for babyson."

And hearing this she gets up from the table. "I sorry I no can think anh oi. I must work now."

"When can I see you?" I ask.

"I come café Majestic Tu-Do Street twelve clock tomorrow I see you," she says, then returns to the stage and I'm left with images of my child, half Vietnamese, half American, dressed in tattered pajamas, picking through Saigon's putrid piles of garbage and eyeing every GI who passes wondering if he is their father, all while I live a comfortable life in America.

CHAPTER 115

Two days later at noon I'm at the Majestic Hotel's sidewalk café waiting for Loan and when I see her get out of a cyclo and walk toward the café I can't help but stare at her belly, thinking that's my baby she's carrying and how can I leave them here in such a place?

"Anh oi, I sorry," she says apologizing as she sits down next to me.

"For what?" I ask?

"When I see you Van Canh I little girl. You, I think Ben right, Vietnam number ten for babyson and I go doctor fini babyson. I sad, buts it better I sad than babyson sad."

Hearing this I am relieved but saddened that during my brief time as a father I failed to give my own child a chance for life, this even though I know ending the pregnancy was best for all.

Realizing how hard this decision must have been for Loan I reach over and take her in my arms not caring that public displays of affection are frowned upon in VN and in doing so feel terrible that she will be left to suffer the devastating effects of the war while I go on with my life in the States. It then crosses my mind I could arrange to take my discharge in-country and get a good paying job with a Saigon based American company and we could live a privileged life together.

While contemplating this, and wanting to bring happiness to her especially after what she just went through, I make a spontaneous decision to take her to Dalat, a resort town in the mountains a couple of hundred miles north of Saigon that was popular with the French elite; thinking this is just what she needs to help heal the emotional wounds of the baby and our relationship, and give me a chance to consider our being together after I leave the military. As a short-timer I know I won't have a problem getting a few days leave. When I ask Loan, having never been out of Saigon except for her family's migration from the North when she was nine years old, and our Honda trips to the villages along highway one, she's excited.

On the day of our trip, we go to the civilian terminal at Tan Son Nhut and wait in the passenger lounge while Air Vietnam's 7:30 A.M. DC3 flight to Dalat is being loaded with cargo. With us in the lounge, are several pajama clad Vietnamese squatting down next to their cloth bundles tied with twine and their crates of live chickens, and a few saffron robed monks, and well-dressed Vietnamese men and women, and one occidental man who I suspect is French since he's carrying a piece of Louis Vuittan luggage.

One of the Vietnamese men wearing a white business suit and accompanied by a young girl, comes over to me and says, "My name is Mr. Chu, this is my daughter. You have been to Dalat before?"

"No, this will be my first time." I tell him.

"Allow me to be of service." He says handing me his business card which identifies him as a jeweler, "Perhaps I can suggest a hotel for you. The best place to stay is the Dalat Palace Hotel where my daughter and I will be staying."

"Thank you," I tell him then wait for the hustle, but none comes. He just nods politely and walks away.

When the flight takes-off, I look out the window and see an Air Force jet loaded with munitions taking off on the parallel runway, something I have seen many times before but not from the prospective of a civilian plane heading on a pleasure trip with a girlfriend, and this fills me with great sorrowfulness and inescapable guilt knowing only minutes from now some poor, loved and valued souls will suffer a terrible fate while am living life to the fullest. Within seconds the fighter jet disappears from view and I turn my attention back to Loan while the Air Vietnam DC3 labors to reach its cruising altitude. Some of the passengers are already battling air sickness, filling the poorly ventilated cabin with the odor of vomit and perspiration.

This being Buddha angel's very first flight I ask her, "How do you like flying?"

"I am with you." She answers and seems surprisingly unfazed by it.

At the airport in Dalat we transfer to a bus for the drive up the mountain to town. Sitting across the aisle from us is Mr. Chu who leans over to inform me, "There are many VC in this area. I am afraid for you if the bus should get stopped, but once we are in the City you will not have to worry, it is well protected by both our countrymen."

Hearing this I reach down and touch the thirty eight revolver in its ankle hostler under my pant leg, then pass the remaining miles my eyes darting in every direction at once. Before we get to town the bus is stopped at a military check point but the soldiers turn out to be ARVN.

At the Dalat Palace Hotel, which stands prominently on a hill above the city like Christ the Redeemer above Rio, we register as Monsieur and Madam Kovner, but the snobby desk clerk eyes us with condescension no doubt because he knows I'm a GI and sees Loan as a common Vietnamese girl, neither of whom belong in his elitist establishment.

It's an elegant place too with French colonial furnishings and a wide winding staircase leading up to generous rooms fitted with crystal chandeliers, original art and Romeo and Juliette balconies that overlook the Hotel's impeccably manicured gardens, orchards, and rolling lawns, beyond which, are breathtaking views of Dalat's magnificent countryside, all of this rivaling the best I've seen anywhere.

The air is chilly and with no heating in the hotel, and my months of living in the steamy lowlands, I feel cold for the first time in almost a year, but surprisingly my Buddha angel Loan isn't bothered by it at all. She immediately fills the bathtub with cold water even though there's hot on tap, then climbs in while I stand over her adding bubble bath from a bottle supplied with the room. Then after a few minutes of soaking, she starts singing acapella, her melodious vibrato reaching out me on the balcony where I've gone to take in deep breathes of the pine-scented air and marvel at the hotel's flower and vegetable gardens and a magnificent lake off in the distance. When I come back inside I towel her off and we lay under the soft quilt of the French provincial bed naked and wrapped in each other's arms, protected by the canopy of mosquito netting, our faces warmed by the sun streaming through the balcony doors.

Following some wonderful love sex, no concerns about PCD with her, we dress and go downstairs to the hotel's ornately decorated dining room for a lunch served at a table set with fine linens and real bone china, with polished silver utensils, and heavy lead crystal glasses. The snobby waiter eying Loan with the same condescending look as the desk clerk, and he's further put out when Loan cannot bring herself to eat the hotel's epicurean French cuisine and sends him into the kitchen for a bowl of rice with fish and nuc mam.

We then set out to explore the city on foot and I'm amazed to see Vietnamese people with rosy cheeks and wearing sweaters, something unthinkable in the sweltering tropical lowlands. At Loan's request I buy two hand knit sweaters from a street vendor as gifts for her parents though I can't imagine them ever making use of them.

Unlike Saigon, the streets of Dalat are spotlessly clean, uncluttered by garbage which makes me wonder what they do with it and facetiously musing to myself they must ship it to Saigon. There's a small contingent of US military based there and the GIs we pass can't help but stare at Loan, not only for her beauty, but unlike Saigon there are few bars in Dalat to provide them with female companionship. Another noticeable difference is the social interaction between GIs and ARVN, walking and talking with each other like friends, something almost unheard of in the rest of Nam outside of actual combat situations.

At a garden beside the city's Xuan Huong Lake, Loan and I pick flowers along with other romantic couples, then sit and watch other romantic couples rowing boats like they do in New York's Central Park and still others on bicycles leisurely peddling around the lake's perimeter path. We then climb the hillside and gaze out at the breath taking views of the countryside before descending to window shop along the city's quaint streets, stopping at a sidewalk cafe for a lunch of Dalat salad; the town's name being synonymous with the lettuce that's grown there. Feeling the effects of the altitude, we head back to the hotel for some more love sex before napping and dressing for dinner, followed by a night's sleep in each other's arms under the quilt with the baloney doors wide open and filling the room with crisp pine scented air.

CHAPTER 116

Waking up in a luxurious bed and new environment with my Buddha Angle sleeping peacefully beside me, I can't help but stare at her and wonder if the whole purpose of me being sent to the Nam was so we could meet and be together forever. Awash in this blissful thought, I watch the tiny slits of her crescent eyes slowly open to my gaze and lure me siren-like, to her lips.

"Good morning Anh noi," she breath whispers to me after our kiss.

"Good morning my little Buddha angel, it's a wonderful day because I am with you."

We kiss again then begin the day as we ended the previous one with some love sex before showering together and going downstairs to the sun-filled dining room for breakfast where I order an Omelette Champignon made with white table wine and fresh mushrooms harvested from the hotel's garden along with slices of freshly baked, crusty baguette and creamy sweet butter, and for Loan a simple bowl of Pho begrudgingly served by the same snobby VN waiter dressed in a Frenchman's tux.

In town we hire a taxi guide with a blue and yellow Puegot 401 and ride through the evergreen forested mountains, climbing up narrow mountainous roads where for the first time ever I see coffee growing, though the driver fails to point this out, likely because they're too familiar to him as are the spectacular views we pass, leaving me to wonder just what he will be showing us.

Occasionally we pass men and boys dressed in black pajamas armed with Chinese assault rifles, unmistakably VC who pan the Peugeot and my European face with enough intensity for me to question the wisdom of letting an unknown driver take us this far out of the protected city. Sensing my concern the driver says, "Plenty VC in Dalat, plenty American, no trouble, both come Dalat for play," confirming what I've heard, that the VC use Dalat for R &R too. Despite this assurance, when he stops the taxi and gets out motioning for us to follow him through the forest, I slip my handgun from its ankle holster into my pocket.

But a short time later we're standing on the top of the world with a view stretching out for countless miles across a great valley, and far below a miniature village of tiny huts, their shiny metal roofs reflecting the sun like glitter on a sequined gown, and looming above the village a massive dam holding back the waters of a vast lake.

"Last year VC blow up dam, fini village, too much peoples die," our driver tells us. "America have ver-ly much money, fix dam, make new village. Army now watch dam."

I take out my camera and snap away knowing the futility of trying to capture the scale of such majesty on a flat piece of film and while I'm doing that Loan runs into the forest and calls back to me, "Anh oi, you come" and when I chase after her she runs off like a kid playing tag until I catch up to her and get a kiss for my reward.

The driver then takes us down the mountain to the village we saw from above and stops long enough for me to snap pictures of simple village life, one of a village girl four or five years old carrying an infant on her hip, another of a bone thin woman shouldering heavy urns of water on a flexi-pole, others of goats, dogs, and oxen roaming free among humans, and one of a toothless old man staring at a group of boys kicking a soccer ball made from tied up rags, his stoic face etched with the remembrance of days past.

The next day our taxi guide takes us back up the mountain to the Van Gogh waterfall that I recognize from the honeymoon photo hanging behind the counter in Mai's tailor shop. There to our surprise, we run into Mr. Chu and his daughter picnicking beside the river adjacent to the falls. Excited to see them Loan runs over and they invite us to join them for lunch. As though expecting us, they have extra bowls, chopsticks, rice and vegetables and the four of us eat in the shade of pine trees serenaded by the sound of water rushing down the mountain; a double rainbow in its mist.

Not seeing another car I ask Mr. Chu how he got there.

"We hired a taxi, same as you," he answers.

"But I don't see it."

"I sent it back because we cannot afford to keep it all day."

"Then how did you expect to get back to town?"

"I knew someone like you would come along and give us a ride."

With that Mr. Chu and his daughter attach themselves to Loan and me and the four of us continue the tour together, stopping next at a tea plantation where rows of mountain tribeswomen sit at a table set with wicker baskets grading tea leaves by hand, placing the leaves one at a time in the appropriate basket, and from there to a pottery factory where Loan and Mr. Chu's daughter run around giggling and touching the unbaked earthenware that crumbles in their hands despite signs in French, English, Chinese and Vietnamese saying "Do Not Touch." In the company of Mr. Chu's daughter my Buddha angel has become like a child and I like a father trying to rein her in and telling her how to behave. And when the factory manager insists we pay for the broken crockery, Mr. Chu is not willing to do so. It's only pennies so rather than let an argument ruin the visit I pay while my Buddha angel doe eyes me with, "I sorry anh oi."

At first I'm embarrassed, then annoyed, by her childish behavior, then ashamed for burdening her with my expectations when she's having such a good time. I realize too, that I'm jealous she's giving her attention to Mr. Chu's daughter and not me, and feel even more ashamed.

That evening the four of us go to the dining room for dinner and the two girls continue to behave like undisciplined children giggling and talking loud to the ire of the snooty staff until I can't help it anymore and blurt out, "Loan, please keep your voice down and sit still" and immediately regretting doing so when she runs out of the room crying and Mr. Chu and his daughter shoot me disapproving looks. I sense they would leave too, but for the food on the table.

Filled with regret I quickly sign the dinner check, which makes Mr. Chu happy, then race after Loan, finding her lying on the bed in our room, tears covering her cheeks.

"I'm sorry," I tell her, but my words do nothing to stop the tears.

"No I sorry anh oi, I no makes you happy. I want be woman for you, buts I child"

"No, you number one girlfriend, I number ten boyfriend, I see you happy I get gen hoa, jealous you no with me, you with daughter Mr. Chu."

Taking her in my arms I hold her wanting want to erase the pain I've caused and salvage the rest of our time together.

CHAPTER 117

When our eyes meet in the morning the regretful events of the night before linger awkwardly behind a simple kiss. I desire sex and know she won't refuse me, but I don't want her to think it is the totality of my feelings for her so I push the thought aside and we shower together, caressing one another, but stopping short of going any further, then dress and go down for breakfast where Loan is a proper Vietnamese lady, understated and genteel, even ordering an omelet against my urging for her to have the Pho she likes so much.

This being our last day in Dalat we stroll the streets then picnic by the lake, ending the day in our room where our kisses lead to tender sex followed by sleep in each other's arms.

CHAPTER 118

W hile getting ready to leave for the airport, Loan surprises me by asking for money something she has
never done before.

"How much do you want?" I ask.

"One thousand Ps," she says, then takes the money saying she'll be right back and returning twenty minutes later
with a bellhop pushing a hand cart loaded with six cardboard trays of strawberries, one stacked upon the other
with those on top pressing the juice from the one's below
and leaving a juice trail down the hallway that fills it and the
room with a sweet aroma. "My family likes dau too much,"
she says to me, then instructs the bellhop to wait while she
gets her things together.

While she's packing I'm wondering how we're going
to get the leaking trays onto the plane, but dare not say

anything for fear of hurting her feelings. It's obvious to me she's beside herself with joy at the thought of bringing the strawberries back to her family.

With the bellhop in tow we go through the lobby trailing juice behind us, then wait outside as he loads the fruit into the taxi that will take us to the airport bus, me dishing out generous tips to him and taxi driver to cover the mess and later to the bus driver, and to worker at the airport who carries them into the passenger lounge where they continue to ooze onto the floor. As we wait to board, Loan is oblivious to the leering judgement of others as she sits proudly beside her precious cargo, guarding it as if were treasure.

Wanting to use the toilet before we board, she asks me to take her place guarding the strawberries and I watch as she enters the bathroom clearly marked for men. Prepared for yet another embarrassing moment I wait as men come and go, surprisingly without incident, until she emerges apparently unaware of her mistake.

CHAPTER 119

With a little more than two weeks to go before my rotation date, I continue to struggle with the idea of taking my discharge in the Nam so Loan and I can be together. But when I have a heated argument with a taxi driver who wants double the fare, then have to fend off some aggressive street kids hustling me for sex, and others trying to steal my watch, I realize I don't want to live in Saigon any more, but in a place where there is more order and less desperation, telling myself I'll gladly pay ten times more for things just so long as I'm not being hustled. The following day I sell the I Honda on the black market, getting more for it than I paid when it was new, and prepare to leave the Nam.

In an effort to feel better about leaving Loan, I remind myself how many times she told me we could never be together once my tour was up, because she would never leave Vietnam. Maybe this was for my benefit, or her own I may never know. Nonetheless, in the taxi to the Van Canh where she's singing, I struggle with how to say good-bye.

When I get there, instead of taking a table, I stand in the back of the room out of sight, listening to her sing, reminding me of the very first time I heard her at the Chinese club and it suddenly crosses my mind the best thing to do is leave her a note, sparing us both the pain of a physical parting, and leaving in its place the wonderful memories of our times together. Those memories escaping via my tears as I ask the receptionist for a pen and paper and write the following, "Em oi, you were right, you cannot leave and I cannot stay. I sad, but I happy too because I will never forget you," then give the receptionist three hundred Ps to deliver it after I leave.

CHAPTER 120

When my replacement reports in a few days early, Captain Stuab approves my rotation orders and I go back to the Hung Dao and pack up my belongings. Then first thing in the morning take a taxi out to Tan Son Nhut and plead with the MAC operations load master and Pan American steward to get me on the freedom bird that's in the process of being boarded by GIs who are on the manifest, my own flight not scheduled until later in the week.

"I'm getting an early out," I tell them, "and have this great job offer that I'll lose if I can't get on this flight."

"I'll see what do what I can," the Steward says, "but there's got to be a seat available. Hang around till everyone's aboard."

His words being all that's needed to stoke an urgency in me as I watch the long line of GIs crossing the tarmac and going up the boarding steps, then disappear into the Jetliner, mentally counting each one and trying to guess the number of seats aboard while telling myself it's hopeless, the plane can't possibly hold that many.

When the last GI disappears into the jet my eyes are locked on the steward and load master as they board with clipboards to make the final tally and I fully expect to see a few GIs being sent back out. But minutes later the steward's arm is waving at me from the doorway to come aboard and I run across the tarmac and up the gangway, still not convinced I'm going to get on the flight.

Once inside I don't see any space in the jam-packed cabin, but the steward leads me down the aisle to an empty seat nearly hidden between two GIs and I quickly take possession of it though fully expecting a manifested GI to come out of the lavatory or running up the steps at the last minute to stake his claim.

Then when the door closes and we start taxiing there's an eerie silence in the cabin and I'm just waiting for a mortar attack while trying to convince myself that when fear knocks at the door and I answer it, nobody will be there. And when the plane turns onto the runway and the brakes are set, and the throttles are advanced, and engines spool up, and the fuselage vibrates I'm still not convinced we're going to make it. And when plane lumbers down the runway and keeps going and going and going I fear we'll run out of runway. And when the nose rotates up and the landing gear retracts into the fuselage with a bang and the engines are grinding and groaning and we're barely climbing, I fear we're too overloaded. And when the jet banks sharply in its departure routing, that the bank is too steep and we're going to stall and fall out of the air.

Not until Tan So Nhut disappears completely from view and we're surrounded by a world of blue do I believe we've made it, and suddenly we're all out of our seats screaming at the top of our lungs, tears pouring uncontrollably from our eyes, hugging each other and the round eye stewardesses who have come to take us home, and they're hugging us back, their faces streaked with mascara, all in one explosive, pandemic of emotion none of us will ever forget.

The end is prelude.

EPILOGUE

Several decades later on a business trip to Washington, D.C. I visited the Vietnam Veterans Memorial. I was certain I had put the whole Vietnam experience behind me, rarely giving it a second thought, and was shocked when tears poured from my eyes leading me to conclude that some things are unforgettable even when you don't remember them.

Carved into the Memorial's black granite are the names of fifty eight thousand three hundred and eighteen American soldiers who were killed or died in Vietnam during the War. Looking at these names I realized for the Memorial to be complete it must tell the whole story of how human beings sent other human beings to kill each other for no other reasons than personal power and greed.

To be complete and tell the whole story, I feel the memorial needs to add the following:

1. The names of the three hundred four thousand American soldiers wounded in Vietnam, seventy five thousand of them severely disabled along with

the names of those who are suffering from life alter-
ing mental/emotional disorders like PTSD.

2. The names of the two million innocent Vietnamese
   civilian men, women and children who were killed
   during the war.

3. The names of the one million one hundred thousand North Vietnamese (NVA) and Viet Cong (VC)
   soldiers who were killed in the line of duty along
   with the names of countless others who were physically and emotionally disabled believing as we did,
   that right was on their side.

4. The names of the two hundred thousand South
   Vietnamese (ARVN) soldiers who were killed along
   with the names of those who were physically and
   emotionally disabled.

5. The names of the four thousand South Korean soldiers whose government for political reasons supported ours and were killed in the Nam along with
   the names of those who were physically and emotionally disabled.

6. The names of the one hundred Canadian soldiers
   whose government for political reasons supported
   ours and were killed along with the names of those
   who were physically and emotionally disabled.

7. The names of the three hundred fifty Thai soldiers
   whose government for political reasons supported
   ours and were killed along with the names of those
   who were physically and emotionally disabled.

8. The names of the five hundred Australian soldiers
   whose government for political reasons supported

ours and were killed along with the names of those who were physically and emotionally disabled.

9. The names of the thirty six New Zealand soldiers whose government for political reasons supported ours and were killed along with the names of those who were physically and emotionally disabled.

10. The names of the tens of thousands of Cambodian and Laotians who were killed and wounded many of them innocent civilian men, women and children, along with the names of those who were physically and emotionally disabled.

11. The names of the millions of the South Vietnamese men, women, children, who were raped, tortured, starved, beaten, imprisoned and lost their homes, farms and livelihood because they were caught in the middle of politics and greed.

12. The names of the millions of families on all sides whose lives were devastated and will never be the same because of the war.

13. A citation listing the three hundred twenty plus un-disputed, documented cases of atrocities and war crimes as defined by international agreement com-mitted by our GIs in all our names including the rape, torture and massacre of innocent civilians ranging from infants to the elderly along with the countless atrocities and war crimes committed by the Viet Cong, NVA and ARVN.

14. A listing of the undisputed cases of flagrant disre-gard for the Geneva Conventions in treatment of captured enemy soldiers which we pledged to abide

by and the same mistreatment by the other side whether signatories or not.

15. The names of the hundreds of thousands of South Vietnamese who allied themselves with the United States and were later abandoned by us and sent to prison camps where they were tortured, starved, beaten and forced into hard labor while their families were left to fend for themselves, branded as traitors and forever relegated to second class citizens in their own country.

16. The names of the tens of thousands Vietnamese who tried to leave for a better life elsewhere and were raped, starved, tortured, beaten and brutally killed for doing so as a result of the War.

17. The names of the countless U.S. military service dogs who despite being credited with saving over ten thousand American GI lives, were at the end of the war, listed by our military as "expendable surplus" and euthanized or left to die.

18. A recognition of the countless domestic and wild animals killed during the war including endangered elephants, tigers and leopards.

19. Before and after photos of the cities, towns and villages that were destroyed by bombs, rockets, mortar, flame throwers and poisonous chemicals that continue to impact the health of people and will do so for generations to come.

20. Before and after photos of the once pristine jungles, mountains, valleys, rivers and rice paddies rendered useless by defoliants and cancer causing substances like Agent Orange.

21. The names of the men, women and children still being killed and maimed a half a century later by unexploded ordinance.

22. An accurate accounting of the one trillion in today's dollars cost of the war as estimated by the Department of Defense, much of it transferred into the pockets of individuals and what it could have accomplished if used to improve the lives of those to whom it belonged and the same for the undetermined cost expended by the opposition.

23. A reminder that we were all one people until race disconnected us, religion separated us, politics divided us and wealth classified us.

24. And the reminder that, "eternal vigilance is the price of liberty."

Post War Communist Vietnam

The official justification for the U.S. involvement in Vietnam was to contain the threat and spread of communism. On April 30, 1975, the war ended when the South Vietnamese government surrendered and the country was unified under a communist government.

On July 11th, 1995, twenty years later, the United States government and the Socialist Republic of Vietnam formally established diplomatic relations.

Here's what the World Bank has to say about Communist Vietnam some 40 plus years after the war: "Vietnam has one of the best performing economies in the world over the last decade. Vietnam's poverty reduction and economic growth achievement in the last 15 years is one of the most spectacular success stories in economic development. It is expected to enter the ranks of other middle-income countries."

In 2018 another World Bank report stated: "Vietnam's development record over the past 30 years is remarkable. Economic and political reforms under Đổi Mới, launched in 1986, have spurred rapid economic growth and development and transformed Vietnam from one of the world's poorest nations to a lower middle-income country."

Every country has a dark side, and every country has a bright side too. We should be aware of the dark side, otherwise we cannot see problems at all. But it is essential to keep our focus always on the bright side. If we lose sight of what is positive, we have no way to change.

Eknath Easwaran

www.ingramcontent.com/pod-product-compliance
Lightning Source LLC
Chambersburg PA
CBHW070801120726
47910CB00001B/251